BESA

Louis Romano

To
Ken Rotner
My "old" friend
all the best.
Louis Romano

ACKNOWLEDGEMENTS

For me to learn about the incredible Albanian culture I needed a lot of help from some wonderful people.

First of all I'm very grateful to Shpresa and Rick Elezi for their constant support, friendship and patience with the writing of this book.

To Gjergj Balaj , Engjëll and Peter Rezaj for putting me on the right track. My dear friend Dino Erbeli for his help with hundreds of questions.

To Louis Gjelaj his wife Lindita Gjelaj for their explanation of Albanian Traditions and for inviting me to various cultural events in New York City. Lindita was an enormous help with language editing.

To Jack Berisha for our long talks and his knowledge of Albanian folklore.

Danny Rivera was my advisor on all police matters. Many thanks to him for keeping the cop stuff real and for being a great fan of Gino Ranno.

To the real Hamdi Nezaj for thirty years of friendship and teaching me what a true gentleman with BESA means.

Janet Garofalow, my business partner for her listening to endless stories, reading the raw chapters, and her encouragement and patience.

To my fabulous editor, Natassia Donohue who is tough as nails and smooth as silk.

Anita Sancinella for her incredible art direction and her husband Joe for the countless hours of listening to my ideas on this book and every other aspect of my life. They are like a sister and brother, even better.

Matt Engel for giving me confidence and for his proof reading and editing.

Thanks to Eugene Duffy for his keen proof reading talent, and his friendship.

Mary Lynn, my part Arbreshe wife, for her support and understanding, and reading the drafts.

To Lekë Dukagjini for writing the Kanun and for Gjergj Kastrioti Skanderbeg for defending Albania against the Ottoman Empire, if only for a brief moment in time.

PREFACE

Land of Albania! Where Iskander rose,
Theme of the young, and beacon of the wise,
And he his namesake, whose oft-baffled foes,
Shrunk from his deeds of chivalrous emprize:
Land of Albania! Let me bend mine eyes
On thee, thou rugged nurse of savage men!
The cross descends, thy minarets arise,
And the pale crescent sparkles in the glen,
Through many a cypress grove within each city's ken."

From Childe Harold's Pilgrimage—circa 1812. Lord Byron

Anon from the castle walls
The crescent banner falls,
And the crowd beholds instead,
Like a portent in the sky,
Iskander's banner fly,
The Black Eagle with double head;
And a shout ascends on high,
For men's souls are tired of the Turks,
And their wicked ways and works,
That have made of Ak-Hissar
A city of the plague;
And the loud, exultant cry
That echoes wide and far
Is: "Long live Scanderbeg!"

From "Scanderbeg," Henry Wadsworth Longfellow

To begin to explain the mind and temperament of the Albanians one has to understand the thousands of years of war, domination, oppression, poverty and clans that formed their mental and emotional DNA.

Kanuni I Lekë Dukagjinit, is the code that the Albanian people have lived by for centuries. These rules of order were highly influenced by the Illyrians, the direct precursors of the Albanians. The Illyrians were over-taken by the Roman Empire in 167 BC and the country formally became a Roman Protectorate. A protectorate was a Roman euphemism for a tax stream. They were such great fighters and strategic military thinkers that they impressed the power thirsty Romans. This region was a source of manpower that was employed by the Romans for hundreds of years. The Illyrians began using their rules to keep their emotional independence from Rome, something that was then and is now of ultimate importance to these proud people.

Saying these codes are old is a gross understatement. They are an-cient and have been tested over an enormous amount of time.

The Kanun is, in short, a compilation of one thousand, two hundred and sixty two articles of laws and rules which determined how people are to behave with family, acquaintances, strangers and enemies. No religious dogma or rules could be held above the Kanun as religion is subordinate to the text within. For the clans in Albania, especially in the northern region, this is their life bible.

Lekë Dukagjini was a contemporary of the Albanian national hero

Gjergi Kastrioti Skanderbeg, who was the "Lord of Albania" in the mid 1400s. Both Skanderbeg and Dukagjini were from the ruling aristocratic class which was eventually replaced by a well defined system of clans throughout Albania. Dukagjini compiled and codified the Kanun which was a major factor in preserving Albanian individuality under the Ottoman Empire. Skanderbeg reigned over Albania for forty Yeahrs until he was killed in 1468. His rule was during a period of European history when the Ottoman Empire was attempting to dominate Eastern Europe, and in fact, the entire known world.

Neither of these men actually authored the Kanun. The Kanun was attributed to them years after their deaths because of their bravery in fighting the invading Turks and their attempts to preserve Albanian faith, virtue, honor, freedom and courage. The laws evolved over time and were tested by family tradition without the interference of religion, although interestingly, the Kanun opens with what role the church plays in the lives of the Albanian people. Never recorded in its entirety, the Kanun is only a part of the customary laws of the Albanians.

The Turks (the Ottoman Empire), eventually dominated and ruled Albania for 450 years after Skanderbeg's death. The Turks, using treachery and death, forced the religion of the Albanians from Christianity, both Orthodox Catholic and Roman Catholic, to the Muslim faith. By 1912 when Albania declared her independence, nearly eighty percent of the population of this country was Muslim. However, if you ask an Albanian-American today they will all tell you that their traditions far outweigh any religion, which in most cases does not have a major influence in their lives. Many will say religion means nothing to them.

The Kanun, ancient as it is, is by no means an antiquated relic of the middle ages. Through the blood of the Albanian people, the Kanun has survived the Turks, the Communists, and even more threatening to its precepts, modern mores. The underlying code of respect and honor are imprinted in the spirit of Albanians throughout the world. Justice, honor, and respect are the backbone of the Albanian character.

Besa is a person's word of honor. The very promise or pledge that makes an Albanian's word a sacred bond that the Kanun has passed on for thousands of years is indisputable. If Besa is not kept, then the mark of dishonor remains with the family for seven generations. Besa is what makes an Albanian Albanian.

The Kanun also depicts Besa as a truce and states, "The law requires a negotiator for the truce; (Besa) to agree to a truce is the obligation of an honorable man."

There are 12 books that make up the Kanun. In book eight, HONOR, there are several passages that depict how important personal honor is viewed by Albanians. "There is no fine for the offense to honor. An offense to honor is never forgiven." And again, "An offense to honor is not paid for with property, but with the spilling of blood or by a magnanimous pardon (through the mediation of good friends)." "A man who has been dishonored is considered dead according to the Kanun."

These are not people who take honor and respect lightly. The Kanun is specific about everyday life including how guests are treated. "The house of the Albanian belongs to God and the guest."

In chapter ninety-seven, "The Conduct of the Master of the House Toward the Guest," there are rules of etiquette that must be followed to avoid dishonoring the guest of the host.

"Coffee is taken first by the guest and then by the master of the house." Then in another passage, "First the master of the house drinks a glass of raki, then the guest drinks one."

The guest must dip his bread and eat before the host. "If the master of the house dips a morsel before his guest he must pay a fine of 500 grosh." Any deviation from the rules opens an offense to a person's honor.

Gjakmarrja is the taking back of blood, the vendetta that is imposed upon the person who kills another. "Blood is paid for with blood." The family of the victim is responsible for the blood feud and the Gjakmarrja "extends to all males in the family of the murderer, even an infant in the cradle, cousins and close nephews..." Blood feuds have been known to go for many years, even decades or just a few hours if the murderer is dispatched quickly. In the 1920s thirty percent of the male population in Albania died violent deaths as a result of blood feuds.

The vicious cycle of Gjakmarrja continues.

In The Kanun, Book Ten, "The Law Regarding Crimes", 128 number 917 states, "Gjaku s' hupe kurre."

Blood is never un-avenged.

1

Lekë Marku's heartbeat was racing as if he ran the whole length of Pelham Parkway. And for good reason. He had almost done that very thing. He was twenty minutes late to meet his wife, Valbona, seven months pregnant and having a sonogram at Albert Einstein Hospital and School of Medicine. As Lekë ran from his office on Williamsbridge Road, just about a quarter mile of concrete pavement, the shade trees along the parkway seemed as if they were zipping by.

Valbona's physician, John Mastrangello, was the Director of OBGYN at the world famous teaching hospital in the Bronx. He wanted some of his students to learn the newest technology in pre-natal care and Valbona agreed to meet at the hospital rather than his office in Scarsdale, 10 miles from the Bronx home on Esplanade where the young couple lived. Usually they would be living with her husband's family but it was agreed that the young couple would have their own place which is unheard of in the Albanian community, especially with Lekë being an only son. Lekë had asked his father for his own home and it was reluctantly agreed upon as a concession to the American way of life.

It was July and going the short distance to the hospital was convenient and much more comfortable with the load Valbona was carrying. Aside from that she was helping Dr. John, whom she trusted with her life. At twenty-eight she was particular about whom she chose to care for her and deliver her baby. Dr. John made her feel comfortable and safe, and had been her doctor since she was eighteen.

Lekë arrived at the hospital and ran up the stairs two at a time, hoping he was not too late. The last thing he wanted to do was disappoint his wife and not be with her for the sonogram. This was something they enjoyed doing together since they heard the first rapid heartbeats during her first trimester.

This day was particularly special. This sonogram would tell what sex the fetus was and they were excited beyond words. They could have known sooner but decided to wait to build their excitement.

Dr. John and four of his medical students were just entering the exam room when Lekë dashed in.

"So here is the proud daddy to be," announced Dr. John with a smile. "And just in time for the big moment. Lekë, when Valbona gives birth I hope that you can break away from business and not make her wait so long."

Lekë bent over and softly kissed his wife, taking her hands in his and making eye contact like the first time they fell in love.

"Don't worry Doc. When she gets into the ninth month I am not leaving her side," Lekë said softly without taking his eyes from his beautiful wife.

Dr. John prepared the jelly that he was about to spread on Valbona's belly.

"Well, let's get this party started,"

As Dr. John gently moved the scope, he began to instruct his students. He spoke of fluids and bone mass, and other technical terms that were meaningful only to the instructor and his pupils.

"Well now. Want to know what you're having kids?" the doctor asked, concentrating on a computer screen that held the secret.

The answer was a fast "YES" from the Markus.

"Let's see. I'm going to move the screen so that you can both see what we need to see at the same time. Okay with you?" Dr. John asked.

Again, "YES" in unison was the answer.

Dr. John nodded to one of the medical students who slowly rotated the screen so that Lekë and Valbona, who were cheek to cheek, could view it.

"Let's see now, there is the cranium, now the shoulders. The chest and abdomen look well developed for seven months; let's go down and check the fetus' legs and feet."

"C'mon Doc, you're killing us here!" Lekë blurted out, the sweat beading up on his forehead.

"There it is. See it, right there? You kids are having a boy, of that there is no doubt," Dr. John said coyly. Truth be told, he knew the sex a few months ago but kept the mystery to himself.

Lekë jumped up with a fist pump to the ceiling as if a goal was scored by the Albanian soccer team at the World Cup.

"Yeah baby...oh Yeah!" Lekë shouted as everyone in the room, including his lovely wife could not help but laugh at his dramatic reaction.

Valbona had a few tears of joy. She and her husband were hugging and kissing while the nurse helped clean the jelly off.

"Okay kids, see you in my office next week. And Lekë, you be on time. Okay?" Dr. John mockingly scolded him.

"You got it Doc, and a bottle of Cristal when I see you," Lekë said with a laugh.

Lekë and Valbona decided to walk a few blocks and chat about the great news. They had already agreed that following tradition, the elders in the family would have the honor of naming the baby. There was no chance the child would be named after his father or grandfather as they were still alive. Superstition was of utmost importance.

Because of the heat they decided to take a taxi to Lekë's father's office and give him the news personally.

Ilir Marku was a man of respect in his community, but not because of his education, business acumen or religious beliefs. He ran the Albanian mob in New York City for decades.

In 1967, Ilir Marku was an Albanian refugee who made his way to Italy with the help of international funds that were provided to him by the Roman Catholic Church. For six months he stood on long lines to get food to feed himself and his sisters and brother. Living in a stone home in Frosinone near Rome, with no heat and skimpy rations provided by the church, Ilir promised himself that he would never again take a cent in charity.

Muslim or Catholic, the refugees were all treated simply as Albanians with only hope to sustain their spirits. Ilir had a choice to immigrate to New Zealand, Australia, or the United States and he knew there was only one place in the world to make his mark.

"I know of no Albanian that came to the United States with money. Everything we have in this country has been earned by our strength," Ilir often said, boasting about his people.

Without understanding English Ilir worked day and night in various jobs. From a laborer in a piano factory to a dishwasher in a Manhattan hotel, to a plasterer in Bronx apartment houses. Each week he would send a bit of his hard earned money to the church in Rome to pay back the $6,000 they said he owed them, and did so until every cent was paid. He appreciated the help but would not accept the assistance as charity.

In late 1969, he and some friends from Tropoja hijacked a truck filled with television sets and his criminal career took off from there. The legitimate real estate holdings that he acquired along the way were the perfect front for his criminal empire.

Ilir Marku's office was very active and was set up to manage his real estate affairs. His portfolio of sixty apartments acted as a perfect front for his illegal activities. The clan was not part of the YACS, which were well known and under constant surveillance by the F.B.I., New York City and New York State Police Anti-Crime units. The YACS were the Yugoslavi-an-Albanian-Croatian-Serbian crime group that was notorious for robbing banks and stores up and down the east coast. The Marku's business was much more sophisticated and profitable than the YACS and both mobs stayed clear of one another.

Lekë and Valbona planned to announce the gender of their baby to the rest of the family when they gathered the next day at the Marku estate in Scarsdale. It would be Ilir Marku's first male grandchild. The continuation of the family name and tradition was monumental news. Lekë was Ilir Marku's last of four children and his *djale shirit*, his only son. His three sisters were Gjuliana, Saranda, and finally Aferdita, who was named after Ilir's sister, a superstition so no more girls would be born. It worked. The daughters were all loved by their father but not like the love he had for his only son, who represented the continuation of the line of the clan. This was truly a spectacular moment for both families.

Ilir Marku knew the minute he saw his son enter his well appointed office that the baby was a boy. The look on Lekë's face and the drops of water in his big, beautiful, green-brown eyes gave him away.

"My son, you have made me very happy this day. You will bring a son into this world and he will make you proud like you have made me." The senior Marku was holding back tears of joy and hugged his son close. He kissed Valbona on both cheeks and looking deeply into her eyes, he said, "*Nuse*, you are carrying this family's blood. For that I am grateful." *Nuse* translates to bride of my son.

"If you will honor me in our tradition I will name the boy after my grandfather who died in battle in Tropoja. His name will be Agron," the boss said softly. They embraced and kissed again, with tears of joy.

Ilir Marku called all of his close associates into his office, to rejoice. His *kumar* started pouring Raki, the Albanian drink, into crystal glasses that he retrieved from the boss' mahogany break-front.

Valbona left the office so that the men could celebrate in their fashion and to call her best friend, Shpresa Metalia, from her cell phone. She was ecstatic at the joy the Marku family was feeling and her heart was soaring.

After an hour of laughing, smoking cigarettes, drinking Raki the Albanian grappa, toasting *Tungjatjeta*, to long life and reminiscing about long dead relatives and friends, Lekë started making his exit to be with his wife who was on her phone the entire time the men were together. From the *kumar*, Pashko Luli, the powerful and loyal underboss, to each trusted member of his father's inner circle, Lekë showed his respects as his father had instructed him since he was a small boy. All of the guests were kissed on both cheeks, the right then the left, and hands were shaken firmly while making eye contact. Then he could show the same affection to his father.

Lekë told them that he had had business to attend to and then planned to take Valbona for dinner to have a private celebration.

Since it was Friday, Lekë and Valbona usually had dinner together in their cousin Niki's Italian restaurant on City Island. One of the men from Ilir's office drove them the few blocks across Pelham Parkway and on to Esplanade so Valbona would be comfortable. The heat had not subsided even though it was nearing nine o'clock in the evening, but they arrived to the coolness of their solid brick house within two minutes. The night was still young.

Valbona wanted to freshen up before dinner and Lekë said he needed a half hour to do some business a few blocks away. They would then take his BMW 725i for the ten minute drive to the restaurant.

"Honey, by ten o'clock we will be eating the best cannelloni in New York at Niki's. See you in a bit," Lekë said as he kissed his wife and ran out the door.

2

It had been three years since Gino Ranno had seen Joey "Clams" Santoro and Charlie "C.C." Constantino. Three years that felt more like
a lifetime ago when the three pals from the James Monroe Projects in
the Bronx nearly lost their lives out at the Fish Farm in Amagansett,
Long Island. Gino had put the experience behind him and was now back
with his family in New Jersey, grateful that his wife Ellen understood
his indiscretions. They were slowly mending their relationship although
Ellen was in various stages of forgiveness. Forgetting was totally out of
the question for her and he deserved every bit of her on-again-off-again
wrath. Forgiving was not in her personality. Ellen's background was both
Sicilian and *Arberesh* Italian, a combination of two societies that did not
do well with letting bygones be bygones. On the contrary, the fact that he
was still able to sleep with both eyes closed was a miracle.

The *Arberesh* were actually Albanians who immigrated as paid mer-
cenaries or who fled the Turks in the later part of the 1400s to the Southern Italian provinces. Ellen's grandmother Sophie only spoke *Arberesh*
and taught the dying language to her children and grandchildren. Ellen
could still remember most of the language but was rusty from lack of
use. After all, how many people could speak this archaic language in
suburban New Jersey?

In many ways Ellen's personality was a throwback to her genealogy.
If she "made the sign of the cross" on someone, they were dead to her
and there would be no reprieve from that banishment. Gino always had

a hard time with her stubborn streak but knew that there was no changing her. After thirty years of marriage, minus two when they were separated, Gino gave up any attempt at it and he was simply trying to live his life in peace and quiet. This want was not in the cards for him.

Gino and Ellen were hosting a July 4th get together at their home in suburban northern New Jersey and Joey and C.C. and a few of the Miceli and Ranno "Cousins" were on the invite list. Gino was thrilled that Joey was coming up from North Carolina to stay in the Ranno home for a week or so. C.C. would drive from Queens and bring Gino's cousin Pete "Babbu" Ranno along for the festivities. They were all planning on staying at Gino and Ellen's house for a few days and breathing the "fresh air of Jersey." Thankfully they lived nowhere near the New Jersey Turnpike.

Joey Clams would take the opportunity to visit his two sons while he was up north, Joey Jr. and Matt, whom he missed terribly. He also wanted to visit his Uncle Vito and Aunt Josephine, his late father's brother and sister who were well into their nineties, both having health issues as expected at their advanced ages. Every time he spoke with them he thought it might be the last conversation they would have so he was anxious to make the visit to Arthur Avenue in the Bronx, the "old neighborhood," where they both lived. Joey knew he could always count on Gino if his boys needed anything and he got reports from Gino on the old folks from time to time. Gino was still active in the neighborhood and would ask one of Joey's cousins about the elder Santoros on a regular basis.

Joey Clams was the first to arrive, in a private car that Gino had arranged to pick him up at Newark Airport. Gino would normally make the pick-up himself but there was too much activity at Casa Ranno to break away. Seventy people, a catered affair, a backyard tent, servers, a DJ, a mandolin player, and clowns and face painters for any kids that came along with their parents, were enough to drive Ellen into a frenzy. Gino knew that it was best to hang around and send a car for his buddy.

Anyhow, it was cheaper to stay around and help than to say he was sorry and feel guilty and have to get her a David Yurman piece. She would get the Yurman anyway but it could certainly wait until their anniversary or Christmas.

Gino was just helping out with the sausage and peppers and onions (helping by tasting a piece or two) when the car carrying his life-long friend pulled up and swung into the driveway.

"Ohhhhh, Jesus Christ Almighty Joey, have I missed seeing your face!" Gino said as he wiped the grease from his hands on a napkin that he quickly grabbed from one of the tables.

"I missed you too pal but I think I missed this lady more," Joey replied as Ellen came out of the house to greet him.

Joey hugged and kissed Ellen first and then grabbed his friend and hugged him tightly. They both got choked up and covered their emotion with quick coughs and laughs.

"Jeez the place looks great and I can smell the food from the airport," Joey said while the driver brought his bags into the house.

"You don't look like you starved down in North Carolina Joey, I'm sure Anita's cooking was just fine," Gino quipped.

"Yeah, she sends her love. She just got to Port St. Lucie to be with her mother for a week. The old dame is still doing great in Florida."

"We miss her a lot," Ellen said and they walked into the cool house.

So far, the summer was brutally hot and it was only the first week of July. Gino was concerned that his guests wouldn't be comfortable outside and made the house like a meat locker. Ellen busied herself with last minute details before the throngs arrived. The caterer was smoking up the deck with two barbeque grills, cooking all sorts of meats, fish, and vegetables that would fill the chafing dishes.

"You okay Clams?" Gino asked Joey, noticing sadness in his eyes.

"I'm as okay as you are Gino. When your kid is having problems you feel it in your blood and I guess it shows on my sleeve," Joey said, again getting a bit choked up.

Both men had known the daily tribulations of having sons that were drug addicts. Joey's oldest son, Joey Jr., and Gino's youngest son, Anthony, were both addicts.

Gino and Clams spoke on the telephone almost daily. For them it was like having their own group therapy session. Neither of them was comfortable with Al-Anon or other support groups as they both trusted very few people in their lives.

"Is Joey Jr. in trouble again?" Gino asked almost afraid to hear the answer.

"Are they ever not in trouble? He just doesn't sound good on the phone. He sounds like he's using again, you know, fucked up," Joey said waiting for Gino to jump in and tell his tale of woe.

"My mutt is in rehab at ten G's a month and my life is quiet...today. You're right; we will never be able to rest with these two boys."

"C'mon Gino, Joey Jr. is thirty-eight years old, not a boy anymore for Christ's sake. Enough already with this shit."

The conversation was interrupted by loud voices from outside.

"Jersey...they made me come all the way to Jersey for a few ravioli and meat balls...Madonna Mia!" It was Babbu making his normal entrance in the front yard. C.C. followed; he seemed to be moving slower these days but Babbu was like a whirling dervish, hugging Ellen and anyone else in sight including the chef and waitresses. Especially the waitresses.

"My Uncle Pete named him right, Clams. Babbu...dummy, but you gotta love him," Gino said and he and Joey had a good laugh.

"We'll catch up later. Let's go say hello," Joey said as they walked with their arms around each other to welcome the new guests.

Babbu kept on being the entertaining character he was and C.C. was lamenting over how sore his prosthesis was and how the V.A. didn't know shit about fitting him right. He complained about that since he lost his leg in Quan Tri Province in Vietnam in 1972, when the Americans got their asses kicked good.

They went on and on about everything and anything except what happened in East Hampton and Amagansett the last time they were all together. Some things were better left for cigar talk when Ellen wasn't around.

The other guests had been arriving and the house and backyard were mobbed, just as Gino liked it. His eldest son Jeff and his wife Ali, his middle boy Arthur and his flavor of the month, along with all of the cousins and kids made the party more like a family reunion. As it should be Gino thought, thanking God that he was here to enjoy it.

Two large sedans pulled up slowly into the cul-de-sac that abutted Gino's property.

Gino immediately know who it was and started walking quickly up the driveway to greet his guests of honor.

The back-up car had four passengers who quickly alighted and smoothly fanned out, walking slowly around the cul-de-sac. They were all wearing jogging suits and sneakers and looked like they were trying to find the nearest Planet Fitness. Gino went directly to the lead car that carried his godfather, Carmine Miceli Sr., his wife Louise, their son Carmine Jr., his wife Angela, and their eighteen month old son, Carmine III.

"*Zio*, how honored I am for you to come to my home with your family," Gino said as he embraced and kissed his "uncle."

"You have honored us Gino by having us here and by being here with your family where you belong," said the Don with a happy smile that showed his pearly white teeth. Gino always thought that the Don's teeth looked like Chiclets gum. Gino kissed his Aunt Louise and told her that she looked younger every time he saw her. It wasn't a lie thanks to plastic surgery.

"Gino, always remember, *La famiglia è la patria del cuore*," the Don said. Gino knew the translation: Your family is the homeland of your heart. Carmine Senior was reminding Gino that his place was with his family and that he made the right choice in returning home.

"Yes Uncle Carmine, I understand and thank you again...but look at this big boy!" Gino picked up Carmine III from the car and nestled his face into the laughing little boy's neck. Like his father Carmine Jr., the baby adored Gino. Gino made him belly laugh with silly faces and noises that looked and sounded like farm animals.

"Gino, did you lose weight? You look great," the ever-gorgeous Angela Miceli said, making Gino blush while patting his stomach.

"I wish Ang. Ellen's cooking is far too hard to resist. Maybe it's the larger size I'm wearing." Ellen then ran out to greet the guests and hug the baby.

Carmine Jr. approached Gino slowly, jutting his jaw out like Don Corleone.

"Gino, my cousin, always remember and never forget, when the cow drinks his own milk, he will have the shits for a week," he whispered to Gino, poking a bit of fun at his serious father.

Gino laughed so hard he saw spots in his eyes.

Having the Micelis at his home was a continuation of generations of Lercara Friddi, Sicily *piasani* getting together for food, laughter, music, and more important, the show of unity. Gino was thrilled to have this opportunity and once again he was thanking God for directing the opera.

The day went by very fast. Everyone raved about the food: sausage and peppers and potatoes, a raw bar with clams and oysters with all the trimmings, stuffed calamari, fried calamari, cold calamari with shrimps and *scungilli, ravioli,* eggplant *parmagiano, linguini carbonara,* the Sicilian specialty *Pasta Con Sarde,* a favorite of Gino and Carmine Senior; seemingly every Italian cold-cut on the planet from *mortadella* to Messina salami to *Prosciutto di Parma* and Speck, a smoked prosciutto, four kinds of olives, and a salad with three different cheeses. Then a cheese table, fresh mozzarella, *Cacciocavallo* from Sicily, even a cheese they make in Catania, near Mount Etna where they coat the cheese in volcanic ash and then bury it for six months in a pot. No hamburgers and hot dogs, but instead there was a roast baby pig on the grill and grilled rabbit, and Wild Boar sausage. Then of course the *piece de resistance:* Ellen's homemade sauce and meatballs. There was the usual debate about whether it should be called sauce or gravy but no one changed their opinion. Five kinds of Italian bread including Don Miceli's favorite *ciccola* bread made with bits of prosciutto made this more like an Italian feast that could ruin any diet and give a cardiologist the fits.

The kids loved the entertainment. And the Mister Softee truck that pulled into the driveway courtesy of Carmine Jr. drove all the way there from Bruckner Boulevard in the Bronx just to make the kids go wild. Gino's neighbors likely never even heard the Softee jingle in their lives until that night.

"The cream-i-est dream-i-est soft ice cream you get from Mis-ter Softee. For a re-freshing de-light su-preme, look for Mis-ter Sof-tee. My milk shakes and my sun-daes and my cones are such a treat. Lis-ten for my store on wheels ding-a-ling down the street. The cream-i-est dream-i-est soft ice cream you get from Mis-ter Sof-tee. For a re-fresh-ing de-light su-preme Look for Mis-ter Sof-tee. S-O-F-T Dub-ble-E Mis-ter Sof-tee!"

All the neighborhood kids got on the ice cream line as their parents gawked in disbelief. When the Rannos had a party it was the real magilla.

The bodyguards were happy to have an easy day in the suburbs and eat a relaxed meal, albeit in the cul-de-sac. Everyone went home happy by ten o'clock in the evening. Gino, Joey Clams, C.C. and Babbu finally had a chance to be alone and have cigars and a few drinks on the deck in the rear of the house.

"Your Uncle Carmine is lookin' old," Joey said as he mouthed his Dominican-made Santa Damiana cigar. Joey was a cigarette smoker and looked uncomfortable with the large Churchill.

"Yeah, he does. Junior is ready to take over when *Zio* decides the time is right," Gino said while he enjoyed the quiet, the cigar, and a light Campari and soda.

"Gino, why you drinkin' that girly color drink instead of scotch like the rest of us?" Babbu piped in, changing the subject.

"Pete, this is what I like to drink. Besides, scotch may make me re-tarded like you," quipped Gino and all four men laughed loudly.

"This ain't no scotch Gino, you should know better. I have my Jack Daniels, in a pony glass like our pal used to have it, rest in peace," Joey said seriously.

"Sal Angrasani is dead?" Gino was wide eyed.

"Years ago, heart attack, bam," Joey said into his drink.

"I wanna go like that—except with two broads in the muff," Babbu added. They all roared with laughter forgetting poor Sally boy.

"Quiet, quiet! If you wake Ellen up she will cut my balls off," Gino said quietly.

"If she didn't cut them off three years ago, I think your nuts are pretty safe," C.C. chimed in to another loud laugh.

"Ya know what, he's right Gino, Anita would have removed my balls and my dick and put them in a Hellman's mayonnaise jar and frozen them for eternity," Joey said almost spitting the cigar on the deck.

"You hear from her?" asked C.C. He was trying to see if Gino had been in touch with Lisa Devlin, the woman who almost cost them all of their lives.

"Yeah we went to the Opera last night, *La Traviata* is her favorite... of course not C. I know I'm crazy but not suicidal. No contact since that night in Amagansett, none," Gino said with a sigh of relief.

"And keep it that way cuz, cause I don't want to be babysitting those two les-boins again, unless I can do my thing," Babbu said thrusting his pelvis up and down. Now Joey did spit the cigar onto the deck and all four men laughed until they had tears in their eyes.

"Don't worry guys I will personally fly up from North Carolina and kick his fucking ass in if I even hear her name again," Joey said with a smile, and a lot of truth behind it.

They drank and talked until two in the morning, polishing off the last of the three-color cookies and the chocolate *cannoli*. The conversation went from the old days, the old girlfriends, who was doing who back then and now, all the sports they played and then the usual debate about who had the better team, The Aces, Soundview Shell, or the Bullets. The conversation got back around to the Fish Farm and how they had all been close to cashing in all the chips. Gino was obviously uncomfortable with rehashing the details. Joey Clams noticed his best friend's leg anxiously bouncing and clicked the glass that he had just emptied the last of the Jack Daniels from.

"Gentlemen, gentlemen please, I have a question of our esteemed colleague, Mr. Peter Ranno." They all looked from Clams to the wide eyed Babbu.

"Pete, tell us the truth now that it's all over. Be honest, did you play stink finger with those two mutts in the hotel room out there in Montauk, yes or no?" They all laughed until they saw Gino's bedroom light go on at the rear of the house.

"Holy shit we woke the sleeping giant!" Gino said spiting the last of a cookie all over his shirt.

"Party's over, see you for brunch guys." They all scampered for their bedrooms.

3

Joey Santoro Jr. was, as his father thought, back in drug trouble. He was using and selling the junk but was street smart enough to always be one step ahead of the cops. He was fighting a six–hundred-dollar-a-day habit so the fastest way to stay ahead of the dealer was to deal. Oxy, heroin, crack, coke... only the hard stuff. Pot was for the kids.

Born and raised in the Bronx, Joey Jr. knew his way around. His two partners in crime, Jimmy Connell and Dennis Birdi, were tough as nails and as strung out as they come. They liked the money but they needed the drugs which made for a dangerous combination. Dangerous for anyone who came between them and the shit. They were real deal junkies and real deal dealers. Not to be fucked with by any stretch of the imagination. Joey Jr., the smartest of the crew, had a charm about him that disarmed people and allowed them to trust and like him almost instantly. Jimmy and Dennis were flat out bad. Both carried 9mm pistols, and both would use them in a New York minute. Joey Jr. was different; his charisma was his weapon of choice and he was never strapped. He never carried a weapon.

This particular Friday night they were going to Pelham Parkway for a big score. Joey Jr.'s Albanian connection had a large amount of Oxy, lifted from a CVS warehouse in Lumberton, New Jersey, and a few kilos of Turkish heroin via the Tropoje connection, the area of Albania where drug trafficking is a way of life. From the poppy fields in Turkey, the distribution system went through Tropoje, Albania then on to Naples, Italy then New York, Boston and Detroit.

The Marku family ran, as part of their illicit operations, the New York-Albanian drug business which was the largest illegal retail drug outlet in the world. The system worked like a charm, and everyone made a fortune.

"We buy the stuff for twenty-five grand and sell it for a hundred. That should make us comfortable for a while, plus we have our own stash to make us straight," Joey Jr. told his two side-kicks.

"Do you trust these fucking Albanians?" Jimmy asked with a hint of fear in his voice.

"Listen to me, the both of you. I've done business with this guy before. His dad is big-time and he's gonna be big-time one day. He loves me. We get in good with him now and we are set, understand?"

"Yeah, yeah Joey, but these guys make me nervous. Look at them, you never can tell what they really are thinking," Dennis replied.

"He's cool. I know his wife's best friend. She got me my apartment last year. His wife is having a baby soon. All he wants to do is make money and not get fucked. He's the man, believe me. Okay?" Joey Jr. said, holding his hands as if he were praying.

"What's his name?" Dennis asked bluntly.

"Ya know Bird, you ask too many fuckin' questions. What? Don't you just fuckin' trust me you douche?"

"What's his name?" Jimmy piped in.

"Jesus Christ you guys, okay, okay. Lekë Marku. You repeat his name and they will be fishing you out of the water under the Throgs Neck Bridge."

Their meeting was set for nine-thirty in the evening at 760 Pelham

Parkway, a building that was owned by Mr. Marku, and Lekë's cousin Zef was the live-in superintendent. At just about this time it started to turn from dusk to dark which was an additional cover for the buy. The building was seven stories high with a large courtyard that was well maintained and divided the building into two separate addresses, with two separate entrances. They would go up to the common roof to make the deal. No one in Lekë's crew knew they were planning to go up to the roof, nor which entrance would be used. Joey Jr. only knew the address and was told to wait on the sidewalk in front of the building.

Joey and his crew arrived at the building at 9:20 p.m. and waited only a few minutes before Ukë Marku, Lekë's first cousin, and two other Albanians approached them. Both were new arrivals from Albania and understood very little English. They spoke even less. They were direct from Tropoje and were seasoned in the drug business. They were here to learn the street side of the business and to do whatever else the Markus commanded. They had sworn their *besa* of loyalty to Ilir and his son Lekë. Not every *besa* was fulfilled.

Ukë Marku's father Afrim was killed in Albania twenty-seven years ago, when Ukë was three years old. Ilir, Afrim's brother, had sent him from New York to Tropoje to coordinate a heroin distribution channel. Afrim was shot in a car twice behind his right ear the day after he arrived. The killer or killers were never indentified but a *Gjakmarrja*, a blood feud, has been in effect against the boss of the powerful Gjonaj family ever since.

Ukë was a tough-guy in every sense of the word, his name fitting his personality perfectly. Ukë is the Albanian word for wolf and his parents named him right. Ukë possessed many of the traits of the canine hunter. Strong, fearless, brutal and cunning, Ukë had a trigger temper. His reputation was what made him feared in the Albanian community. Aside from his drug dealing and other nefarious activities, Ukë owned a dozen pizza shops in the Bronx and Manhattan, marking him as a legitimate business man. Proud of his Albanian heritage, every shop Ukë owned, along with the usual Italian pizza, served authentic *burek* made from scratch. This pizza-like food, a remnant of the Turkish influence on the Albanian culture, is made with fresh dough and filled with spinach, cheese, meat, or a combination of all three.

"'Sup Joey how ya doin?" Ukë asked Joey Jr.

"S'all good Ukë, good to see ya," replied Joey Jr., falling into street-speak, and shaking Ukë's hand.

"You came with your boys I see."

"And you came with yours."

"They my cousins from the other side. They don't know shit and they speak no English, they cool," Ukë said, pronouncing 'they' as 'day' every time. He eyed Jimmy and Dennis.

"They aw-right Ukë, we partners. They cool. Let's get this thing done," Joey Jr. responded, referring to his crew.

"Just waitin' on my main man is all," Ukë said still looking at the two strangers, and eyeing the Nike sports bag that Jimmy was carrying.

"We ain't gonna deal right here on Pelham right Ukë?"

"Relax bro, it's all worked out."

"When's he comin'?" Joey Jr. asked hastily.

"Dude, relax, he gets here when he gets here. You wired or some shit?" Ukë asked in a nasty tone.

"Fuck that shit Ukë, I'm no narc. We got business to do so let's do it." Joey Jr. matched the aggressive tone. Ukë glared at him, sending a chill down Joey Jr.'s spine. Joey Jr. was no match for the wolf.

With that the blue BMW pulled up, Lekë driving and his cousin Zef riding shotgun. Zef had the keys to the doors to enter the building and roof top.

"Yo Joey, how ya doin?" Lekë approached Joey and made a full embrace—feeling his back for a wire or weapon.

"S'all good Lekë, s'all good. Dude these are my partners Jimmy and Dennis. Been with me from the beginning," Joey Jr. said with a hand signal to indicate his seal of approval.

"If you say they good, they good to me," Lekë said giving Jimmy and Dennis the same friendly pat down.

"Are we ready to make the deal Lekë?" Joey was chomping at the bit to get the deal done and get going.

"Dude, we ain't doin' it right here on Pelham Parkway. We might as well just go down and exchange in front of the four-nine," Lekë said referring to the NYPD precinct that covered the area.

"Let's go inside and upstairs where it's private," he continued, leading the way to the doorway on the left side of the building, with his arm around Joey Jr. in mock friendship. The rest of the group followed them with Ukë still eyeballing Dennis and Jimmy. Engjëll and Gjergj, the Albanians brought in by Ukë, took up the rear glancing back toward the parkway and up and down the sidewalk to see if anyone was following and to notice any out-of-the-norm activity.

As they approached the building entrance Lekë suddenly made an abrupt change and directed Joey Jr. to the right entrance of the property. Joey was momentarily startled as were Jimmy and Dennis, but they recovered quickly understanding Lekë's caution. The move was made for the protection of everyone in the deal.

They quickly entered the building using Zef's pass-key. Lekë ignored the elevator and began ascending the stairwell towards the roof.

Zef and Gjergj took the elevator to the basement to get two large knapsacks that were stored in his office containing the cocaine. They then took the elevator to the seventh floor and walked up one short flight to the door of the locked roof. The rest of the group went up the fourteen flights in silence, so as not to disturb any pain-in-the-ass tenant who might call the police.

If someone did call, the buyers would possibly still have a full half-hour before any cops showed, so it was still safe. The patrol cars in the four-nine were not at all famous for their rapid response time. Worst case scenario, Zef was the building superintendent showing the roofers his leak problems. They were covered.

The timing was perfect as Zef and Gjergj reached the roof just as the rest of the group came up the last few flights.

Once on the roof they got down to business. The roof was dark except for one 40 watt light bulb over the exterior roof door. It was tough to see more than fifteen feet in the distance. Lekë's cadence changed from street talk to financial analyst.

"Joey, we've agreed that you will pay us thirty percent of our asking price for the product. We get another thirty percent in two weeks and the balance, paid in full in thirty days with ten points vig. Any questions?"

"No problem on the money. We have the thirty. We just need to test the stuff," Joey Jr. replied.

"Test the stuff? What the fuck is that dude? Our shit is always top quality and you know it. You have the balls to treat me like a *zezak*?" Ukë interrupted, raising his voice, almost screaming the Albanian word that refers to a black person.

Lekë tried to disarm the argument.

"Calm down Ukë, this is a business transaction and he has the right-"

"Fuck these mother fuckers, he has no right to shit, that is disrespecting us. I'll put a cap in his fucking eye!" Ukë reached under his Nat Nast shirt into his belt.

Jimmy and Dennis instinctively separated and Joey Jr. froze, not processing the scene. Jimmy drew the 9MM Glock from his ankle holster, where Lekë never checked, and started shooting wildly in Ukë's direction, hitting only the roof wall behind his target. Mass confusion took over as the Albanians, Engjëll and Gjergj, drew their weapons and began randomly shooting up the roof. It was difficult to see a target as everyone ran for whatever cover they could see. Exhaust fans, water tower stanchions, chimney brick, anything. Dennis was hit in his shoulder and was screaming like a stuck pig.

Joey Jr. ran for the roof door just as Ukë raised his gun and put two bullets into his first cousin Lekë's brain. The young Santoro never actually saw Ukë do the hit but the blood, bone and brains splattered all over him. Joey Jr. ran down the stairs six at a time. Ukë immediately started sobbing that his cousin was dead.

"That fucking piece of shit....that fucking guinea....he killed my cousin....he killed Lekë!" Ukë dropped to his knees and was cradling Lekë's head in his lap.

Jimmy and Dennis fled down the stairs behind Joey Jr. while the Albanians all stood around Lekë, already knowing what their role was. Zef, unaware of the planned hit, took all of the guns and the knapsacks filled with drugs and made his way down the stairs into his basement office. In the distance the wailing of police cars could be heard. Lekë was stone dead; his blood formed a puddle around his head on the gravel and tar roof.

Chapter Eight, of the *Kanun* under The Rights of Inheritance specifically states neither a wife nor daughters are recognized as heirs. It also spells out the line of inheritance: "A household without heirs passes to the cousins, who have equal rights; the property of the extinct house is divided among them in common." The power and position of the Marku family would pass, according to tradition, to Ukë Marku.

4

NYPD's finest arrived en masse with guns drawn, ready to blast anyone with a handgun. When they arrived on the roof they were met with an Oscar winning performance by Ukë, wailing about his poor dead cousin. His dramatic monologue went from English to Albanian and back to English nonstop until his voice was raspy. The acting was supported by Zef's sincere tears and the two Albanian visitors looking baffled and confused. A perfect scene for the first responders to arrive to. Ukë had to be physically pried from his cousin's body as the police tried their best to preserve the crime scene.

Joey Jr. and his two druggy friends ran down Pelham Parkway for a few blocks and made a right on Muliner Avenue toward Lydig Avenue to retrieve their car and make their escape. They never dreamed the buy would end up with shots fired. They all wanted, and indeed needed, the drugs. Jimmy still held the bag of money that was meant to buy the junk from Lekë. In the dark and confusion none of them actually saw Ukë do the deed and they were now in shock and shaking uncontrollably, not yet processing the events, and with no idea that Lekë was even dead. The only evidence of injury was Dennis' wounded shoulder and the mess all over Joey Jr.'s face and clothing.

The scene at the Marku building was pandemonium. The emergency lights from the police cars bathed the scene in swirls of red, white and blue, bouncing off the parked cars and the surrounding apartment buildings. A crowd gathered quickly on the sidewalk on both sides of the double building, held back by that famous white crime scene tape with blue lettering, used on every cop show since Jack Lord's Hawaii Five-0. Every window in both buildings was open and the tenants, with an aerial view, were gaping down at the scene taking place below. All the crowd knew was that there was a shoot-out on the roof and a dead guy was up there. That information was enough to keep them glued to the scene on this hot and humid night. The police were keeping a tight lid on any information about the murder.

Traffic on both sides of the Parkway was diverted from White Plains Road to Eastchester Avenue. Only emergency vehicles that were going to Jacobi Hospital, just down Pelham Parkway from the crime scene, were permitted access.

By the time the homicide squad and the coroner arrived it was a little past ten o'clock. Valbona was getting impatient as Lekë was not back at home to take her for dinner. More tired than hungry, Valbona made herself some fresh iced tea and went into her bedroom to lie down for a few minutes. She fell fast asleep, as so many expectant mothers often do in the last trimester. The baby boy inside her had been moving a lot over the past few nights interrupting her sleep. *Anxious to come into the world,* she thought and smiled to herself when he woke her. Between the baby moving and the torrid heat Valbona was exhausted. The short rest would do her good.

When homicide Detective Lieutenant Carlo Del Greco arrived it looked like any other gunshot murder. As usual he spoke to the first officers on the scene getting their take of things and asking if they secured the complete crime scene. In his thirty years on the force, twenty-two of them in Bronx homicide, he had seen countless murders of all descriptions. Long ago he stopped counting the cases and no longer got that little tingle in his stomach when he saw a body sprawled out dead and bloodied. But this time was different from all of the rest. When he looked at the body, his heart skipped a beat. This time he recognized the victim and for good reason. Del Greco wasn't the most ethical of police-men, to put it mildly. He had a long association with the Marku family throughout his entire career with the NYPD. He and Ilir were as close as a cop and a crime boss could be without raising suspicions and hav-ing internal affairs give him the proverbial enema. His luxurious condo apartment in Punta Cana, Dominican Republic, along with a few other nice toys and loads of hidden cash were courtesy of the Marku clan. The moment he saw that the victim was the son of his benefactor he knew this murder was going to test the relationship. He was now second guess-ing himself for not putting his retirement papers in and thinking about going for thirty-five years. Why him, why now?

As the highest ranking Homicide Squad officer on the scene Del Greco knew the drill. The Emergency Services Unit was already on site and had started placing the flood-lights to illuminate the crime scene. ESU had also started marking the shell casings and bullet fragments they found on the rooftop with small cones and were in the midst of the total perimeter search as they were safeguarding the crime scene. The night duty captain made his visit, checked the scene, saw that Del Greco had everything under control, and quickly exited to leave the rest of the job to the experienced Detective Lieutenant. Everyone that was on the roof would be taken to the Four-Nine on Eastchester Avenue for questioning. Ukë, Zef, and the two foreigners would be brought in separate police cars for the short three minute ride and kept in individual holding areas so detectives could get statements and sort things out. Del Greco had the only Albanian speaking detective they had, Detective First Class Jimmy Gojcaj, paged with orders to get down to the house to interview the wit-nesses on the double.

Photographs, measurements, ballistics, body fluids, hair particles and fingerprints were being collected by the Crime Scene Unit and a door-to-door interview with the building's tenants was already under-way by plain clothes and uniformed police. Who saw anything, who heard anything, what time did they see or hear anything, were there any suspicious people hanging around, and how is the landlord, and the rest of the normal run-down of questions at a major crime scene. Two things were next on his list before he began personally interrogating the witnesses: get the Coroner's Office field personnel to examine the body to determine time of death and other basic information, and to notify next of kin. That job he was not looking forward to. This was much too close to home.

"Detective can I use my cell phone to call someone?" Ukë asked between sucking in air from his incessant sobbing.

"The rule is absolutely not. Who did you want to call? Your lawyer? There is plenty of time for that," Del Greco replied a bit sarcastically so the other detectives heard him clearly.

"No, no, no, I had nothing to do with this. This man is my cousin. I don't need a damned lawyer. I wanted to call my family and tell them what has happened. His wife... poor woman is pregnant and I don't want her to-"

Del Greco cut him off. "No calls. I will contact the family myself after I finish up here. Right now just go with these officers. I will see you a bit later and I'm sorry for your loss young man."

"That fucking guinea Joey killed my cousin," Ukë began his rant, sobbing.

Del Greco knew Ukë well from his dealings with the Marku clan but needed to stay in character as a homicide detective for the sake of the other cops at the scene. It was going to be a very long night.

5

Joey Jr., Jimmy, and Dennis were quickly out of the neighborhood in Jr.'s car and headed north toward the Major Deegan Expressway to make their way to Washingtonville in Orange County, New York, about an hour and a half drive from the Bronx. Joey drove at the speed limit knowing any fast or erratic driving would be the end for them all. Dennis' wound was bloody and painful but not life threatening. Ukë's bullet passed right through the meaty part of his shoulder, seeming to have missed any bones or major arteries. Jimmy sat in the back seat holding an old sweatshirt that Joey Jr. had in the trunk as a compress to stem the blood flow. Dennis was moaning like a woman in labor. Other than getting Dennis to a friend in Washingtonville who was an EMT, their second biggest problem was all three were starting to jones from the lack of having their narcotic of preference. They would have to wait until reaching their destination before they could get straightened out and remove the drug longing that had begun to take over.

The three men all relocated for a few years to Washingtonville when they were in their late teens so getting the shit was not a problem. They knew the lay of the land as all drug addicts do. Obviously money wasn't an issue as they had a bag full of hundreds from the busted drug deal that they were fleeing from. Thirty-thousand dollars worth of pictures of dead presidents.

As they approached the New York State Thruway some thirty minutes after the rooftop shootout, Joey Jr.'s cell phone played his theme song, "Eye of the Tiger."

"Joey...what the fuck? Are you all right?" one of his asshole pals said on the line.

"Yeah, fine...sup Butchie?"

"Motherfucker, they're saying that you popped that Albanian dude Lekë."

"Get the fuck outta here, no way. I didn't even have a gun."

"Hey, my cousin is a cop in the four-nine and he just called me. They are keeping it under wraps right now but he knows I'm close to you. He thought I might have been one of the two guys that was with you. Whatever you do get the fuck out of here, he's fucking DOA bro. Maybe move to fuckin' Chile or South America or somethin'. You and your boys are toast dude," the Rhodes Scholar advised.

"He's fuckin' dead?" Joey yelled into the receiver.

"As dead as Kelsey's nuts bro, and you are the one they're saying did the job."

"Fuck that. None of us killed nobody, understand? Don't tell no one you reached me, understand? I'll straighten this shit out in a day or so," Joey said with a cocky attitude.

"Yeah right dude. The only way this will be straightened out is when you and your crew are at St. Raymond's in a box. These fuckin' Albanians don't play."

Joey Jr. hit the red button on his phone ending the conversation. He felt the blood drain from his head and became woozy from both the stress of the news and missing his fix.

"What the hell was that about? Who's dead?" Jimmy asked.

"Butchie said Lekë is dead and word is I shot him. What did I shoot him with, my dick?" Joey Jr. floated the question.

"Dead? Can't be! We couldn't see shit up there never mind hit someone," Jimmy said dismissing the possibility.

"Right genius, look at Dennis, he got hit, what if the fuckin' bullet hit his heart or his head? He'd be dead right? You were shooting the place up too remember?" Joey Jr. shot back.

"Fuck you Joey. What, you blamin' me now?" Jimmy pushed a bit too hard on Dennis' shoulder causing him to scream out in pain.

"No douche bag. I'm just sayin' who knows how he got hit? Now what the fuck do we do?" Joey Jr.'s voice gave a hint of a tremble.

"Those Albanians will skin us alive, man. We got to lam it big-time," Dennis piped in.

"Lam it to where? Those fuckers will hunt us down like animals. We are fucked unless we can prove we didn't do it," Jimmy said quickly.

"And how we gonna do that Sherlock? Ask for ballistics and a video tape? Hire O. J.'s lawyers? If the word on the street is that I popped Lekë in a drug deal we are all dead meat. We can't prove shit, we can't turn ourselves in to the cops, the Albanians will kill us in jail and we can't go...I don't know. We are just done man, just done," Joey Jr. said on the verge of tears.

"Dude, what about your Uncle Gino, you're always saying he's connected right? He knows who's who. Call your old man and ask for help Joey," Jimmy said, making the most sense so far.

"Dude, my father is at his house in Jersey right now. What do I say? 'Hey pop they're blaming me for killing the Albanian boss' kid. Tell Uncle Gino to make it go away.' Are you fuckin' high or what?" Joey said, the trembling in his voice subsiding.

"You got a better idea Joey?" Dennis replied stiffing a moan. They went silent as they continued the long ride to the sticks.

6

Detective Lieutenant Carlo Del Greco finished supervising the removal of Lekë's body and orchestrating the homicide squad's activities for the major crime scene on the roof and around the building. It was after one o'clock in the morning and he decided it was time to go see his benefactor, Ilir Marku, in his usual hangout on Arthur Avenue, *Djelt E Shqipes*, the Sons of the Eagle social club. He began dreading the task as he took the ten minute drive to the neighborhood that was a stronghold of Italian restaurants, stores, and the Italian wise-guys for the last hundred and ten years.

The Italians and the Albanians found a way to peacefully coexist on Arthur Avenue for the past forty years, when tough Albanians started immigrating to the states in large numbers. There was a mutual respect if not fear of each other's temperaments and traditions that somehow allowed them to live and work side by side.

The Italians were not always so liberal and understanding of people other than themselves. As near ago as the 1970s, a black or Hispanic would be chased out of the neighborhood, running for their lives in a ten block radius of East 187th Street and Arthur Avenue. The decade before that saw the locals stop the City from running its buses from Southern Boulevard to 3rd Avenue. Control of the entire neighborhood was in the hands of the tough Italian guys and they were controlled by the mob. Yet, the power of the Italian mob was waning and minorities had taken grasp of the Bronx as a whole. Even the Bronx District Attorney was black.

For Christ's sake, so was the President of the United States. The day of chasing people out of the neighborhood with baseball bats and crowbars was just a vague memory.

Del Greco pulled his unmarked Ford SUV into a fire zone adjacent to the crowded Albanian men's club. The double eagle symbol and the club's name were written in Albanian on the front window; there was no sign above the storefront.

The detective entered the club and was met by a few of the members who knew his affiliation with the boss and he was pointed to the rear of the room. Coffee and drinks were being served from a small bar and the no smoking sign that the New York City Department of Health required be posted was ignored. Those rules were made for someone else.

Del Greco took a long deep breath, tasting the cigarette smoke as he made his way to a table of six men, one being Ilir Marku. He quit smoking six years ago but wanted to light a cigarette so bad his hands were shaking.

Ilir saw him and immediately stood as a sign of respect for a guest. The men kissed on both cheeks and Ilir immediately called for the bartender to see to the needs of his guest.

"My friend, coffee? Perhaps a drink? Come sit with me here," the boss pointed to a chair beside him.

"My dear friend I must speak to you in private," the grim faced cop said, almost risking an insult to the others at the table, the boss' inner circle.

Ilir Marku knew from Del Greco's face that there was something seriously wrong and quickly dismissed his entourage.

"What is on your mind my friend?" Ilir asked, searching Del Greco's face and eyes for a hint of the news he was about to hear.

"Ilir, I have terrible news for you. There was a shooting at 740 Pelham Parkway tonight. I don't yet have all of the specifics. Your son Lekë was shot and killed in the shooting. I am so sorry to have to bring this news to you," Del Greco said, his eyes welling up with tears.

The boss of the Albanian mob dropped his head, needing time to process the disastrous news. The room went silent as all eyes were upon the boss. They could not hear what was said but could tell Ilir was shocked. The men in the room could only imagine the gravity of news that the detective brought with him.

"Who did this thing Carlo?" Ilir asked solemnly with true hatred in his eyes.

"I do not know yet. The investigation has started," the cop said in a dry voice.

"Where is my son now?"

"His remains will be sent to the coroner's office and will be released to you sometime late tomorrow."

"Who closed his eyes?" Marku asked. A perplexed Del Greco did not understand the question.

"I'm sorry sir?"

"Who closed his eyes and his mouth? In our tradition this must be done to stop death from coming to us again." Del Greco was taken aback but rallied quickly.

"I'm certain that this was done. I will check if you like."

Marku ignored the response and leaned over and whispered to him so as not to be overheard.

"I want you to do your investigation. I want you to find out who did this thing to my family. I do not want the people who killed my only son to be apprehended or harmed in any way. You will give me their names and turn your back. Will you do this for me Carlo?"

Detective Lieutenant Carlo Del Greco, with over thirty years on the NYPD, a beautiful life, a hot new wife, and a great pension, knew that he had no choice in the matter.

"Yes my friend. I will do exactly as you ask."

"Good, now I must go and tell his wife and his mother. Arrangements must be made."

"Sir, your nephew Ukë is being held as a witness. As are three other Albanians, two from Europe. He asked that I contact a Shpresa Metalia, who is your daughter-in-law's best friend. What do you wish me to do?" the detective asked.

"First, release my nephew. You can hold the others for now. My people will contact Mrs. Metalia. Thank you for your help my good friend."

Shpresa Metalia was indeed Valbona Marku's best friend. They were both born in Albania, and came to the States within a month of each other. Ilir Marku and Shpresa's father knew each other from working in the same Park Avenue buildings as porters and handymen. Once they learned to speak English and found that the American system of doing business was no less corrupt than it was in Albania, they moved up their individual ladders quickly. Within ten years they were both resident managers of two of the finest Fifth Avenue apartment buildings in New York City.

Shpresa and Valbona went to the best public schools in Manhattan together and found escape from their over protective fathers, who were strict, old-school Albanians. Their friendship grew into more of a sisterhood; they truly loved each other without the petty jealousies that some women seem to manufacture. After college, Valbona went on to teach while Shpresa made her name in the big ticket world of New York real estate. She quickly became a major earner in the dog-eat-dog residential apartment rental and sales business. Both young women married their husbands within six months of one another.

Yet Shpresa, unlike many Albanian women even today, married a man that she absolutely fell in love with. Rick Metalia started out working for Shpresa's father as a doorman at a luxury apartment building. Rick watched the young girl leave the building early every morning and come back in the late afternoon, their first shy hellos building into a distant romance. The old man would have fired his ass and then thrown him piece by piece into the boiler if he only knew what Rick was thinking. But of all the eligible men that wanted to date her, Shpresa found a warmth and kindness in Rick, things she saw in no other, and knew she had found her soul mate. Rick moved on, became a resident manager himself, and soon fulfilled his ultimate dream, to own a Property Management firm. By the time they married, the young Metalias put their skills together and were a one-two punch in management and brokerage. Life was very good.

Shpresa's name in Albanian translates to Hope in English and she fulfilled her parent's dream of optimism for their beautiful daughter. And she was beautiful indeed. A stunner, both in looks and personality which when you add brains and street smarts, the latter taught in part by her father, was her recipe for success.

Everyone who was anyone in real estate knew Shpresa, or Hope from developers, property managers, on site and resident managers to competitive brokers. They knew her by the name that she introduced herself. The ultra wealthy WASP's might think her name was too ethnic so to them she was Hope. To the more down to earth buyers, who went for her chic style and straight-forward manner she was Shpresa. She knew when to use her arsenal of attitude and played the role well. Sadje told her many times that she should be herself with friends and family but be a chameleon with the people she worked with. His credo was, "Get the money and walk to the bank." Her charm and sophistication saw that she made many trips to that bank.

There were times that clients, both male and female would hit on Shpresa confusing her friendly demeanor with availability. Shpresa was cool under this kind of pressure and would let them down softly, explaining that her marriage vows really meant something to her. If they persisted or tried a second time, her icy eyes froze them in their tracks and the flirtation was over. Business was strictly business. Sleeping with a client to close a deal was for someone else, and in Shpresa's world that kind of woman was called a prostitute not a broker.

As a broker, one of her favorite people in the industry was none other than Gino Ranno.

Shpresa adored Gino from the time she was a little girl. Her father and Gino knew each other for thirty years from Gino's salad days in real estate development. Gino watched Shpresa grow up from a baby to a married woman by way of the wallet sized photos that her dad showed him every time they got together for lunch or at one of the industry functions. The first time Gino had the pleasure to meet Shpresa he was dumbfounded by her looks. Her dad laughed at Gino fumbling for words.

"I told you she is more beautiful in person," Sadje said as he hugged his friend closely.

"Sadje my friend, you said your daughter was cute...not gorgeous. Thanks to God she takes after her beautiful mother," Gino said while kissing Shpresa's mother's hand.

They sat at the same table that night and Gino was hooked for life. Shpresa became his go-to broker from that night forward and he did everything he could to get her name to his friends in the industry. Not that she needed his help as she was destined for success, but one more advocate couldn't hurt. Especially if that sponsor was Gino Ranno, who was connected from A to Z. Shpresa would never reveal the small crush she had on Gino. His quick wit and Sicilian charm were attractive to her and she was grateful for their close relationship.

Over the past five years they had not seen much of each other at industry functions. Gino was winding things down and then he had that two year thing with that *Kurvë* as Shpresa would call her, a slut, the biggest insult a woman can be called in Albanian. She was not happy with Gino's choices then but didn't judge him. She was more disappointed for Gino and his family but she still adored him. They kept in touch by e-mail and an occasional phone call to check in and see that everyone was doing well. Little did they know that the next time Shpresa called Gino it would be a matter of life and death.

7

Ilir Marku dispatched two of his men to Shpresa Metalia's home in Westchester County, to have her brought to his office. He would attend to the funeral arrangements later that afternoon with Frank Farenga at the Farenga Brothers Funeral Home on Allerton Avenue in the Bronx. Before he returned to his home in Scarsdale to break the news to his wife, his daughters, and the rest of the immediate family, he needed to see his daughter-in-law Valbona and inform her that her husband was dead.

From the time Ilir was a child in Albania his life was very difficult. Death was around him throughout his entire life. He saw killings from wars, street battles, assassinations, even killed himself many times, and ordered men to their deaths to get to his position of power, but he had no experience with the murder of his only son. A lesser man would have broken down but Ilir knew that he needed to be strong for the family and to protect his affairs. There was plenty of time to grieve. He was prepared to mourn his son for the rest of his days.

Shpresa and Rick were entertaining guests in their home when Rick's cell phone rang interrupting the evening. Rick took the call and after a few seconds of conversation in Albanian he turned ashen.

"Rick, this is Ilir Marku."

"Yes, Mr. Marku...ah how are you...ah how can I help you?" Rick answered awkwardly, never in a million years thinking that he would receive a call from this man.

"Rick, I need your help with a delicate matter. With all respect to you and to your family I need for your wife to come to my office. There has been a tragedy in my family. I would never impose upon you like this but the matter is urgent. With your permission I am sending a car for Shpresa now. She will be safe," Ilir Marku said in a serious and monotone manner.

"May I ask what this is about sir?" Rick was baffled as to what the tragedy could possibly be that Shpresa was needed at nearly midnight.

"I cannot discuss this now. Just know that I am grateful to you and you will soon understand why Shpresa is needed."

"Of course Mr. Marku. May I come along with her?"

"Best if you stayed at home my friend," Rick heard the telephone click and go silent.

Shpresa could see the strain on Rick's face.

"Rick, is everything all right? Honey you look..."

"Shpres, that was Mr. Marku. He needs you to go to his office right now. He wouldn't say the reason but said there was a tragedy."

"Oh no...It must be Valbona...the baby..." Shpresa gasped.

Before she could ask further the door bell rang. The two Marku men came to collect Shpresa. They were respectful and comforting to Rick and Shpresa.

"Mrs. Metalia, Mr. Marku asked that you come to his office as quickly as you can. A matter of great importance," the larger of the two oversized men said softly.

"Yes, I just spoke with him. Do you know what happened?" Rick responded.

"There has been an accident and Mrs. Metalia is needed now."

"Okay I will come; let me say goodnight to my guests." Shaken, Shpresa responded only in her mind which was going in a hundred directions. *What kind of accident? Is Valbona sick...the baby...a car accident? Oh my God, what could have happened?* She thought to herself as she made the motions of excusing herself and headed for the front door of her home to go with the Marku soldiers.

Rick knew he had no choice in the matter and felt helpless that he could not accompany his wife. He knew the best thing for him to do was remain calm and wait to hear from Shpresa.

Within the hour of Ilir Marku hearing the news of his son's death, Shpresa walked into the Marku office with the two men. Their entire ride had been silent. She knew better than to ask any questions of the pair just by their severe countenance. She entered Ilir Marku's office white as a sheet.

"My God, Mr. Marku what has happened?" Shpresa said with a trembling voice.

"My dear Shpresa, Fridays have always been a bad luck day for our people. Tonight my son....my Lekë was shot and killed not far from where we sit."

Shpresa felt her knees give way and she was caught by the two men who remained by her side. Ilir motioned to the sofa in his office and the men gently helped her onto it, while another man brought her water.

"Oh no...no...my... God how did this happen? Who would have done such a terrible thing?" Shpresa asked, her hands on her face.

"The important thing is that we now go see Valbona and bring this news to her. I thought you were best to join me," Ilir said ignoring her questions.

They drove together silently in a caravan of six vehicles. Ilir's bodyguards were on full alert in case there was a move against the clan by any enemy or opportunist that saw this as a moment to gain power.

As they entered the home on Esplanade using Ilir's key, Shpresa was trying to find the words to comfort her best friend, knowing that there were no words that could suffice. Valbona was still asleep, curled up with both hands around her large abdomen, cradling her unborn son. Shpresa sat softly on the bed next to her friend and gently touched her hair. Ilir stayed in the doorway, not to invade the women's privacy. His men encircled the home and two bodyguards waited in the living room. Valbona was startled and came awake quickly.

"Shpresa, what are you doing here? What time is it? Oh God I fell asleep? Lekë didn't come home we were supposed to-"

"Val, I am here with Mr. Marku. Please come out of the bedroom, he needs to speak with you." Shpresa's face was stone as she knew the job of telling Valbona the tragic news could only come from the eldest man in the family.

"What are you talking about? Is this a dream? My God where is my husband?" Valbona said wide eyed, looking from Ilir to Shpresa and back again.

Shpresa walked her friend into the living room of her home where Ilir stood waiting, his men waiting outside surrounding the home.

"*Nuse*, you must be strong now, you are carrying the blood of this family and you must have courage. Lekë was shot tonight. He is dead." Ilir Marku addressed her as his son's wife and spoke slowly so she could grasp the meaning of his words.

Valbona looked blankly at her father-in-law, without blinking, and then pleadingly to Shpresa, who held her hands to her own mouth. Ilir Marku had a look on his face she had never seen before. Her Lekë was dead. This was no dream.

The sound of her wailing sent shivers up the spines of the hardened Marku soldiers around the perimeter of the house. Ilir felt his blood surging in his head and walked from the living room into the bathroom to compose himself. Shpresa held and rocked the young widow in her arms and they began sobbing together uncontrollably. Shpresa's thoughts jumped to the baby as she futilely attempted to suppress Valbona's moaning and screaming that pierced her ear drums.

"Val the baby, honey you must think of the baby, please take deep breaths...someone bring me some water and call an ambulance," Shpresa called to a few of the men who had entered the house.

"Val you have to calm yourself for your son, please you must settle down," Shpresa asked her friend as she commanded the men in the next room.

"Get an ambulance and have Doctor Mastrangello called, now!"

Valbona's body began to shake uncontrollably and her screaming continued until her face was reddened and her screams became gasps for breath. Shpresa led her friend to the bedroom and back onto her bed. Suddenly Valbona felt a gush of water and pointed to Shpresa who saw the stains coming through her friend's sun dress.

"Jesus Christ where the fuck is the ambulance?" Shpresa screamed out but it was only a few minutes since she called for one.

"She's going into labor, fuck the ambulance let's get her to Einstein NOW!" Shpresa hollered at the top of her lungs.

Ilir Marku was paralyzed on the sofa in the living room, in shock from the events that were befalling his family. His men moved like lightening. One soldier picked Valbona off the bed like she was a small child and ran with her to a waiting car. Shpresa was by her side every moment. Ilir Marku was led to another car by his *kumar* Pashko Luli, his underboss, who just arrived at Esplanade from his home in Armonk. Luli would now take over the particulars for his boss and *probatin*, his blood brother from when they were children in Albania. He could never imagine that any God could have allowed this to happen to this family, to the man that he honored and respected as the leader of this clan.

They arrived at the emergency room of Einstein Hospital in less than four minutes. Traffic lights and stop signs were disregarded as was the rent-a-cop directing the caravan of cars to move out of the ambulance entrance. He was pushed aside and somehow knew he should not resist these swarthy, powerful men.

Dr. John Mastrangello arrived within thirty-five minutes of being paged by the Einstein Hospital ER. Valbona was already being prepped for a premature delivery in the maternity ward. The nurses could tell from the monitors and sounds on the fetal stethoscope that the baby was in distress. Valbona was catatonic and non-responsive, clearly in shock. Shpresa was exhausted and alone in the hallway with her hands in her hair, praying for her friend and the baby boy.

Dr. John did not like what he was seeing and wanted to have Valbona somewhat responsive and alert before he could determine if the baby should be taken. The obvious measures were being taken. Additional liquids were being pumped into the patient via IV, an oxygen mask was attached to Valbona almost from the moment she arrived, and the nurses rolled her on her left side as required in cases of fetal distress. Dr. John was trying to bring her back to reality by talking softly and reassuring her that he was there and everything would be fine. She did not respond. He had seen Shpresa in the hallway and asked the nurse to have her put into a surgical gown and mask and get into the operating room, stat.

"Shpresa, talk to her in Albanian please, tell her she will be fine and that the baby is okay. It would be better if she was conscious but I can take the baby anyway. Let's give it a try. It looks like I'm going to have to take the baby out soon from the looks of things."

"It's okay to take that mask off," Dr John instructed Shpresa in a calm voice.

"Of course Doctor, anything, anything you say," Shpresa said taking a deep breath and composing herself.

She leaned down so that her mouth was almost touching her friend's right ear.

"Valbona, my dearest friend. I am here with you. Everything will be fine. The baby is good but he wants to come out and see his mommy and his *teze* Shpres and the world. You know that there is nothing for you to worry about. You and he will be taken care of for the rest of your lives and you will be happy with this baby boy. He needs you to be strong so you can help Doctor John. Val, wake now and be brave. I love you my sister."

Nothing. No response. Shpresa tried again talking about when they were girls and how they pretended to make tea for their fathers and how much fun they had torturing their high school teachers. Still nothing. One of the fetal monitors suddenly made a shrill noise and Dr. John asked Shpresa to leave and began giving instructions to the other doctors and the nurses that were attending to Valbona Marku and her baby.

The baby that was to be called Agron Marku was taken by Caesarian section from his mother but did not survive the trauma. As much as Dr. John tried, the baby was non-responsive. He needed to attend to his patient and do everything he could to save her life. It would take over one hour to stabilize Valbona and for Dr. John to meet with Ilir Marku and pass on the dreadful news.

Shpresa stood behind Ilir Marku as Dr. John approached them in one of the waiting rooms. The Marku bodyguards were trying to be inconspicuous lining the corridor of the maternity ward.

"Mr. Marku, your daughter-in-law will be fine. Unfortunately I could not save the baby. I am terribly, terribly sorry. I did everything possible to save him."

Shpresa gasped and crying softly she slowly crouched down until her knees were both on the floor.

Mr. Marku did not reply to the doctor. He turned and walked out of the waiting room and looking up to the ceiling said, *"Kush, a fiki Deren."* The light has been taken from my life.

8

The news of any death in the Albanian community travels very rapidly. The news of the death of Ilir Marku's son Lekë and his unborn son moved at the speed of light. As is their tradition, any time of the day or night when a death is reported, the Albanians rush to the house to pay their initial respects. Unlike any condolence call that most Americans are accustomed to there are rules of etiquette that must be followed that have been used for centuries in Albania. These customs are followed by even the most liberal of Albanian families. In times of strife and sorrow the Albanian people come together as one. They have century upon century of practice.

The crowds that converged on the Marku estate in Scarsdale were enormous. Into the thousands the procession of people, friends, business associates and family to the "seventh blood" came to show solidarity and respect for the deceased and the family. For the Markus, this rush to the home would take days.

Upon entering the house the line of men, dressed in muted colors, from the eldest to the youngest male, consisting of the father, uncles and cousins can be as many as fifty to seventy. This is followed by a line of women all wearing scarves to cover their heads in respect for the deceased. The line begins outside the home where usually shoes are left before entering, but in this case, because of the sheer mass of people attending, this tradition is forgiven. In general it can take an hour to get through the hand shaking and the verbal offering of "May God leave you in peace" or "May God give you strength," while the visitors place their right hand over their heart in a show of reverence.

Long tables of Raki and feta cheese and olives are offered. The people do not come to eat but rather to mourn along with the family. Trays of a variety of cigarettes are offered as well as coffee with no sugar. The guests are still guests in the home and are treated according to the precept of the *Kanun*. "May we return this visit with you for a happy occasion," or something to that effect is told to virtually every visitor as a sign of the family's honor and respect to their visitors.

In front of the line, like a lion, stood Ilir Marku, unshaven, his eyes black with grief and the awaiting vengeance that needed to be taken on the murderers of his son and grandson. Ukë Marku continued his Operetta and continued to wail about his cousin's death. Unshaven and slovenly, Ukë made sure everyone knew how despondent he was. He made sure his drama continued until he collapsed and had to be taken to a bedroom and attended to by a physician who came to pay respects at the Marku home.

"It should have been me! Lekë was about to become a father and he leaves a wife. Now the baby is dead because of these animals. I will not rest; I will never rest until the blood is avenged."

The *Kanun* is clear about how the killer of Lekë is responsible for the death of his child. A story is told about two men who were arguing and brandishing weapons. A pregnant woman tried to intervene and mediate the argument to no avail. The two men fired their guns but no one was hurt. The men left and the woman returned to her house where she then gave birth to a stillborn child. The men in her household went to demand satisfaction after the woman told them why she believed the baby died. The elders of the clan were asked to give a judgment but could not agree on which way to rule.

The most experienced elder took his colleagues to a milk shed, where there was a pail in which cream had risen to the top and was undisturbed. The elders all agreed that the cream was undisturbed. The first elder closed the milk shed, walked a short distance away and fired two pistol shots. When they entered the shed again they found the cream and the milk had completely mixed in the pail. The elder stated, "A pregnant woman is like the cream of the milk." The elders agreed that the shock of the shots led to the frightening of the mother, leading to the child's death. The men were held responsible for murder.

Joey Jr. Santoro was liable for the murder of Lekë and his son.

It would be days before the *Pamje*, or the memorial meeting after a wake would be held for Lekë and his son. The medical examiner needed time to do their investigation into the homicide and then confer with Detective Lieutenant Carlo Del Greco and his staff. In the interim, the mourning process continued day and night. Lekë died late Friday night, the baby early the next morning. It would not be until Wednesday that the *hater* would be held with burial the next day.

Del Greco had an All Points Bulletin circulated for the apprehension of Joey Jr. Santoro and his side-kicks as persons of interest in the killing of Lekë Marku. No evidence except for the testimony of Ukë Marku and the two Albanian toughs tied them to the murder. Del Greco was hoping that he would get to Joey Jr. and his crew first to fulfill his promise to his benefactor Ilir Marku. Either way this Santoro kid was dead meat, he thought, so his conscience was clear in helping to satisfy his friends.

There was however some evidence about the crime scene that troubled him. More importantly his sixth sense was gnawing at him telling him something was amiss with this murder. He needed time and needed to do more homework so he could at least look at himself in the mirror when he shaved. He did lots of underhanded things but none of them amounted to anyone getting murdered. Providing confidential police information, tampering with evidence, working with his pals in narcotics to help the Markus was one thing but murder was taking things to the next level and not giving him the warm and fuzzy.

Del Greco began working the evidence gathered at the scene and studied the interrogations of Ukë, Zef, and the two Albanian nationals.

Shpresa left the hospital at six o'clock in the morning with Valbona still in a state of shock. Val was unaware of her surroundings and had not yet realized that her baby was no longer inside her. The worst was yet to come for her best friend she thought as she left her in the loving care of her grief stricken mothers and aunts.

Rick waited for Shpresa to make the visit to the Marku estate. She was exhausted both physically and mentally from the experience she just lived through but her sense of obligation kept her going. The Marku home was only a few minutes away from their home and Rick just listened to his wife as she told him of the horrible events that occurred. When they arrived Ilir's men ushered them to the front of the receiving line. Again the emotions were almost unbearable as she faced Ilir and saw the misery lines that were now etched in his face. As they progressed down the line of Marku family men they could not help but hear the sobbing of Ukë Marku.

In the mid 1400s in Albania, when Skanderbeg died, the men pounded their chests and scratched their faces to demonstrate the pain they were suffering at the loss of their great leader. This was a practice that was still followed for funerals in obscure villages in Northern Albania but not at all followed among Albanian-Americans. This was far too arcane for the modern world in which they were living.

But Ukë was indeed pounding on his chest, pacing up and down the receiving line and swearing that he would avenge the death of his two cousins. His eyes were wild with the terror that he was pleading to perform. Ukë was not shy about mentioning the name of the person who took Lekë's life and indirectly the life of the baby boy.

"I will kill this fucking Joey Santoro and his two fucking pieces of shit pig pals. I will hunt them down and kill them where they breathe. Nothing will stop me...nothing," Ukë was saying to anyone who would listen in what seemed like a speech for everyone to hear. A few times when Ilir Marku heard his nephew invoking *Gjakmarrja* and raging about justice he asked Pashko to settle the young man down, telling him this was not the time or place for such behavior.

"Rick, is he saying that Joey Santoro was the murderer? Oh my God I know that guy. I leased him an apartment as a favor to Gino Ranno. Gino is like an uncle to that kid. What the fuck? What do I do?"

"You need to tell Gino but be careful that we don't look disloyal to our own people Shpresa. This is not going to go down easy," Rick said, and his advice to his wife was right on point.

"I'll call Gino when we get home. I don't even know what day it is? I really need a shower and some sleep Rick, if I can ever sleep again."

Rick let her know it was Saturday and just after eight o'clock in the morning. They drove back to Eastchester in silence, each with their own thoughts reviewing the tragic events that occurred in their community. Things would never be the same in their lives.

9

Even though he had stayed up until after two o'clock in the morning and the Mister Softee jingle kept playing over and over in his head for almost an hour, Gino was up and having coffee with Ellen by eight a.m. Ellen had already been out to get fresh bagels and lox and three different kinds of cream cheeses, and the great crumb cake from B & G Bakery in Hackensack for breakfast for the men. Gino laughed thinking they wouldn't be awake until nearly noon. She had that covered also and was planning on serving leftover sauce and meatballs and everyone's favorite raviolis from Borgotti's on East 187th Street. When it came to food the Rannos were most particular. What a great wife, Gino thought when the phone rang and startled them both. Gino answered, and it was Shpresa.

"Honey what's the matter, you sound awful, what's wrong?" Gino could tell she was stressed to the maximum.

"Oh, Gino there is big, big trouble here and you need to know what has happened. Ilir Marku's son Lekë was killed in a shoot-out yesterday... it's awful."

"Jesus Christ Shpresa I had no idea."

"The story gets worse. Lekë's wife went into shock and lost the baby. There is a problem for you in this but please you have to behave like I didn't call you. Please I am begging you on this."

"Honey, you are like my blood, tell me what's going on."

"They are saying that your nephew, Joey, the one I rented an apartment to, is the killer."

"Oh my God. The kid is screwed up but I can't see him doing this." Gino sat down on a chair in the kitchen while signaling a curious Ellen to be quiet.

"Ilir's nephew, that psycho Ukë, witnessed the murder. Gino they are calling for *Gjakmarrja*," Shpresa said in a whisper, as if someone could overhear her.

"Honey, what the hell is that?" Gino asked

"It is the taking back of blood, blood retribution against all of the men in Joey's family. His father, his brother, anyone they can get their hands on will be killed for sure. What you Sicilians call a vendetta."

"Where is the kid now? What do I need to do?" Gino said feeling his adrenaline soaring and his heart beat faster.

"I have no idea and I couldn't tell you even if I knew. I would be betraying the Markus. The Albanians are rushing to Mr. Marku's home. There will be a *Hater*—I'm sorry, a wake—for Lekë and the baby on Wednesday, then they will be buried. After that there will be hell to pay for Joey and two of his friends," Shpresa said with sincere sadness in her voice.

"Okay Shpresa, we never spoke, don't even tell your father. If Rick knows you are calling tell him not to repeat a word. I will do what I have to do on my end."

"Gino, please do me a big favor, okay?" Shpresa asked holding back the last tears she had left.

"What honey? Anything for you."

"Gino...be careful." Shpresa hung up and cried into her hands.

Gino's mind went into overdrive. He had to sit for a few minutes and think things out and compose himself. Ellen could surmise what was going on from hearing the one-sided conversation and just waited for her husband to react. She was stunned as much as Gino.

"Ellen, things are going to be rough for a while around here. Be patient and do whatever I ask of you okay?"

"Of course, you know I'm here for you Gino, just don't get too involved. You always make others people's problems your own. How many times have I told you that?" Ellen warned.

"I am involved. This is my problem. This is family," Gino tried to say as gently as he could but it still came out a bit harsh.

"I understand, just be careful all right?"

"You are the second woman in five minutes to give me that warning. I appreciate it. Now I have to break the news to Joe. Oh boy!" Gino inhaled deeply and headed for the guest room where Joey was sound asleep.

Gino knocked on the door and Joey Clams responded fast.

"What's up?" Joey said with some alarm in his voice.

"Joey, get dressed we have a headache. Coffee is ready," Gino replied to his friend and proceeded to wake C.C. and Babbu in the same manner.

In a few minutes all four men were in the kitchen and fixing the coffee their way. Ellen made herself scarce, more out of fear that she would break down than being the old fashioned Sicilian wife. They stood in the kitchen and Gino broke the news to all three but addressed Joey.

"Joe, I just got a call from a friend of mine. It seems that that Albanian wise-guy Marku's son was shot dead yesterday in the Bronx. They are blaming Joey Jr. as the shooter. It's not good." Gino did not beat around the bush.

"What! How the fuck did this happen? Where is my son?" Joey asked.

"No idea. The only information that I have is that they are looking for Jr. and two of his pals and no one in your family is safe."

"Fuck that Gino, I need to find the kid." Joey put his coffee cup down and started for the kitchen door.

"No. You sit down and listen to me," Gino said as C.C. grabbed Joey by his arm to slow his down.

Gino continued, "I will go to the Bronx right now and see what's going on. I have to call a dear friend and find out what steps need to be taken. He's a well respected Albanian and we will be guided by his advice. We need to keep cool, level headed and take the right steps. Understand?"

"Christ Gino, when will this ever end?" Joey asked.

"When we close our eyes pal. They are your kids for life. Good or bad, they are your blood. Now relax here with C.C. Pete will come with me and I will call you when I know more. Just two things you have to do. Call your son Matty and tell him to stay put and you stay right here. Give me your word," Gino commanded.

"Okay, you got my word," Joey said meekly.

Just then Joey Clams' cell phone rang with a distinctive musical rendition of a "Meringue." The caller I.D. Joey read Jr.

"Jr., are you okay?"

"Yeah Pop what's up?"

"What's up? That's what you ask, what's up? They are saying you killed this guy!" Joey Clams blurted out.

"Pop, I was there Yeah but I never killed nobody. I don't even have a freaking gun," Jr. replied.

"Where are you now?" the elder Santoro asked.

Gino interrupted, "Don't talk on the phone, and don't ask him any more questions."

Joey Jr. heard Gino and knew better than to give a destination.

"He's right pop. Right now I'm safe. Up north somewhere. I called to see if Uncle Gino could help me out with this."

Joey put his son on the cell with Gino.

"Jr., I'm just going to tell you one thing. Everything you tell me has to be the truth. I don't want to hear any bullshit, no lies no manipulation. Whatever I ask you I want one hundred percent truth. I can't help you if you lie to me. Do you understand me?"

"But Uncle Gino-"

"Jr., do you understand what I am saying to you? This is not some chicken shit drug game. This is life and death. Do you fucking understand me or not?"

"Yes Uncle Gino."

"Okay. Did you pop this guy, yes or no?"

"No."

"Did one of your boys pop this guy, yes or no?"

"No."

"Then who did? The guy is dead so somebody killed him," Gino asked dispassionately.

"Unc it was on a roof. It was so dark you couldn't see shit. Three of these Albanian dudes started shooting at us over bullshit. I had two of my friends with me. They fired back, one of my guys was hit in the shoulder. He's okay. We ran outta' there and they were still shooting," Jr. said.

"Could one of your guys have hit this guy?"

"I doubt it. Look, I got blood and shit all over me and it wasn't my boy so I have no idea where it came from. Maybe he was shot accidently by his own people, I don't know...all's I know is I did not shoot no-body period."

"Let me guess. Drugs were involved? Did you try to rip them off?" Gino asked.

"No fuckin' way Uncle Gino. This wacko Ukë started a beef over nothin', we had the money they had the shit. Straight up."

"You're slurring your words Jr."

"Yeah, I'm just tired."

"What did I say about lying to me Jr.," Gino snapped.

"Sorry. I'm a little high Uncle Gino, I need help. Can you help me?"

"I'm reaching out to see what needs to be done. In the meantime if you are in a safe place stay there. Don't call anyone. Tell your momo friends not to call anyone. We have your number. Keep your phone charged and stay inside. Can you do that?"

"Yeah, I have a charger in my car, otherwise we will stay in."

"Say good-bye to your father and get off the phone quick."

Gino handed the phone to his friend and turned toward the door.

"So, Pete, I'll drive," Gino said to his cousin. Joey Clams told his son he loved him and hit the red button.

"Gino, one thing though...please be careful," Joey warned.

"Christ Almighty, another careful warning. That's three this morning. *Madonna Mio*, everyone is a friggin' crossing guard today," he said over his shoulder as he made his way to his garage. He didn't even take the time to kiss Ellen. He knew, or at least he hoped, she would understand.

From his cell phone Gino called the home of his oldest Albanian friend Hamdi Nezaj. Gino respected Hamdi and knew that he would get the proper information that he needed to try to sort out this mess. Hamdi was a client of Gino's but more important a true friend. Gino and Ellen were at two of the Nezaj children's weddings and got a real taste of the Albanian culture. They were both enchanted by it and Ellen felt a familiarity with these people. After all, half of her heritage was *Arberesh* so the civilization was in her blood.

Hamdi was at his home in Armonk, and agreed to meet Gino at his basement office in one of the buildings he owned in the Bronx. Hamdi knew what the call from Gino was about and wanted to keep their meeting only between them. This was a very smart move as the Albanian community was on high alert.

10

Detective Lieutenant Carlo Del Greco was in his office at Bronx Homicide staring at the ceiling deep in thought when Detective First Class Jimmy Gojcaj tapped on his window and walked into the room.

"You looked stressed out Lieutenant, what's eating you?" the Albanian-born Gojcaj asked.

"Is it me? Something just does not smell right on this Marku case. It's been eating at me for two days."

"Like what?" Gojcaj asked

"Like how, if they were facing each other and shooting straight in that direction, how did the Marku kid get it on the side of his head, more toward the back of his skull and with two shots? And what about the powder burns on his hair? Were they just a few feet away from each other? If someone was shooting at me I would have the sense to duck and cover. What am I missing Detective?" Del Greco asked.

"Yeah that occurred to me too. But Ukë Marku saw it happen. When I spoke to the two Albanians they kept saying they couldn't see anything, it was too dark on the roof. Also, the perps ran and are on the lam. Makes them look bad, no?" the young cop asked.

"Listen, pretend you are involved in whatever the fuck they were involved with. I don't buy that they were up there to smoke pot like they all said. Christ, you can smell pot on every block in the Bronx. They were up there because they were up to no good. So whatever they were doing, this Santoro kid and his pals ran because he has a nice rap sheet for petty stuff and he doesn't want to get busted and do a year on Rikers' on a gun or narcotics rap. Wouldn't you run if you were in a shootout with a Marku? I would run back to Naples for Christ's sake. And if it was so dark how in the fuck did Ukë see the shooter but the super and the foreigners didn't?"

"You got a point there."

"Okay, let me ask you something else. How did the Albanians seem to you? You know, the two from the other side. How did they react to questioning?" Del Greco was fishing.

"Pretty cool customers those two. They both had an identical story; they both said they were trying to get a work visa so they could start as house painters or porters. They had no idea why they were on the roof, and saw nothing after the shooting started."

"Coached perhaps?" Del Greco was now staring intently into the eyes of Gojcaj.

"Maybe, just maybe, yeah. These guys were ice cold. If I just saw someone killed, even if I never saw them in my life I think I might have been a bit rattled. Certainly more nervous than these two. You bring up a great point Lieutenant."

"That's why my pay grade is so high," he said with a laugh. "Let's get those two mutts in here again and bring that super in also. I want to see what else they have. I'm off for a couple days, taking my gal to the beach, the Hamptons. Bring them in after the Marku funeral on Thursday."

11

Gino Ranno left his cousin Babbu in his car outside of Hamdi Nezaj's building. The old friends met and kissed and embraced in the hallway of the building with somber faces, both knowing the difficulty and severity of the situation.

"My dear friend Hamdi, I wish that our meeting would have been for more of a festive occasion," Gino began.

"Gino my friend, I have prepared coffee for you, please join me inside my office."

Hamdi's office was a portal to the past. No computer on the desk, no creature comforts, nothing to show the significant wealth that the man had amassed since his arrival in the United States almost forty years ago. His old school mentality and his belief in the ways of his ancestors made him a man of honor and respect in the Albanian community. His word was his bond, his *besa*, and was above reproach as was his interpretation of the *Kanun* in a fast changing world.

"Gino, this young man who killed the Marku is your nephew?"

"He is my best friend's son. I am his uncle out of respect for the friendship that his father and I have. Yes, I consider him my nephew."

"So he is not your blood?" Hamdi asked almost in a whisper.

"No he is not," Gino replied looking deeply into his friend's eyes.

"I am glad for that blessing for you and your children. Gino, this thing that is called a *Gjakmarrja* in my language is the most serious of all oaths. Nothing can prevent the Marku family from taking back the blood that was spilled. There is no money, no property, no sympathy, there is nothing to prevent the death of this boy and maybe even the other male members of his family. Your friend himself is in great danger. It is written and it will not go away."

"Hamdi, I spoke to this boy a short while ago. I know this boy. Yes he is involved with drugs and yes he has a troubled life but he is not a killer. He did not shoot and kill this man. He has no gun and his past crimes were never serious. Stupid perhaps but never would he take a life. He tells me he's innocent of this horrible act and did not even know that the Marku boy was dead when he fled the scene. I believe him."

"Lekë Marku's cousin witnessed the murder." Hamdi raised his open hands indicating that the testimony was enough for the Markus.

"Perhaps when they were shooting at one another the boy was accidently shot?" Gino was clutching at straws.

"They are not burying an accident Gino, they are burying a murdered man and his murdered baby. The end of Ilir Marku's family. This crime is unforgivable and must be avenged."

"Hamdi, in this country a man is innocent until proven guilty. There is no proof other than the word of this cousin that my nephew killed this boy. He should have a fair trial to determine if he is guilty or innocent."

"Gino, we are not in this country. The country has no say in this. The police have no say in this. The religion has no say in this. The law here has no say in this. What must be done will be done. How far and how deep into this boy's family the *Gjakmarrja* will go is up to the Marku family and no one else. I'm sorry."

"Hamdi, tell me what can be done," Gino asked.

"Nothing can be done."

Gino clasped his hands together as if in prayer and paused.

"Can I meet with the family? Can I bring the boy's father, can I bring my godfather to speak on this boy's behalf and explain our position with all respect? You know that my family is respected in this world. I am asking as a friend."

"I'm telling you it will do no good. For you I will mediate a meeting with Ilir. You may bring whom you like. I will get the promise from the Markus that you will all be safe for this meeting but there is no offering that can be made that will not insult the family. Do you understand that Gino?"

"I do, yes I understand."

"Go home and wait for my call. I will wait until after the funeral to approach the father. I can make no promises but I will try for you. I will try to get his *besa,* his word of honor on this meeting," Hamdi said as he stood to say goodbye.

"Gino, please for the sake of your family be careful with this. You are playing with a loaded gun my friend," Hamdi said as he held Gino's hands in his own.

Gino thought, Again with the 'be careful;' I get it, I'll be careful.

"Thank you my friend. I am in your debt." The words just came out of Gino and he knew they were not appropriate.

"You owe me nothing Gino. You only owe your sons their father and your wife her husband," Hamdi said firmly.

As he always did in the past, Hamdi walked Gino to his car and kissed him on both cheeks. This time however, Hamdi was not smiling.

"How'd you make out cuz?" Babbu asked when Gino got behind the wheel and started the car.

"We are in a different world Pete. I feel like we are caught in the ninth century. We are way out of our league here." Gino's stomach was in a knot as he tried to get his bearings and get out of the Bronx and head toward Manhattan.

"Jesus Gino, you don't look so good, what are you gonna do?" Babbu asked with a look that was comically quizzical.

"Only one thing to do cuz. We have to go see *Zio* Carmine. Let's get out of here and get into the city." Gino used his cell phone to dial his Uncle Carmine Miceli Senior as they drove toward Bruckner Boulevard. But he would have to wait until the next day, he was told, until Sunday to see the Don.

Uncle Carmine had just came from The Church of St. Ignatius Loyola on Park Avenue where he attended a morning mass. Carmine didn't miss mass on Sunday anymore and enjoyed the walk to his townhouse on East 79th Street. The five block walk in the fresh air did him good, his two bodyguards walking closely behind as his driver coasted nearby in a black sedan along the storied avenue. Gino and Babbu were waiting in front of his home when Carmine Sr. spotted them as he turned right on Park Avenue. His broad white smile showed his happiness at seeing his godson. He opened his arms to embrace Gino and then Babbu.

"What a treat. I get to see you a lot recently. You should have come earlier; we could have had breakfast with me and gone to mass. I bet you guys don't go to church any more right?" the elder mob boss asked. It always amazed Gino how the wise guys found their way back to the church in their latter years as if they were looking for a loophole, an angle with God himself.

"You know how it is Uncle Carmine, I usually play golf on Sunday with my regular foursome. No time for church when you're trying to make a buck on the course." Gino laughed with his godfather as the joke went right over Babbu's head.

"Come inside, let's have some *demitasse* and anisette, what d 'ya say? Like me and your papa did years ago." Carmine was beaming.

"Sure *Zio*, that would be great," Gino said.

The old man knew there was a reason for the visit from his godson so he sent Babbu on an errand.

"Peter, go with my driver to Rocco's Pastry Shop down Bleeker and tell them I want an assortment, they know what to send. Then we all can have a nice dessert."

Babbu was tickled to run down to the old neighborhood for Carmine and rushed into the waiting car.

Carmine Sr. was moving slower these days; each step seemed deliberate, almost planned. His strength seemed to be diminishing a bit each day and the once powerful of all mob bosses was just another old man waiting for his time to die. Hopefully he would die peacefully and naturally; that was the reason for the security detail that Carmine Jr. selected and insisted upon.

"So godson, you look a bit worried. Don't bring bad news about your household to me please. I thought you outgrew this by now." The Don was referring to Gino's near divorce a couple of years prior.

"*Zio* Carmine, yes that is behind me thank you. I have another headache. My *gumbada* Joey Santoro, you remember him from the old days and when he helped me with the trouble I had out on Long Island, yes?" Gino asked.

"Of course I do Gino, he was always around you when you were kids. I knew his uncle very well. Stand up guy Joey and his uncle Vito."

"Well, it seems that his son got mixed up with some bad things with drugs, Uncle, but that is not the worst of it. The kid, who is like a nephew to me as you know, is being blamed for shooting and killing Ilir Marku's son up in the Bronx. The kid swears he's innocent. I believe him. My friends in the Albanian world tell me they will kill this boy and his brother and my *gumbada* Joey and nothing can be done to stop it. This is how they live. Eye-for-an eye and that's it." Gino felt as if he was rambling.

"Gino, first of all, why do you believe the word of a drug dealer, drug addict, and I don't know what else?" The old man asked while lighting a Churchill cigar in his study.

"I know the kid has problems but I know this kid. Never would he use violence like this. He is what you say but his background is all petty stuff, nothing too serious," Gino said.

"So now you tell me drug dealing is not serious? I'm surprised at you Gino."

"Please don't misunderstand me *Zio*. He is a problem. I spoke with him by phone today. He's scared, he's confused, but he didn't shoot this Marku kid, on that I would bet my life. Joey Jr. didn't even have a gun *Zio mio*. Maybe someone else shot this guy or maybe he's being set up, I don't know. All I know is that he could not have killed." Gino was pleading his flimsy case.

"Look Gino, these Albanians are very serious people. We have worked with them for many years. We have lived with them with no real trouble except when one of their bad seeds killed a friend of ours' son. That was a bad time and we want to go forward not backward. I know Ilir Marku; he is a very tough cookie and is by the book when it comes to this stuff. Talking to him will not help. Best we can do is hide the kid in the old country and the same with the rest of the family but even then they are not safe. I think you need to tell them this is the best they can expect."

"*Zio*, I want to go and speak with Mr. Marku. I have a friend that will see that I am safe as a condition of honor. I want them to understand this is not the person who they think killed their son."

"Gino, all I can do is send a message to Marku that you are with me and you need to have his time. I will send Carmine Jr. with you to show him that I am sincere. You are wasting your time here. They must have *sangue per sangue come in Sicilia*. You know this from your own family history. Blood for blood, nothing can change this, nothing."

"I would appreciate the message to Mr. Marku. Coming from you he will know that I treat this matter with respect. This is more than I can ask from you *Zio* Carmine," Gino said and kissed his uncle's hand.

"One more thing Gino. Be careful with this. This is very dangerous waters that your boat is in. For me, and for your family, be careful."

Here we go again with the 'be careful' stuff. I guess I better be careful, Gino thought.

They talked about the old times, in Sicily and New York, the families and friends, good times and bad. After a short while Babbu returned with a large stringed box of pastries and the three men enjoyed their time together. Gino's mind was racing in a hundred directions.

12

Farenga Brothers Funeral Home has not ever been known to have ample parking for its visitors. They were and still are to some degree the funeral parlor of choice for Italians that lived in the Bronx and Manhattan for many years. They are now one of the funeral homes that cater to the needs of the Albanian community. As the population in the Bronx changed so did the venerable Farenga Brothers.

The Tuesday after Lekë Marku was murdered and his infant son died at birth the funeral home collected the remains from the coroner and the Einstein Hospital morgue to prepare for one of the most heart wrenching wakes in the history of the Albanian community. Lekë never said if he wanted to be buried in the United States or in Albania. Without an *Amanet*, a death oath promise that would be made by a friend and family member, Lekë and the baby son he had never met would be buried alongside each other, in separate coffins in a cemetery in Valhalla, New York. They would not be returned to Albania.

Valbona was beginning to recognize her mother and aunts at the hospital but would not be attending the wake or the funeral for her husband or son. She had still not grasped that her world was in pieces. The doctors felt it best to continue sedation and to gently wean her away until she was strong enough to cope with reality.

The throngs of visitors that visited the Marku home to pay their respects were ascending on Allenton Avenue for the one day viewing. Visitors were parked as much as fifteen blocks away. Some parked illegally and decided to take the parking tickets rather than aggravate themselves driving around in a futile attempt to find a nearby spot. The police were told to be lenient issuing summonses and several patrol cars were dispatched from the Four-Nine Precinct House to manage pedestrian and vehicular traffic near Farenga's.

The immediate Marku family arrived at one in the afternoon and prepared to meet visitors for the entire day and evening. Ilir Marku's men were strategically positioned in and around the funeral home as the possibility always existed for a person with a blood feud against the Marku family to take action in a public setting. It was unlikely as that person or persons would also immediately forfeit their lives but Mr. Marku's protectors remained vigilant.

As at the home the reception line began with Ilir Marku's father who was flown in from Albania to attend the funeral, followed by Ilir and the rest of the many male relatives that would greet the guests as they had at the estate. The long line of women family members, all standing with their heads covered in scarves, followed behind the row of men. The procession would take nearly a half hour to complete and the visitors would be waiting on a line that snaked around the block. No one would complain about the hours' long wait in the hot and humid Bronx streets.

The two caskets were placed with the bodies angled head-to-head to each other. Lekë's coffin was open, the baby's, thankfully, was closed with a male cousin standing sentry at the head and foot of both of their dead relatives. The four young men were the only males in the extended viewing room where every seat and every foot of available standing room was taken by crying and weeping women, all with heads shrouded, all wearing muted colors.

A woman who is known as a *Vajtore* expressed the life of Lekë and lamented over the possible life of the baby in song. This *Vajtim* could reduce the strongest willed person into a sobbing wreck. The singing is only in Albanian and done only a few lines at a time so that new visitors can hear the song of grief. The *Vajtore* also would stop if the weeping became overwhelming and begin again when the mourners quieted down. In this case there was no seam to the hysteria.

The *Vajtore* began her lamentation in a strong and beautiful voice filled with emotion.

"Lekë wake up your father and mother are here to see you...what are you doing lying there...get up and kiss them and show them baby Agron." That alone was enough to make several women pass out; the smelling salts were at the ready. When things calmed down she continued her work.

"Lekë, get up you are the only son of the Marku family. Your family is crying for you Lekë. Your three sisters are here to kiss you and hold you... oh Lekë, how anyone could hurt you is terrible. You are a good man who always smiled and worked hard for the family." Again, the sobbing reached a crescendo. Occasionally a family member, caught up in the moment, would also lend their voice to the *Vajtim*.

"Lekë you are leaving your beloved nephews and nieces behind you are their only *Daje* so how can you go?" A *Daje* is an uncle from the mother's side.

The *Vajtim* tore at the hearts of the family and friends alike and went on and on into the night. The family remained at the receiving line holding their honor in place.

Ukë Marku, the cause of all of the sadness and grief, in his quest for power, played the wake for all it was worth. It became like a stage for his histrionics. Several times during the day, Pashko Luli noticed the still unshaven and unkempt Ukë carrying on and taking his hysteria a bit too far. Still pounding his face and pulling at his face and hair, Ukë had to be reminded to keep his talk of *Gjakmarrja* to himself. This was not his place and not honorable. Pashko at first thought that the young man was acting poorly because of the trauma of seeing his first cousin murdered in front of him. Now the underboss was beginning to have second thoughts but kept them to himself. Thinking that Ukë could have been involved with Lekë's death was not at all possible. In fact, it was unthinkable.

Platters of cigarettes were offered to the men who smoked in a special room or outside on the street while they heard the *Vajtore* singing of Lekë's life and the women in the viewing room continue their abundant wailing. In general this kind of outpouring of grief would wear on the men and they would look forward to leaving quickly but this time was different. The funeral home was devoid of flowers as the Marku family was very specific that any monies that would be spent on flowers should be contributed to the villages and towns in need of help in the homeland.

The next morning, the funeral procession left Farenga Brothers promptly at nine. The ride to Valhalla took just about an hour with over a hundred vehicles escorted by New York City and County of Westchester police cars and motorcycles.

The coffins were carried to the grave site by male family members with assistance and direction of funeral home personnel. The somber feeling at the cemetery was made even sadder by the continued sobbing of the women. Just as in the Marku home and at the funeral parlor the receiving lines were in place and the procession of handshakes and embracing was done once again. The platters of cigarettes were also offered at the end of the line of grieving women. The gravesite prayers were minimal and an announcement was made in Albanian by Pashko Luli.

"I have been asked by the Marku family to represent them and speak on their behalf. The unjust blood that was spilled and the death of these two clan members will not go un-avenged. The *Gjakmarrja* is open and will continue. We will not rest until those responsible for these two deaths are brought to justice, on this we swear upon our honor. Let it be known that these deaths will only be settled with blood. The family invites everyone to join us at the Eastwood Manor directly after the services." The *probatin* of Ilir Marku then led the crowd to their vehicles.

The funeral repast was held in the very same room at the Eastwood where Lekë and Valbona celebrated their wedding day.

13

Joey Jr. and his two drug addict buddies were holed up in a Days Inn in Newburgh, New York, a bit over sixty miles north of the murder scene. Jimmy was feeding both his alcohol and drug addiction with a McDonalds Big Mac as a chaser and Dennis was nursing the boo-boo on his shoulder with Oxycontin that they procured from their friendly EMT buddy. Joey was doing exactly what he was told probably for the first time in his life. Laying low and keeping his big mouth shut. The realization that the entire Albanian population in the United States was probably out looking for him and his junkie friends kept them from leaving the hotel room to go to the nearby titty bars of the rough and tumble town of Newburgh. The hotel, nestled between Routes 84 and 87 was perfect for a quick escape if the need arose. They could flee west on Route 84 into Pennsylvania, or east into Connecticut or jump on Route 87 north and go long to Canada. South on Route 87 was not an option. In their minds south took them back to the Albanians and sudden death.

The day after the funeral Detective Del Greco had his detectives from Bronx Homicide pick up Ukë Marku and the hear-no-evil, see-no-evil, speak-no-English Engjëll and Gjergj for further questioning. They were brought to their squad room at Bronx Homicide Headquarters. Detective Del Greco and Detective Gojcaj were prepared to lean hard on the Albanians but in the back of his mind the senior detective knew that Ukë was a protected species. He would question Ukë himself almost as a formality in deference to his benefactor, the grieving Ilir Marku.

Gojcaj took Engjëll into a small interrogation room and brought along his Turkish coffee maker for effect. The men chatted about the old country in a friendly fashion but Engjëll was savvy enough to know he was being set up for a rough time. After a while of pleasantries the interrogation in Albanian began.

"So Engjëll my friend, what did you see on that rooftop when poor Lekë was shot?" Gojcaj asked to get warmed up.

"Nothing, nothing at all. It was too dark to see," the Albanian responded looking into his coffee cup.

"Did you see shots fired?"

"Yes of course but I could not tell who was firing."

"Did you fire back Engjëll?"

"How could I without a gun?"

"Just answer my question. Did you fire back and at whom?"

"The punk kid who killed Lekë was firing and I did not shoot back."

"So you did have a gun?"

"No I had no gun."

"How do you know if the punk kid was shooting if you could not see because of the dark Engjëll?"

"I guess it was him who was firing. The gun was going off and we jumped to hide from the bullets," Engjëll said, shifting in his seat and looking now at Detective Gojcaj.

"So you hid from the bullets and you saw Lekë hit?"

"No, I did not see Lekë hit, but it had to be the punk American, who else could it be?"

"Well now let me see. It could have been you. It could have been Gjergj, he seems a little bit off to me, no? It could have been, perhaps Ukë. Or the two other American punks, yes?" Detective Gojcaj asked.

"Well...well yes, I mean no. It could not have been me or Gjergj or Ukë... we did not have guns," the wide eyed Albanian answered.

"So you stabbed one of them then?"

"Stabbed, what stabbed? What are you saying stabbed?" Engjëll was losing his cool.

"Fucking stabbed like with a knife is how people get stabbed," the detective raised his voice now.

"No stabbing. I had no knife."

"You had no knife but maybe Lekë or your partner from the mountains had a knife."

"Look, you don't know what you are saying. Who said anyone was stabbed?" the Albanian laughed.

"The way I see it, there were bullet chips in the roof wall behind where the American punks were standing. There where shell casings all over the place and there was blood that was different from Lekë's on the roof. Did one of the Americans have a bloody nose Engjëll my friend?" Gojcaj said smiling at the foreigner. At any moment the detective thought Engjëll would ask for the intercession of a lawyer to protect him from this interrogation.

"I saw nothing."

"But you saw the American punk shoot Lekë dead correct?"

"No, I saw nothing."

"So you lied to me when you said you saw... wait a second Engjëll, why would you go against your honor and lie to me? Are you perhaps protecting the real shooter? Are you trying to tell me that Gjergj shot Lekë?" Detective Gojcaj was purposely trying to confuse and irritate his charge.

"I never told you shit. I want to see someone from the Albanian Embassy, this is bullshit. Why are you treating me like one of your *zezaks*?" Engjëll stood quickly from his chair.

"Sit down cowboy. You can wait here. I think you have told me what I needed to know. Thank you for the cooperation. More coffee?" The detective pointed to the long handled pot on a hotplate.

"Fuck you and your coffee. I told you shit cop."

Detective Gojcaj looked his straight in his eyes and said, "One of the three of you killed your own kind. I know it. I feel it in my bones."

"You don't know dick."

Detective Del Greco was amazed when he saw Ukë. Unshaven and unkempt, his clothing appeared as if he had slept in them for days and the dark circles around his eyes made him look as if he was ill. His demeanor was even more disturbing. He was more hyper and jumpy than he was at the murder scene where the detective saw him last.

Detective Gojcaj had joined Del Greco for the interrogation which was held after Gjergj had been interviewed. Other detectives monitored the proceedings from behind one way glass.

"Mr. Marku, smoking isn't allowed in this room," Del Greco began in an officious tone, setting Ukë off like a Roman candle.

"Fuck that shit man. I'm a nervous wreck since my cousin was killed right in front of me. You should be out finding that cocksucker who shot Lekë point blank in his head. Instead you break my balls. It's always the same with you guys. Waste time so that prick can get away."

"Would you like some coffee?" Gojcaj asked, ignoring the rant.

"Thanks, the last fuckin' thing I need...coffee. How about some nice burek you Albanian asshole? I'm surprised at you breaking my balls when my cousin's killer is on the loose." Ukë's voice was strained from his incessant crying and chain-smoking over the last few days.

"Look Mr. Marku, we have a few questions to help put the pieces of the puzzle together. Relax and calm down and just answer our questions," Del Greco said in a soothing voice. He continued.

"When we briefly interviewed you on the night of the murder you said you saw Joseph Santoro shoot Lekë is that correct?"

"Yes, I saw him shoot and kill him."

"You also said, and so did the other witnesses, that it was very dark on the roof and you could barely see a few feet in front of you, isn't that correct?"

"Yeah it was dark but the gun flashed right in front of me."

"So could one of the other men on the roof have been the shooter?" Gojcaj asked.

"No way, that fucking guinea was standing right there; he shot Lekë in cold blood." Ukë drew hard on his cigarette.

"Did Lekë have a gun?" Del Greco asked

"Lekë never had a gun in his life," Ukë responded quickly with a smirk.

"Did you have a gun?" Gojcaj asked

"Fuck no."

"Did either or both Engjëll or Gjergj have a gun with them or fire a gun?" Del Greco asked quickly.

"Look you guys were there, did you see a gun on any of us?" Ukë said defensively.

"Just a simple question Mr. Marku, please answer it," Gojcaj said.

"No, none of us had guns," Ukë responded.

"Did any of the other men on the roof have guns or fire guns?" Del Greco was leaning in, his eyes intent on the nervous Ukë who now held his head while staring down at his hands.

"They shot the whole place up, yes they all had guns," Ukë's voice rose again as if he were annoyed at the question.

"What were you all doing on the roof Mr. Marku?" Del Greco continued.

"Jesus Christ, we…I already told you we went up there to smoke some weed and chill. So arrest me for smoking weed so I can go home to my family," Ukë said offering his wrists for cuffing.

"C'mon Ukë, you expect us to believe that bullshit," Gojcaj blurted out with a hint of sarcasm in his voice.

"I don't give a fuck what you believe you Albanian pig." Ukë looked at Detective Gojcaj with a menacing glare.

"So then tell me something Mr. Marku. What caused Santoro to shoot Lekë? An argument about the Yankees? Why would friends go up to a roof to smoke pot and bam—shoot a guy dead like that?" Del Greco queried.

"It was probably a hit all along I guess. These Italians are crazy motherfuckers, who knows why? Maybe a vengeance thing, I really don't know," Ukë said, more subdued when speaking to the older detective.

"How can you explain the bullet holes behind where you say the other three men were standing and the different shell casings that we found all over the rooftop?" Gojcaj asked.

"What the fuck am I, CSI or something? *Ta qift bota nanen,*" Ukë said in Albanian to Gojcaj, loosely meaning 'may the entire world fuck your mother.' The young detective's first instinct was to lunge at Ukë and kick his face in for him but he knew better and held his composure.

"Mr. Marku, your story is not adding up. We are going to hold the other two men for more questioning as witnesses to felony murder. You are free to go. We will be in touch. I would greatly appreciate it if you would drop by and surrender your passport to me." Del Greco tried to shake Ukë up a bit.

"Unless you are accusing me of murdering my own cousin and arrest me now, my passport stays in my safe at home. If you are accusing me then I want my lawyer here," Ukë challenged the detectives.

"No one is accusing you, Ukë. Your story is bullshit and is not matching up with your two *kumar*. We will get to the bottom of this and get back to you. Just stick around the area, okay," Detective Gojcaj said in a matter-of-fact tone.

"*Ma hanksh mutin,*" Ukë responded. Again an insult, albeit not as grave as the first one. 'Eat my shit' was a compliment compared to cursing out his mother. *This guy has a real problem with authority,* Gojcaj thought to himself rather than rap Ukë across his dirty mouth.

As Ukë left the office and flicked another in a chain of three cigarettes at a water cooler, Del Greco and Gojcaj looked at one another in disbelief.

"Lieutenant, this guy is...I don't know Lieutenant, I just get the feeling..."

"Don't jump to conclusions, Detective. There is a lot more work to be done here," Del Greco said, like the older uncle to his nephew.

"Lieutenant, there is no evidence that Santoro was the shooter. The bullets marks, the casings, the entry wounds...nothing makes sense except Lekë was killed by one of his own. Maybe friendly fire?" Gojcaj posed an obvious question.

"Go ahead and interview the other Albanian. I'm going to hold them both and contact the D.A. so they can notify the Albanian Embassy as a courtesy if they want. I've never called an embassy in all my years on the job but I want to follow the book on this one." Del Greco was nervous about his relationship with Ilir Marku and how this whole mess would play out but his experience was telling him that Santoro was not the shooter. He didn't yet know who was.

14

Hamdi Nezaj had gone to see Ilir Marku at his home in Scarsdale the day after the funeral of his son and unborn grandson. The Albanian mobster was still in a state of grief and permitted by the *Kanun* to mourn for a period of one year. Ilir would indeed mourn for whatever years he had left on earth but would begin planning to take back the blood of his family without haste.

When Hamdi arrived at the Marku Estate he was met by Pashko Luli who greeted him as a friend and escorted Hamdi into Ilir's study. They spoke only in their native tongue. Coffee was poured by the women attending to the family.

"My friend Ilir, may God give you strength! May you be well from this day on!" Hamdi greeted his friend with traditional and deserved respect.

"I am happy to see you my old friend. I think I know why you are paying me this visit. Don Carmine Miceli called to ask that I see his son and godson and the father of the murderer to discuss the events of my son's death. I have not given him my answer as my blood is yet too hot to think clearly," Ilir said, his voice just above a whisper.

"Yes friend. I have asked to discuss with you a truce for the family of the murderer. They are saying he is innocent. I am not here to judge that but to get your *besa* for their safety."

"Pashko, you are my son's godfather. You gave him his first haircut. Guide me in this as my mind is clouded with my vengeance."

"A man of honor is always obligated to agree to a truce. This is written in the *Kanun*. We are not dealing with our own kind here so I am not certain that this obligation should be fulfilled. To show respect for Don Miceli I would advise that a truce of only a few days be accepted. Let them come and tell their story. We will make arrangements for a meeting place where everyone will feel comfortable," Pashko said.

"Hamdi, you have my word. Bring them here to my home where they are my guests and nothing bad can happen to them. Explain the importance of having a guest in our home. The truce will be for three days and no more. Explain that to your friend. Also explain that the taken will be avenged at all costs." Ilir Marku needed to rest and politely excused himself, bidding goodbye to Hamdi.

Pashko Luli walked with Hamdi to his car to show respect for his *Kumar's* guest. The two men had a brief but telling chat.

"Pashko, they are saying this Italian boy did not shoot Lekë. He is not that kind of person to hurt anyone. These people understand what *Gjakmarrja* is about. They too have a history of blood-for-blood and would respect our obligation. I am disturbed by what they are saying," Hamdi said solemnly.

"We will listen to what they have to say but we have two murders in the house of Marku. The act was witnessed by a first-blood relative and our need for justice is absolute," Pashko replied.

"What if, and I chose my words carefully, what if it was one of our people who shot Lekë even if by accident? What would be then?"

"My friend, don't let your thoughts be swayed by friendship. What you are saying is not within the realm of possibility. Go tell your friends that we will meet them here tomorrow or the day after but the window will not remain open. Let me know what arrangements are being made. I hope we can meet soon at a better occasion." The men kissed on each cheek and Pashko opened the car door for Hamdi.

Hamdi did not have a cell phone as that was an ostentatious and unnecessary luxury to him. For the whole twenty-five minute drive back to his home in Armonk he kept mulling the information over and over in his mind. He was certain of one thing: this story would have a sad ending. How sad, was known only to God.

Gino had returned to his home in New Jersey on Sunday night with Babbu and filled Joey Clams and C.C. in on the events of their meeting Carmine Miceli Jr. Everyone was very tense about the entire situation and Clams was pacing back and forth waiting to hear from Joey Jr. Evidently his cell phone was out of battery power or he was in a poor cell zone and he was incommunicado. Clams did however reach his Uncle Vito, the one-time mob soldier who did serious time in federal prison for drug trafficking in the 1960s. Vito was ninety-one years old but still sharp and still connected as he took a fall for some major players and was always provided for by the family. Clams was not necessarily close to Vito Santoro but he called him for his advice and help. Surprisingly the old gangster lived by the code of honor and family that the old Sicilians had instilled in him. He would not discuss anything over the telephone as he learned his lesson well. The telephone helped to put him into the Atlanta Federal Penitentiary for fourteen years. They were to meet that evening, at Vito's sister's apartment on Arthur Avenue. She was ninety-two and lived in the same apartment in the neighborhood since 1952. She was under death watch from two people, her landlord because she was paying $205 a month in the rent controlled apartment and Di Bari's funeral home because she prepaid for her wake and burial ten years ago.

Joey Clams was safe as the Albanians had no idea who Joey Jr.'s father was nor what he looked like so meeting across the street from the Son's of the Eagle club was not an issue. Gino thought that perhaps it would be a good idea if they rented an apartment in the Bronx to be closer to the action. Back and forth to New Jersey was not a wise use of vital time to manage the problems that they were facing. Gino had a friend close to the Miceli family with a two family house in the Country Club section of the Bronx on Ohm Avenue that was available and secure. He would pay cash and no questions would be asked. The still mostly Italian area was safe as the neighbors tended to their own affairs. Unless of course blacks or Hispanics moved in. Then it became personal. All four agreed that having a headquarters closer to enemy territory would be the smart way to get things done. They all had their suitcases and clothing and all Gino had to do was pack his things for a week or so. Gino also thought it wise if Ellen went to visit his cousins in Clearwater, Florida until things were settled. It was unlikely that the Albanians would disturb Gino's home because of his relationship with the Miceli family but there was no need to take unnecessary chances and besides, Ellen could use the vacation.

Hamdi called Gino as they were making the necessary moves and plans to discuss the negotiated sit-down with Ilir Marku. The meeting was set for the next morning at eleven o'clock at the Marku Estate. Hamdi explained again what the *besa* meant and told Gino that he would meet him, Joey Santoro Sr. and Carmine Miceli Jr. at the Scarsdale home. Gino was concerned that he was bringing his friend into mortal danger going to the Marku home but Hamdi allayed any fears. The safest place for Joey Clams to meet Ilir was in his home as shame and dishonor would befall the Marku family if harm came to a guest. The conversation was short, sweet and to the point—all business.

The men decided to go to the Bronx, settle into the apartment on Ohm Avenue and try to see Vito Santoro early that evening. They would be fresh and ready to meet the Markus the next day and hoped for a good resolution to the problem. Things were moving fast and furious and Joey was getting that thousand yard stare again. He was thinking four steps ahead, as he was trained to do in the military and how he survived in Vietnam as an assassin and combat soldier.

They packed quickly; Gino kissed Ellen and told her not to worry and to please don't say be careful. That got a big laugh as the men headed for the cars.

"I'll go in with Gino and you guys ride together. C.C. I think you need to go to Queens and get the duffle bag," Joey said as he was already taking over command of the 'operation.'

"Woah Joey, we can't show up at the Marku house with weapons. Are you crazy? This is a discussion to let them know that they have marked an innocent man. We're not attacking the Fish Farm again bud," Gino said

"Gino, listen to me. No one said we are going to Marku's to shoot up the place. I'm just preparing for after the sit-down if things don't go the way we want. The stuff will be at the apartment just in case we have to mobilize," Joey Clams said while putting out a cigarette before getting into Gino's car.

"What's this talk about mobilizing? We're not at war Joey, you need to come back to reality here," Gino said a little bit preachy.

"If they think my son killed their son and they don't believe that he didn't, I'm in a shit storm of a war my friend. Maybe you want to just come to the meeting and back away. No hard feelings," Joey said without thinking about who he was talking to.

"What's the matter with you? I'm in this until the last dog dies and I would never turn my back on you. I wasn't clear about your plan is all. Relax pal, we are in this together." Gino hugged his friend and motioned to the other two to join in.

"Yeah c'mon Joey, I know this is tough but we win or lose together," C.C. said.

"What lose? Lose what? No way we lose! And no dogs are gonna die over here," Babbu added a typical Babbu-ism.

They all cracked up laughing at the serious look on Babbu's face and stared out for their appointed destinations.

15

Shpresa had visited her dear friend Valbona at Einstein Hospital every day since she lost her husband and son. She sat with the elder Albanian women, all in dark headscarves tending to her needs. They sang softly to her, applied lotion to keep her skin soft and hydrated, read stories to her, and talked about the place that she was born in Albania. Shpresa would sit beside her and talk about the fun times they had when they were girls and how they studied together every day after school. She would remind her of how they would sneak into movies that their fathers forbade them to see and how they had to make up a story about where they had been for three hours. The library, shopping for clothes, at the Central Park Zoo. They made up a different event every time they saw an R-rated film and made sure their stories were in sync.

There was no reaction to anything. Valbona was conscious but in a "catatonic stupor" that the doctors felt would diminish with time. The severe shock brought on acute depression that Valbona experienced sending her into this state. Dr. John, who felt that he should have done more to save the baby and was also in his own world of depression, came by twice daily for a visit. He brought in the best psychiatric physicians he knew. They all agreed that her condition was temporary but just how temporary would be just a guess.

The doctors advised that she should be moved to a sanitarium as there was no medical reason to keep her at Einstein. These doctors did not know the Marku family and the traditions that they lived by. So long as Valbona lived, and did not remarry, she would be provided for. Her every need would be met, every want would be made available. She would never worry for a day in her life about her comfort. The Markus were making arrangements for Valbona to return to their estate with round-the-clock nurses and daily visits from her psychiatrists and physical therapist. A hospital room was quickly being assembled in the massive home in the event that it was needed for Valbona's care. She was to be brought to the home in a day or two. The doctors thought it would be therapeutic for her to be in a familiar setting, hearing her first language, hearing Albanian music, smelling the distinctive aroma of home cooking, and being around the normal activities of the family.

What her long-term mental health would be was a question that could not be answered. Her future was of serious concern for her family and friends. Just thinking about her brought the women to tears and the men to anger.

16

Gino and Joey Clams made it to the three bedroom Ohm Avenue apartment in forty minutes from New Jersey. The place was neat, clean and fully furnished in 'Bronx-Italian.' The living room furniture was from the 1950s and looked like it just came from the furniture store. The Italian Provincial sofa and chairs were all covered in thick fitted plastic so that they would last the millennium. The furniture was in the room for show and not for sitting. The large dining room and bedroom furniture were a throwback to when these sixty year old men visited their grandmothers. Ornate was an understatement with the large square Capo Di Monte lamps and chandeliers, all adorned with cherubs and prince- and princess-like figurines. The two bathrooms in the upstairs each had bidets like in the old country. The window treatments were regal beige and brown with gold brocades.

Despite the safe and protected neighborhood—which had its own vigilante patrol car with tough-guy volunteers—every window on the ground and first floors were protected by strong, black iron window guards. The house was like an impenetrable fortress with the front and rear door equipped with Fox Police locks, the kind that have the iron bar bolted into the floor. Whoever owned this house was serious about keeping unwanted visitors out. The *maganette,* the old fashioned *demitasse* coffee pot, was on the stove with a supply of *Medaglia D'Oro* coffee, anisette, and sugar. Gino put the pot on before he even brought his suitcase to a bedroom. The "entertainment center" consisted of a twenty-seven inch Motorola color television set from the 1960s and a few faded TV Guides. HBO and Showtime were alien to this house.

C.C. and Babbu got to the hideout within an hour after Gino and Joey Clams arrived. C.C. carried a heavy looking, green canvas Army issue duffle bag filled with an assortment of weapons from M-16s to a hand held rocket launcher, .45 caliber pistols, an Uzi, a sawed off shot gun and other assorted tools of the killing trade. Babbu entered the house with a square metal box that housed a few hand-grenades, an assortment of ominous looking knives, and a few sophisticated looking communication devices. Gino made note that the equipment looked refreshed from the last time he saw his buddies when they did battle with the Colombians out in East Hampton. He just shook his head and thought of Hyman Roth's line in Godfather II, "stupid thugs, behaving like that with guns." Gino thought that violence never truly solved an issue. He always believed that negotiating a deal so that both parties could believe they won something was better than using violence. Perhaps that was why he never entered the area of organized crime; he just didn't have the stomach for killing.

Joey Clams and Gino left C.C. and Babbu to their own devices and set off to Clams' aunt's apartment on Arthur Avenue. They were going to meet Joey's true life gangster Uncle Vito and see if he could be of any help with the Albanians. After Joey explained the details as he knew them, about the drug deal gone bad and the murder of Lekë Marku, a quietly listening Vito Santoro spoke.

"Joseph this is not good. These people are like the old time Mustache Petes from the mountains of Sicily, but worse. They understand one thing and that's revenge. It's as simple as that. You kill one of us we kill you back. You have three choices as I see it. Have your son surrender and be killed, that ain't happening. Run and hide so you can never be found, and they will eventually find you or your grandchildren, or fight them until you kill them all."

"But Uncle Vito, can't we explain that there is no hard evidence that Joey Jr. even fired a gun that night? They won't listen to reason?" Clams questioned.

"They have their witness. That's all they need to kill you and your two boys as payback. So run and hide or stand and fight. Me? At your age I would go away and live a simple life back in Italy, nice and easy, start over and keep your sons alive. A war with these people will be next to impossible to win. They are too many and too strong," the old man said to his nephew.

"But Uncle Vito, this meeting tomorrow, what do I say to Marku? Your witness is full of crap?" Vito turned to Gino.

"I'm an old man. My friends are all dead. I'm living on a memory of how things used to be. We don't have loyalty among our people, everyone rats on everyone. No more stand up guys. My day is over, the old ways of our life are gone forever. What does your godfather say Gino? He knows these people, can anything be done?"

"Mr. Santoro, I'm afraid he agrees with you. Even he with all his power knows that this is a fight we won't win. When you can't win you must retreat or face sure death. Either way, we lose," Gino said looking from the old man to Joey Clams.

"So, Joseph you should follow the advice of us old guys. If your father was alive he would tell you the same. Get your boys and get under the protection of some of our friends where you will at least be alive. I wish I could help you more."

"I'm sorry to bring this problem to you. I didn't really know you much when I was growing up. I wish that I had...."

"Joseph, your father kept you away for a reason. A very good reason. My life is really not a good life at all but it was all that I knew and what I chose to do. My brother was right to keep you away as he did. We are still family, the few of us that are left and I am sorry that you are in this mess. Go take care of your family, and don't look back."

Joey and Gino said their good-byes and left the apartment and didn't speak one word on the ten minute ride back to the apartment where C.C. and Babbu were polishing off a bottle of Dewar's they found in a kitchen cabinet.

"Pizza or chinks?" Babbu asked when they walked into the house.

"I'm not hungry right now," Joey Clams said his voice stale from cigarettes and pent up emotion.

"Okay White Castle or a hero sangwich then," Babbu replied.

The other three laughed again at the way Babbu pronounced sandwich, C.C. gagging on his drink.

"I say we get some veal parm sangwiches from Louis' on Tremont Avenue. They make the best veal cutlet in the Bronx," C.C. said holding back a cough.

There was a knock on the door and Joey and C.C. instinctively moved for the trove of weapons in the duffle bag. Why would anyone be knocking on the door? Gino and Babbu were startled by their reaction momentarily then realized that they were in danger. They were likely followed out of the neighborhood, giving up their hideout.

Joey hand signaled to C.C., never forgetting their military training. Gino was dumbfounded and looked at Joey for direction.

"Gino, answer the door, but don't stand in front of it," Joey said as he leveled a Beretta shotgun at the center of the door. C.C. had an M-16 ready to light the place up. Babbu picked up a .45 and stood behind a wall leading to the kitchen.

Gino had seen enough stupid cop movies to know how to stand

aside of a door. He slowly made his move to the door, but never thought of taking a weapon, and suddenly felt naked and vulnerable.

"Who's there?" Gino said in a deliberate, deep voice so as not to sound like a scared *funnuccio*.

"I have a pizza delivery from Patsy's on First Avenue for the Goldberg pajama party," said a familiar voice. Gino opened the door and there stood Carmine Miceli Jr. and two of his men, all carrying boxes of the famous pizza from Harlem.

"Jesus Christ, Carmine I almost shit my pants," Gino said as he walked his nephew into the dining room. "How the hell did you know where we were?" Gino asked as they embraced.

"C'mon Gino, you think for a minute the friend of ours who rented this place to you wasn't gonna tell me?" Carmine Jr. said with a reserved half-smile.

The men all greeted each other and like all self respecting Italian-Americans went directly for the pizza.

"It's like we never saw a pizza. It's like if you put beer down in front of the Irish, they drink it. Wit us it's eatin'. That's our booze," Babbu offered.

"I wish this was for fun guys. Joey, I'm very sorry for your headache. I figured we would get together and make a plan for tomorrow with these Albanians," Carmine Jr. began the reason for his visit with a hint of displeasure in the word Albanian.

"Thanks Carmine, sorry to bring you guys into this but I got nowhere to turn on this one," Joey Clams said with a lot of humility.

"C'mon Joey. You think we forgot about what you did for this *strunzo* over here? Besides we are family, no?" Carmine Jr. said, referring lovingly to his "Uncle" Gino.

"So now I'm a *strunzo*, an asshole...okay I get it, the kid's getting ready to take over the family and it's time to throw the old guy under the bus," Gino said laughing to break the tension.

"Never in a million years Gino. Look, every time I hear the word 'Albanian' a fly becomes an elephant. These fucks are nothing but a stone in my shoe. They are pushing us out of a lot of our businesses *piano e piano*. Little by little we are losing ground with restaurant action, gambling, broads, a few small unions. They are starting to infiltrate some big jobs that we are involved with now and I'm getting tired of it. I understand they are the new immigrants and they are a tough bunch but do they have to eat our lunch AND dinner too?"

Gino jumped in, "Carmine, all we want to say to them is that Joey's kid did not shoot this Albanian kid. Yes they were doing a drug deal but from what Joey Jr. has told me, he didn't have a gun and it was so dark on that roof he could hardly see his hand in front of his face."

"I understand all that Gino and that's all true but when is enough, enough? They have this ancient, what, eight thousand year old blood thing? They are hunting people close to me and I don't like running scared. All respect Joey, business is business and if your kid killed this guy we would have to deliver him to the cops or to them. Either way he's fucked right? We are saying they don't have proof except for the word of that maniac Ukë. How the fuck do we know that it wasn't him who did the Marku kid? Show me more proof or sit down and shut the fuck up you fuckin' mountain hillbillies." Carmine was on a roll and unlike his father he was showing he was hot and angry. Gino thought for a second about Santino Corleone and what happened to him.

"Carmine, all I want is to be able to state my case to Mr. Marku and his people and see if we can come to an agreement. If my son killed this kid, he needs to stand trial for his actions, not be hunted like a wild animal and killed in the street. We are still in the United States am I right or wrong Carmine?" Joey pled his case.

"The United States is a fairy tale Joey. A real nice story like the three wise men and the manger with Jesus, Mary, and Joseph. A real nice story. Justice has many faces and we have to look for it ourselves."

"Guys listen. We can't go in there tomorrow with a 'fuck you attitude,' that would be a mistake. I know these people, they believe in honor and respect, a lot like our families did in Sicily. Carmine let's not forget how our families came to this country. It was because of La Vendetta. We need to respect this man, his home, be respectful about the death of his son and grandson and reason with him. Tell him the facts as we know them," Gino said trying to keep the mood more even tempered.

Carmine looked at him for a few seconds. "You sound like my father Gino. And what happens when he says 'fuck you we want Joey's kid,' then what?"

"And your father is always right. We cross that bridge when we come to it. In the meantime we go into this man's home with dignity and respect as we would expect him to do to us if the roles were reversed," Gino said taking the lead.

Carmine again took a few seconds before responding.

"Not for nothing Gino, but you're right. I'm still hot over how they conduct business and over the murder of a friend of ours kid that was never answered. I have to put that aside for now. Let's see what tomorrow brings. Right now, pass me a slice with the *salsice*."

17

The Bronx homicide squad was getting busier by the day. In the week since Lekë was killed there had been seven murders in the borough. It was summer, drugs were flowing in the streets like the waves on a beach and a gang war was erupting between the Crips and the Latin Kings. Fun and games in the borough named after Jonas Bronck, the great Dutch farmer rolling in his grave somewhere.

Ilir Marku had asked Pashko Luli to find out what Detective Del Greco was doing with the Albanians whom he was holding in custody. Why was he holding these two men and treating his nephew Ukë so harshly? Pashko made contact with Del Greco and they met at Niki Balaj's restaurant on City Island, early that morning before the place was open.

"Coffee Carlo?" Pashko asked, already pouring a cup for Del Greco as they sat at the bar.

"Thank you, just what I needed."

"These are tough and terrible times my friend. There is no more honor, no more respect among these young ones. They want everything in a hurry and they don't want to earn their stripes. This kid that killed Lekë, do you have any idea where he is?"

"He could be anywhere by now. We are doing what we normally do to find someone. None of it is easy. They normally make a mistake and slip up or someone drops a dime and we pounce. Right now it's cold," Del Greco said sipping the hot coffee.

"So why are you holding our people?" Pashko got to the real point of why they called.

"They are what I would call persons of interest," the detective answered.

"And this means?"

"This means that we are not yet convinced that Santoro was the shooter." Del Greco swallowed hard.

"So this is why you and your Albanian detective have upset a family member who witnessed the murder of his cousin?" Pashko was pressing.

"If asking simple questions to get simple answers is upsetting to someone then perhaps that someone has something to hide Pashko."

"Ridiculous. This is our family you are talking about. Our friend made it very clear to you that we want to handle this matter ourselves. Why are you not cooperating with us?"

"Look, there are some doubts that we have about the testimony of the witnesses, serious doubts. If they cooperate and we are comfortable with their stories we will proceed with an indictment of the Santoro kid. Until then this case still must be investigated like any other."

"Do you suffer from amnesia Carlo?" Pashko asked with a serious tone.

"Amnesia? I don't get it," Del Greco shot back.

"Are you forgetting about our relationship, our friendship?"

"On the contrary Pashko, and with all due respect, if you are interested in a murder for a murder I can easily turn my back. But an unjust murder I cannot live with. I understand the idea of an eye for an eye. I get it! What I don't want to see is the wrong eye for an eye," Del Greco said and poured the second cup of coffee himself.

"You don't believe that Ukë is telling the truth about the murder of his own blood? Something he saw with his own eyes?" Pashko asked incredulously.

"Please Pashko, give me some time to do my job. There are questions about the crime scene that I would prefer not to get into with you right now. You and our friend and I have trusted each other for years. Please understand that I'm trying to do the right thing for all concerned here."

"Yes Carlo, we have trusted one another and you were paid well for that trust. Let's remember that and understand that our blood was spilled and we will have justice with or without your help," Pashko replied with an even voice and tone.

"I just need some time," Del Greco said a bit exasperated.

"And you will release our men and back away from our Ukë?" Pashko's question was more like an order. Detective Carlo Del Greco came to a defining moment in his life. Now or never, do or die, all of the cards on the table, shit or get off the pot time.

"I will release your men and stop interviewing Ukë Marku when I am fully convinced that they had no culpability in this murder. Please send my respects and deepest sympathy to our friend."

Detective Lieutenant Carlo Del Greco, at that moment, was a liberated man in his mind and soul. If he was in any danger from his decision it was of no consequence. The veteran homicide detective shook hands with the underboss and left the restaurant.

Del Greco headed toward the homicide squad office to begin the questioning of the Albanians. He thought about bringing Ukë in again for a brief moment and decided against it. A quick decision like that would perhaps be taken as an insult. Ukë would likely bring a lawyer so he was best to work on the two weak links. He phoned Detective Jimmy Gojcaj telling him to be ready to grill Engjëll and Gjergj when he arrived, starting from jump street.

On his drive over to the office Del Greco played and replayed the crime scene and what he had gathered from the witnesses in his head. He was still convinced from the physical evidence that Joey Santoro Jr. may not have been the shooter. He wasn't yet sure who was and he was not going to buckle under pressure. The vise he felt that he was in convinced him that this would be his last case. Time to get out of Dodge City.

The senior and junior detectives started this time with Gjergj, who seemed to be the tougher nut to crack. The Turkish coffee pot with steaming hot brew was brought in by Jimmy with sugar packets and small plastic cups.

"How do you people drink that stuff. It's so damn strong and when you get to the bottom it's like you're drinking mud," Del Greco said pleasantly. Gojcaj translated for Gjergj, who didn't find it a bit amusing.

"*Rrac Mutit,*" was all Gjergj said to the Albanian detective and he gestured with a flip of his hand toward Del Greco.

"What's that Gojcaj?" the Detective Lieutenant asked.

"Well boss if you really want to know, he thinks you are a shit race, but please don't shoot the messenger."

"I'm curious if he means the Americans or Italians...don't ask him that," Del Greco said jokingly.

"Gjergj, so tell me again how Lekë was hit in the side of the head with two bullets. Was he running away?" Gojcaj translated for Detective

Del Greco.

"No Albanian with honor runs away. We face our enemies and fight like men."

"So he was shot from the side, from close range. Did Santoro run up next to him, in the dark, not being able to see his hand in front of him, as you stated the other day, and pop two bullets into the rear side of his head? You expect me to believe this garbage?" Del Greco said

"And the only one that witnessed this was Ukë who was standing next to Lekë when you all entered the rooftop. This is what your pal Engjëll told us," Gojcaj was shaking his hands and making his eyes wide, imitating that Engjëll was nervous.

"Engjëll and me dove for cover when the shots started," Gjergj replied as if the cop should have assumed they were not standing there like sitting ducks.

"So what if I tell you that Ukë and Engjëll have said maybe you accidently shot Lekë in the confusion?" Gojcaj asked.

"I would say you were full of shit because I had no gun with me. Sell this bad smelling fish to someone else. I am not some dumb fucking zezak," Gjergj replied with a laugh.

They sparred for the better part of three hours, never once did Gjergj sway from his original story or show the slightest crack under pressure. Del Greco and Gojcaj flipped-flopped the bad-guy-good-guy routine until they were worn down. It was apparent that this witness was not going to make a misstep and break under any conditions.

Like two bees, Del Greco and Gojcaj went to the next flower. This time Gojcaj asked that he take the lead with a different approach.

They entered the interrogation room without the coffee. That didn't seem to be working for them and Gojcaj was racing because of the huge amount of caffeine he was taking. Truth be told, Jimmy preferred brewed tea anyway.

After several hours of interrogation going over the events of the murder several times, step-by-step in rapid fire Albanian, Detective Jimmy Gojcaj got down to business.

"Engjëll, we are convinced from our discussions with both of your so called 'friends' that one of you shot Lekë Marku. We are prepared to make you a deal and get you out of this mess and either back to Albania or to resettle you here somewhere in the United States."

"I have no idea what you are saying. I did not have a gun to shoot anyone," the jumpy Engjëll said.

"Which one of the others had guns Engjëll? C'mon you need to save yourself or be an accessory to felony murder. I'm trying real hard to be a friend to you here but you are making it very difficult for me. You can spend the rest of your life here in prison or be a free man. That is all up to you my friend," Gojcaj said.

"Life is still life. If I tell you what I saw I will be a disgraced dead man. I will not speak further about this; I will not betray my *besa*."

Bam, the noose worked on the unsuspecting and not overly bright Engjëll. The two detectives knew at that moment they were on the right track. Their instincts were correct and they had some additional time to keep both men on ice. They still had no proof and that would be the hard part. The forensics on the bullets and casings were not yet complete and Del Greco needed to make a few more moves of his own.

18

They arrived at Ilir Marku's Estate at ten minutes to eleven o'clock so as not to show the disrespect of being late. Carmine Miceli Jr., Joey Clams, and Gino all in Gino's car. No bodyguards, no follow-up car, no two-way radio, no GPS tracking system, nothing that would insult Ilir Marku or indicate that they had nothing but honorable intentions. Joey Clams was visibly nervous. Not for the fear of being waylaid, he had ice in his veins since Vietnam, not at the possibility of being held hostage or seeing his friend harmed. He was at a loss for words for Ilir, who thought Joey Jr. killed his only son and was responsible for the death of his unborn grandson.

Talk about an awkward moment, this was worse than having to go to his ex-wife's wake and face her five sisters and half-dozen friends who always blamed him for leaving her twenty years prior to her death. Clams was never timid when it came to playing sports as a kid, during a rumble with the Puerto Ricans, doing his job in Vietnam, in his working career, or in any other tough life circumstance. He was, however, socially timid. High school dances, asking a girl out on a date, speaking to a group in public, things like that sent him spinning. Now he was about to face Ilir Marku and try to explain how his son was innocent of murdering the man's family. He was not even sure he could speak.

Gino and Carmine Jr. didn't share his fears. Hamdi Nezaj came from inside the house to greet the three guests of the Marku home. As always Hamdi greeted Gino in the Albanian-European fashion before he was formally introduced to Carmine Jr. and the especially reserved Joey Clams. Hamdi led the way into the Marku home where there were no signs of swarthy security guards or Albanian goons mulling around the property. This was Marku's home and his guests were to be treated as the *Kanun* dictated, with honor and respect. Hamdi led the men into a large living room that was elegantly appointed with a magnificent Louis IV style grand piano, exquisite European furniture with fabulous Persian rugs, and a breathtaking mural depicting Skanderbeg, the hero of the Albanian people fighting the Turks, a copy of the original that is in the Skanderbeg Museum in Albania.

Ilir Marku came to the doorway of the room to welcome the men into his home. Hamdi formally introduced each man individually and Ilir shook both of their hands in his own. When Joey Clams was introduced intentionally last, Ilir embraced the man and declared, "Welcome, Mr. Santoro my home is yours," with such sincerity that Joey had to hold back his tears. Ilir led them to a sofa and winged chairs as women, adorned in muted colors and head scarves, served coffee in vintage red porcelain demitasse cups with cubes of sugar that were mounted on a pure gold platter. The women did not make eye contact with the guests, served the coffee in silence and left the room without turning their backs on the guests. Pashko Luli entered the room and greeted the men with equal welcome and sat in a chair next to his boss and blood-brother Ilir. They chatted for a few minutes about the World Cup which had just ended and how Spain was the odds-on favorite to win from the beginning. It was idle talk that all three Americans found bizarre to say the least, and only Gino contributed to the conversation by saying how he was looking forward to the next cup matches in Brazil. Ilir Marku, mindful of not being rude to his guests, broke the ice to lead to the necessary discussion.

"Mr. Miceli, how is your father? It's been too long since I have broken bread with him," Ilir said with a broad smile.

"Thank you Mr. Marku. He is well and sends his best wishes to you and remembers you in his prayers." Carmine Jr. thought that would be the most polite way of offering his father's sympathy and opening up the recent wound so early in the conversation.

"A true gentleman, that man. I'm sure that he has prepared you well to follow in his footsteps." Ilir spoke with reverence of Don Miceli.

"My father casts a large shadow Mr. Marku and I could only hope to be half the man that he is. Luckily for me he is still around and teaches me something daily. I am thankful for that," Carmine Jr. said with true adoration of the Don.

"I see he has taught you well. Please send him my best wishes."

"I will do that Mr. Marku, when I see him later today."

"I am saddened by the reason for today's visit. I know this must be difficult for all of you, especially you Mr. Santoro. I also know one of your relatives quite well. You are related to Vito Santoro, yes?" Ilir asked, taking in the full picture of the father of his son's murderer in his living room.

"Ah, yes sir, he is my uncle?" Joey Clams' answer came out awkwardly, sounding like a question.

"I did business with him many years ago. An old fashioned and brave man of honor your uncle. Please send my regards to him." Marku smiled again.

"Ah, yes sir, I will." Joey was as awkward as he ever was.

"Mr. Ranno, my dear friend Hamdi tells me that you are a respectful friend to him and to the Albanian community. We are all grateful for the fundraiser that you sponsored for the floods in our country last January. I know that you are the god son of my friend Don Miceli and you are here as a friend to discuss the horrible events that my family has recently endured."

"Mr. Marku, thank you for your kind words and for seeing us today. We all share in your grief and hope that God gives you and your family strength," Gino said his practiced words perfectly.

"So, tell me what is on your mind," Ilir said with a sudden stone face.

Gino glanced at Carmine Jr. to give him the first opportunity to speak. Carmine nodded sending the responsibility back to Gino.

"Mr. Marku, with all due respect, we do not believe that Mr. Santoro's son was the man who killed your son," Gino stated with conviction.

"Then who did?" Ilir shot back.

"I wish we knew the answer to that question sir," Gino replied.

"I am going on the word of my nephew, my brother's son, who witnessed the killing. How do I not believe a man with the same blood that flows through my own veins Gino?" Ilir took the liberty of speaking in the familiar. "I'm to believe the man who took the light from my life simply because he said he did not do it?"

"This is a very difficult question to answer. Mr. Santoro's son is not a man of violence. Yes, he is in the drug world and yes he has had problems, but this boy's character is not able to commit murder. He did not even have a weapon with which to commit such a terrible crime. We are asking that you allow the time to be taken to prove that he is indeed the killer of your son. We believe that the facts are not being considered."

"We are not dealing with the character of a little boy. When someone is taken over by drugs they are no longer the person that you knew, they become the drug," Ilir interrupted, giving Gino a wave of his hand.

Carmine Jr.'s left leg was bouncing, a sign that he was losing his patience and Gino glanced at him for a moment to get his attention.

Carmine took it as his cue to speak up.

"So how do you know it wasn't one of your boys that shot your son? They are dealing the same drugs, for all we know they could be using too."

Ilir Marku ignored the impetuous answer and looked at his *kumar,* Pashko Luli, who spoke for the family.

"Gentlemen, first of all we are not talking about one death we are talking about two. The baby died as a result of the murder of his father, of that we are certain. We must have our satisfaction in these deaths. We believe what we have been told by a family member who was an eye-witness. What else can be said?"

"What other proof do you have? If you can prove to us what you are saying we have no issue with you pursuing your way of justice. We simply don't agree with your position. Look, what can be done here? We've done business for many, many years and lived beside each other in peace. There is no reason to upset the balance of things. We will make any reasonable restitution that you request," Carmine Jr. said holding his real feelings back. Hamdi looked up at the mural of the great Skander-beg and his men in battle with the Turks and knew that this discussion would not lead to a good ending.

"Our proof is the word of our family. The *besa* that we all adhere to means everything to us. There is nothing that can change that. And you must understand...you all must understand that no deal, no property, no money can be a settlement for these deaths. The deaths cannot go un-avenged. This is our law for centuries." Pashko had a twinge of irritation in his voice.

"So even if this man is innocent as he's claiming, he still needs to die to satisfy you?" Carmine Jr. now personalized the issue. He was showing his anger at the unwillingness of the Albanians to be open minded at the very least.

"There is nothing that can be done. Until the murderer is illuminated every male of the Santoro family can be killed. This is very clear in our laws." Pashko said standing on the principles of the *Kanun* and the history of the Albanian people.

"You are wrong if you think that we will sit by and watch as you kill our friends, those that we believe are innocent of these things that you are claiming, you are very wrong Mr. Luli. We are also a people of principles, our country was also victims for many centuries but we listen to reason. You are shutting your eyes and ears to our request to judge this man by the laws of this country. Here, he is innocent until proven guilty and you are ignoring the law and live by an ancient standard that we simply cannot abide. The result of your decision will put a strain on our long relationship to say the least," Carmine said.

"Gentlemen, I have been a poor host. Let us all have some food and then drink some homemade Raki. You have heard our position; there is nothing more that can be said." Ilir Marku was ending the conversation.

"I don't think we will join you Mr. Marku. Under the circumstances it's best if we leave." Carmine Jr. stood and offered his hand to the stunned Ilir and continued.

"I will discuss this with my family and decide what course of action will be taken."

Carmine Jr. walked out without the ceremonial good-byes as were customary. Knowing that they could not show any disloyalty to the family, Joey Clams and Gino followed quickly on his heels. Hamdi and Pashko stood in silence and disbelief at the manner in which the Italians departed.

His brashness was an insult. Carmine Jr. could care less at that point as he knew there was no sense in begging for them to change their position on the matter. His feelings for the "crazy Albanian bullshit," as he was fond of calling their unmoving ideals, was evident. He felt that it was time they stopped thinking that the world, his world, was all theirs.

19

Joey Jr. and his two knucklehead pals were growing restless, watching television, eating fast food, getting high and listening to the planes in the landing pattern of nearby Stewart International Airport. The boredom was getting to them and they all wanted to get back to their lives, as shallow as they were. They had no clear idea of the certain death sentence that they were all facing. Joey Jr. was now looking for a way to get back into action. Never one to listen to the advice of anyone, especially his father, he began making plans to move his hideaway down into the Yonkers area. There are as many Albanians in Westchester County as in Tirana. Not actually but it's pretty close. The point being that if you are trying to avoid the alligators, stay out of the water. Yonkers is no place to be hiding from the Albanians, that's for sure. His cell phone battery was full and he made a call to his father.

"Hi pop what's up?"

"Nothing real good Joey, these people not only want you they want me and your brother too. Don't tell me where you are, just tell me if you're safe and laying low," Joey Clams said, annoyed with the 'what's up' question.

"Pop, I swear on mom's grave I did not shoot anyone. Do you believe me?"

"Your history of lying and bullshitting goes back to when you were a teenager and I always told you never to lie to me. I just don't know if you're being honest or just adding to the thousand lies that you've told me. This time it's not a game. You're dealing with our lives. I need the truth Joey. If I find out you're lying, I will turn my back and you will be dead. I'm going to ask once more...did you kill Lekë Marku?"

"I understand that you're having a tough time believing me. I've screwed up a lot in my life. This time I swear I did not shoot anyone. I had no gun. Yeah, I was dealing shit with these guys and that crazy fuck Ukë started shooting at us, and yes the guys with me shot a few back but nobody killed this guy. If I would have shot Lekë Marku, of all people, I would have jumped off the roof and saved all this trouble. Dad, I didn't do it," Joey Jr. said sincerely.

"So if your friends returned fire could they have shot him?"

"I doubt it. They were shooting at Ukë and the two mutts that were with him. They were not shooting to kill anyone. We had no beef with them, it was that maniac who started acting all big and stuff. He started a fight over bullshit. Could it have happened, Yeah, but they only fired a clip each and when they stopped firing and I ran for the door I saw Lekë still standing. When I ran by him he was hit. That's all I could see. All's I can say is I never shot no gun that night, period," Joey Jr. said.

"Okay, somehow I believe you but you have to stay put and keep yourself low key. These are tough guys and they want you dead. Do you understand what I'm saying Joey?" Clams asked.

"But pop, I didn't do anything."

"Let's try this again. Man, are you thickheaded. They believe that you killed their kid. They are also saying the baby died because of you. If you show one hair on your ass you are dead. This isn't a bullshit game. Stay put for a while so we can sort things out. They don't want to hear a thing. To them you are guilty and that's that. Joey, you brought this on yourself with this drug world you live in. Lay low and see how things play out."

Clams was exasperated by his son's insistence. He always debated every point his father made and resisted any advice that was given. Joey Clams could never tell if it was the drugs or just his personality that made him this know-it-all who was in trouble all the time.

"This is bullshit. It's so boring here. I'm going nuts and I'm feeling shitty. I think I need to go to the doctor," Joey Jr. whined like a spoiled sixth grader.

"Suck it up. It's much more boring at St. Raymond's cemetery Mr. I-know-everything. That's if they leave enough of you to even bury. Stay put Joey, do you understand?"

"Yeah, I get it." With that he hung up on his father.

There was no doubt in Joey Clams' mind what his idiot son would do next.

Just about the time that Joey Clams was talking with his son, Gino and Carmine Miceli Jr. were at the 79th Street townhouse of the senior Carmine Miceli. They waited for a while for the Don to return from a doctor visit. When Carmine Sr. returned he seemed a bit out of sorts. He entered his home and was greeted by the two men.

"I don't know, I go from one doctor to another. My days are filled with doctor visits. Eyes, stomach, heart, head, name it and I'm seeing some other quack on Park Avenue. I've been to more doctors in the last month than I saw in the first seventy years of my life. This old age is no fun boys. But, it beats the alternative, no?"

"Pop, just take it easy and do what the doctors say. They are all tops in their field. Maybe a nice vacation or a cruise or something like that will make you feel better."

"My grandmother used to say, *Lu medicu piatusu fa la chiaja virminusa*. The doctor has feelings but his cure is not enough." The elder Carmine laughed.

Carmine Jr. hugged his dad and rubbed his back affectionately. "Pop we need some advice."

"I see my god son is keeping quiet so I assume it's about these Albanians."

"Yes *Zio*, we have a major problem." Gino kissed his godfather and walked with him from the parlor to his favorite chair in his den.

"Tell me," the Don said while opening his humidor, picking out a fat Churchill.

"Pop, these people will not listen to reason. You know how they are, all full of this old time law that they go by without using any common sense. They want this kid dead and they could even go after his kid brother or his father. All they want is blood and will not talk about any other way. This kid says he's innocent. We're not really sure one way or another but a friend of ours on the job up in the Bronx says that no final word has come down on who the shooter was. Look, if the kid did the deed then we have to back away, no problem but they just want to whack him now, case closed. I tried to reason with them and buy some time but they will hear nothing. Besides, over the past year or so they are running us into the ground in a lot of our interests. When does it stop?" Carmine Jr. waited for his father to respond as he was slowly lighting his cigar, twirling it around his lighter.

"Gino, what's your take on this thing?" the Don asked his godson.

"*Zio*, they are not looking at this like a business deal. They don't care what happens, they want *la vendetta*. They have another name for it but that's what it comes down to. They will not rest until the kid and other people we know are dead. I agree with your son, they will not listen to any reason or wait for the police report. They want bodies now. Marku was respectful and sent his regards to you but his mouthpiece handled the talking. Would not budge an inch," Gino said trying to paint a picture for his godfather.

Carmine Miceli Sr. blew out a long stream of smoke and glanced from his son to Gino in deep thought. His reply was more of a lecture than advice.

"We can't mix apples and oranges. There is no sense in bringing up how they have muscled into our affairs over the last thirty years. We let that happen because we were weak. All of the mess we have today is because the old ways that made us successful, powerful, were destroyed in ten maybe twelve years. That was our fault and that is a separate issue. The Albanians are not dumb mountain *cafones*. They are strong because they stay with what worked for them for centuries. Their rules are not easily broken. No way will they treat this as a business, so don't expect that for one minute. We got soft, our leadership became celebrities and thumbed their noses into the faces of the Feds. They don't behave like these low-lives that we let take over our thing. They want justice and they will have justice, on their terms. I admire them for keeping their traditions above all else. Gino, I know this is tough for you to hear, but your friends, who are our friends, are not safe here. If we step in only violence will happen and then we and almost every area of our business will be affected. If you wanted to play tough because these people were hurting our business I would be the first to agree. This is different. It's not our fight. Hear what I'm telling you both. Ilir will not, he cannot negotiate over the blood of his family so stop wasting your time. The only way I can help is as I said to you before. We can give them safe passage to Sicily and wish them a long life. Anything else is foolish. *Cui scerri cerca, scerri trova.*"

"I know pop, you told me this a thousand times, who looks for a quarrel finds a quarrel." Carmine Jr. knew that a debate with his father on this matter was fruitless. Gino also understood that the old man's words on the subject were final.

Gino headed back to the Bronx and the hideaway to talk to his best friend and had no idea how to break this news to him.

2 0

Ukë Marku was making a scene everywhere he went. Anyone who would listen to his rants about *Gjakmarrja* and how the Italians killed his cousin got a description of how his poor cousin died in his arms, the baby, the wife in a coma, the whole drama played like an opera. In his warped and violent mind he wanted to prove to everyone that he could take power and control of the family whenever his Uncle Ilir was ready to pass the torch. After all, by tradition and birthright he was to obtain the position of head of the family, so illustrating how he would avenge the blood of his family would make the immediate world respect and fear him. Fear is what he really wanted and respect would follow. And what better way was there than to show Ilir Marku that he would quickly dispatch those who killed the family members.

Beyond the killing he wanted to show the Italian mob that there would soon be a new sheriff in town. He was already making moves with cousins in Detroit to set up a system of hydroponic marijuana farms as part of a comprehensive drug distribution network that he wanted to manage. The heroin from Turkey, and the hydroponic weed from the states was a one-two punch in capturing the market share in several American cities, with the New York Metropolitan Area as the crown jewel and major source of income to the family. When the family was all his, the lion's share of the profit would also be his and the Italians would go whimpering into obscurity. So he thought.

Hydroponics introduces the water, nutrients and oxygen to plants bypassing the spider web of roots. The end result is faster plant growth and more potent cannabis. One of the big secrets of success is stealing the great amount of water and electricity for the lights without red flagging the location of the factory to the utilities provider. Ukë's system was to pirate the water and electricity by opening the indoor pot farms near large manufacturing plants using sophisticated energy reducing technology, stealing from both the energy company and the neighboring factory so that the amount used would reflect as a small increase in the plants costs. His system would avoid the surge of power and water required to grow the hydroponic weed and at the same time bring his cost of manufacturing to next to nothing. Grow the pot, grow a powerful product, grow it faster and sell it cheaper than anyone else and slaughter the competition. His distribution model would include the sale of any and all illicit drugs that his dealers could push. His distribution system, expanding his pizza shops, taking union business, lending hard money, controlling the best strip clubs and whore houses, would send rival mobs packing. In his mind the day of the Italian mob had long passed and the Russian mob in Brooklyn were merely goons that he could work with and control. He thought he had the brains and balls that his cousin Lekë lacked and he, Ukë Marku, was fearless, ergo whacking his cousin was good for the business and in the long run good for the family.

The Miceli family had been put on notice that their want to save the Santoros was not an option. Ukë figured that Don Carmine Miceli would not let business be affected by the murder of some punk ass American kid, and the two asshole accessories to murder. They way it was looking Ukë had figured the chess board correctly. Now, he wanted to double the ante and bring things to a head, in effect flexing his muscles.

Ukë used his Uncle Ilir's grieving period to his advantage. It was time to show him and everyone else in their world what he was all about. Under normal circumstances he would have had to confer with Ilir and Pashko to make the street moves he was contemplating. Instead of seeking their advice and support, he planned on surprising the elders by making their piece of the underworld pie a much larger portion. In thirty days he would be king of the organized crime hill in New York.

He knew that he could pull it all off with the support of a group of rogue Albanians that already had sworn their allegiance to him. They would provide the muscle and be handsomely rewarded as major operatives in his criminal cabinet going forward. Of minor concern were Engjëll and Gjergj, still in custody as material witnesses in his cousin's death. He could wait out the system knowing that their loyalty to him was unwavering or simply have them whacked at his first opportunity. Either way, that problem would take care of itself. In his mind they were a temporary and small stone in his shoe.

Three days after the meeting between Carmine Jr., Gino Ranno, Joey Clams Santoro, and the Marku clan, two events occurred that changed the course of the peace that the Albanians and Italians had enjoyed in New York for decades. One was an act of man, the other an act of God.

21

"Hey Clams, I'm gettin' tired of doing the dishes around here, you never take me out to dinner, you don't listen when I talk. It just ain't right ya know." Babbu was trying to break the tension in the hideout on Ohm Avenue. The guys all chuckled but no one was ready for the typical quick comeback.

It was three days since Gino met with his godfather Carmine Miceli Sr. and got the unpleasant news that the Don didn't think the situation with Joey Clams' son warranted an interruption of business and a war with the Albanians. Clams was eerily quiet since Gino broke the news to him, C.C. and Babbu. They were staying put to see how things would play out for a while. The place was clean and comfortable. Gino went out and got a plasma television so that they could at least see a Yankee game; the cable was rigged by a buddy of his that was trusted not to say anything about their whereabouts. C.C. and Babbu took turns getting the great food that the Bronx had to offer and stayed far away from Arthur Avenue. Ronnie's Pizza, Patricia's, Louis Seafood, bagel shops, Italian delis, Chinese, everything that you wanted and the cardiologist said was bad were available within minutes for pick up.

There was no word from Joey Jr. and they all agreed that no news was good news. They limited cell phone use as there was no way of knowing if the Albanians or the police for that matter could trace calls. C.C.'s phone was the only really safe one to use as it was in his sister's name. Babbu didn't have a phone for fear that the radioactive waves would kill the six brain cells that were in his head.

They were watching a repeat of the movie Zulu on the A & E Network and feeling as if they could relate to the British soldiers held up in that small fort where the men awaited the Zulu onslaught when C.C.'s phone rang. It was Carmine Jr. asking to speak to Gino.

"Hey bud how's it going?" Gino asked, his voice sounding tired from lack of use over the past three days.

"Gino...I have some bad news pal. My father passed away this morning," Carmine Jr. said holding back his tears.

"Oh no, Carmine. Oh Jesus, what happened?" Gino was stunned, his voice quivered, his already sallow complexion going paler.

"He never woke up Gino. Massive heart attack I guess. Good way to go for him I guess but we are all in shock over here. Some fuck leaked the news to the media and 79th Street is packed with those trucks and asshole reporters. They can't even let this man rest in peace for an hour these whores," Carmine Jr. said.

"How's your mom handling it?" Gino asked

"Hey, a lot better than me. I guess she was always prepared for this day since they were kids. And she knew he was feeling crappy the past month or so. Besides, she's a Sicilian woman, she's stronger than steel, you know."

"Carmine, I'll be there within the hour. Don't get too involved with those *strunzos* outside. Stay calm," Gino warned.

"Thanks pal, I need you here with me." Carmine Jr. broke down and hung up.

"Mother of Christ, just when you think shit can't get any worse my godfather drops dead. What the fuck?" Gino said to the guys. They all mumbled their condolences and felt the loss in their own way, most of all they felt for Gino. They witnessed the end of an era through him.

"Want us to go with you?" Joey Clams asked knowing the answer.

"No, no, you guys stay put and follow the plan. I'll take my car and you still have an escape car if you need one. Don't take any chances. Remember we are in the Bronx and these Albanians are everywhere. I'll use a safe phone to call you C.C. and in the meantime if anything pops call me. Don't even think about leaving here and you will miss the wake. Both Carmines will understand, trust me," Gino said as he went to pack a few things in case he couldn't get back for a day or two.

On his way from the country club section of the Bronx to East 79th Street, Gino was remembering his childhood, his parents and grandparents, the Sunday picnics at Peach Lake in Putnam County, New York. They would all get there around nine o'clock in the morning, Aunt Pat would already have the coffee percolating. Aunts, uncles, cousins, the Micelis from the old country, friends forever, cousin Patti's girlfriend with the big hair and small bikini. The huge pot of water was on the Coleman burner so it would boil by noon and everyone would be eating like it was any other Sunday at home, with two kinds of cheese, locatelli and parmigiano reggiano with two separate graters. All the comforts of home except there were no fried meatballs on the stove when you got home from church because the sauce was made the night before to be ready for the "picnic." The fresh ricotta, beef braciole, pork skin braciole, sausage, meatballs and a big piece of pork were all put on the table with wine for the adults, soda for the kids, all on real plates. No bologna and yellow American on Wonder Bread sandwiches with yellow mustard and paper plates for this bunch. Then after, the macaroni, he laughed when they started to call it pasta, the sausage and peppers on the grill, chicken and hot dogs so we knew that we were in America. Loaves of Italian bread, pastries, cookies and the demitasse coffee and anisette. No beer, none at all. Gino had to laugh again at that image. The food was for us and the beer was for the *midigans*. The most important thing was the families all being together, swimming, playing bocce, drinking wine, playing catch, cards and then a big Po-Ke-No game. Gino saw everyone's face in his mind and his eyes filled up with tears. For a second he reached to turn the knob on his steering column to start the windshield wipers and realized that he needed a handkerchief.

Zio Carmine was the last one left from those summers at Peach Lake and now Gino moved into the front row to wait for his time to go. It was just yesterday that he asked his mother if he could move from the kids table to the adult table. "No Gino, you're only twelve. Maybe next year, sit with your cousin Thomas and watch the baby. And don't go in the water for thirty minutes after you eat, understand, thirty minutes, wipe your chin you have sauce on it." He heard his mother's voice as if she were in the car next to him.

This was going to be a tough one for him. He had to be strong for Carmine Jr. and his Aunt Louise. They expected him to be strong, after all he was a man, a Sicilian man. He got off the FDR Drive at 71st Street and made the left on 79th Street heading west.

When he got to Lexington Avenue he could see the satellite dishes raised from the roofs of the television news trucks in front of the Miceli brownstone. He parked his car in a lot and walked the two blocks through the crowd of reporters and police to the front door. Two of the Miceli crew members guarding the door saw Gino and let him in without exchanging a word. Soft music was playing throughout the home. It sounded like Ella Fitzgerald to him but he couldn't tell for sure. He was still thinking about the old times that they all had together and felt empty that those days were gone.

"Gino, doll...oh how he loved you Gino," Aunt Louise Miceli greeted him from up one flight of stairs.

"Come up honey, they didn't take him yet. I was waiting for you to see him before they fix him up," she said with no hint of tears.

"Aunt Louise, I loved him like he was my own father," Gino said swallowing hard.

"You know, he wasn't feeling so well the past few months but he wanted to come to your house no matter what. Somehow he knew Gino, your Uncle Carmine knew this was the last party he was going to. And who better to have it with than you and your family. He was so happy that things worked out for you and Ellen. We all were honey. Now come on, let's go see *Zio* Carmine. My son is in the room with his father." Aunt Louise looked very old to him for the first time.

Carmine Miceli Sr. looked like he was sleeping. He was tucked under the beautiful bedding, his hair looked like it was just combed and his cheeks still had a rosy hue. Carmine Jr. was sitting in a chair next to the bed just to the left of his father's body. He looked as if he had been crying and he needed a shave. The old man looked better dead than the son did alive at that moment. Gino was taken aback by the small smile on the Don's face. He looked like he died happy, and that was comforting to Gino. Without any illusions Gino wondered if indeed there was a heaven, would a gangster like his *Zio* Carmine, who had killed and ordered men to their deaths, be accepted and spend eternity with his own grandfather and father and play those card games and holler and laugh as they did. Gino really didn't buy those myths but he couldn't help thinking about it at that moment.

What if it is true? Would God let Uncle Carmine through the gates of heaven? Gino thought and quickly put the questions out of his mind.

Carmine Jr. was concentrating on his father's face and felt the presence of someone in the room. He rose from the chair and went to Gino, the two men embraced and hugged each other without words. No words were needed. They both lost a man that they loved and respected. It was his time, his life was full and his death was good.

22

The word of Don Carmine Miceli's sudden and natural death traveled fast. Every wise-guy from East Harlem to California, from Brooklyn to Sicily, got the news from the very effective word-of-mouth network. The news reporters were broadcasting live from the townhouse so the whole world would know that the New York Don was dead and that his son would be taking over the "family." No waiting for the white smoke like the Vatican, no Senate hearings, no voting, no coronation. Carmine Jr.'s birthright was all that was needed. That and the fact that his father started his tough-guy training almost when he was in his bassinet would make for a successful transition of power. The other families in New York and around the country expected the change of power and respected Carmine Jr. so there was no immediate concern of a hostile takeover or trouble on the horizon. What Carmine Miceli Jr., the heir to the largest New York mob family was not aware of was the plan of one rogue Albanian gangster, Ukë Marku.

The Morris Park section of the Bronx had not changed much from the 1950s and 1960s. The old timers would not agree with that statement but the neighborhood was still going strong. Clean streets, low crime rate, excellent nearby hospitals, good schools, stable property values, a strong neighborhood association, great bakeries, wonderful pastry shops and cafes, good Bronx pizza and a few very good Italian family restaurants. One of the last safe Italian neighborhoods that had not fallen to the urban decay and drug dealing that most of the borough had suffered. Most apartments and homes were rented or sold before there was ever a realty listing made. The neighborhood was well known for its pre-approval of potential renters and home buyers.

One of those very good Italian family restaurants was Patricia's on Morris Park Avenue. The two biggest problems the restaurant faced were the long lines on weekends and the traffic department giving thirty five dollar parking violations at lunch time. They needed more seating and a parking lot but this was Morris Park Avenue and you played the cards that were dealt. Their reputation for great food at reasonable prices was about to experience an added star, and not from Zagat.

Johnny "Canada" Toronto and Fred "Ro" La Rosa ate at Patricia's at least twice a week for the past five years. Their large bellies were an indication of their love for good food and their distaste for any physical exercise. They always took the same table for four as that's what they needed to be comfortably seated and enjoy their long lunch. From the first dish of homemade pasta to their espresso Johnny and Freddy savored their meal. The owners didn't care much about the table being for four because the checks for these two were always big. The wait staff loved the generous tip; everything was paid in cash. Johnny Canada and Freddy Ro were made guys who ran a variety of gambling rooms and handled loan-sharking for the Miceli family in the Bronx. They also oversaw a piece of an internet poker site out of Costa Rica for the family without bringing any unwanted attention to them. Both were low key guys which was how Carmine Miceli Sr. wanted things. "A fish dies by its open mouth," was one of the Don's favorite expressions so Johnny and Freddy kept *sotto voce*, a soft voice. They were deciding on the best way for them to handle the Don's wake and funeral. Should they go? What would the Don have wanted? What would the new Don want? Keeping a low profile was not in step with going to a mob boss' wake, with the F.B.I. snapping photos of everyone who paid their respects. It would become a carnival, but they decided they could not stay away. Fuck the F.B.I. they loved this man and were planning to attend as soon as the arrangements were announced. Right now, business was business and lunch was lunch and neither could suffer because someone died.

They had just been served a nice bowl of gnocchi bolognese, family style, when two very large and very tough looking white guys calmly walked into the restaurant and pumped nine shots into both men, killing them on the spot. Everyone in the place jumped under a table or a counter or just on the floor and saw nothing. The exploding Glock 33, .357 subcompact handguns were enough to scare the shit out of anyone. The shooters placed both of their black pistols on the table where Johnny and Freddy missed their last meal. They also left a calling card: a bumper sticker with a double-headed eagle.

Fuck you Miceli's. Fuck your dead Don. Fuck those guys who killed our family. It's our turn. That was the message that Ukë Marku was sending to the Italians and anyone else who needed to know his intentions.

The *Gjakmarrja* had reared its ugly head.

23

The Bronx homicide office had another major crime scene on their hands in the forty-ninth precinct. Some of the work fell upon Detective Lieutenant Carlo Del Greco and his staff, who felt that the murder of the two Miceli crew members was not going to be an isolated incident. On the heels of the Marku murder, the double-headed eagle calling card was a sure sign of a possible conflict between the Italian and Albanian wise guys.

Engjëll and Gjergj were still being held for additional questioning which was put off a few days just to break balls and make them think things over, let them worry about their future of lack of one. Del Greco and Gojcaj were now chomping at the bit to start from scratch with Engjëll. Both Engjëll and Gjergj were without legal representation so Del Greco was pushing the envelope on their rights. The Albanian Embassy was never called and so far the Markus were not making any fuss to get these guys from under the magnifying glass of Bronx Homicide. The Marku family, especially Ukë, was not making noise nor were they sending any legal help for their fellow Albanians.

"Engjëll, I brought you coffee, the way we make it at home. I thought you might need some," Detective Gojcaj began the interrogation with feigned sympathy on his face. Gojcaj brought along his *xheze*, the coffee pot and burner to make Turkish coffee for the questioning. Both he and Del Greco agreed that if they did not get anywhere with Engjëll they would need to release them soon. Releasing them was as good as taking them back to Tirana in a box.

"What do you mean I might need some, what are you talking about?" Engjëll said more jumpy than ever.

"We're not sure how we will handle this Engjëll. Whatever happens, you will come up a big loser and I'm trying to be fair to you," Gojcaj said again, intentionally not making eye contact to show Engjëll that he felt badly. Del Greco sat there with a blank stare, not understanding one word in Albanian but his look was enough to add more drama and mystery to the moment. They were playing their prey for all he was worth.

"Detective, tell him that we know the gun that killed Lekë was not from the Italian kid or his crew. We know it was from him." Del Greco was just playing his hunches. Gojcaj translated Del Greco's bullshit story and the look on Engjëll's face was that of a trapped and desperate man.

"No fucking way. Not my gun. Who is saying I shot Lekë? That's bullshit, fucking bullshit! Not me, no fucking way!" The rapid response further confirmed Engjëll's shaky emotional state.

"We have evidence from the bullets and other information and a witness. I'm sorry I said too much already. I feel sorry for you Engjëll," Gojcaj said while pouring the hot coffee. Engjëll sipped the coffee too quickly and scalded his lips.

"Fuck...Look, I told you many times, I did not shoot him. Maybe someone else did, but it was not me, this is all I know."

"Engjëll, you are in a bad position my friend. You are the one that we think did the shooting. You will be sent to prison here and that is a death sentence for sure. If we let you go, you may return to Albania and be killed there, or they will ship your body back to your family in a casket. So this *besa* thing that we Albanians have has you caught in a death trap. In the meantime your pals get to continue their lives free to do whatever they and you, the idiot Engjëll takes the fall. Not so smart?"

Gojcaj ended his appeal to common sense with a question.

"Do I get to see a lawyer? I have seen American television."

"Sure, you get a lawyer. Do you want me to ask Ukë for the bail and to pay the lawyer? So you talk to a lawyer, you get out from our protection, we release you and you die quickly. This is what you want? Sure, I will contact the Markus and tell them you need help." Gojcaj pretended to stand and end the conversation.

"Wait! So if I say what I saw, what happens then?" a shaken and confused Engjëll asked the detective.

"If it's not bullshit and we follow the information and can trace it to the real killer, we will do our best to help you and protect you. The District Attorney, who is the one that can make this happen, is growing impatient with this. I need to tell him what you decide. He could give a fuck about *besa*. He is not Albanian my friend, he is black and has no patience for this. He wants this case finished now," Gojcaj said. Del Greco was just getting bits and pieces through body language and the sweat that was beading up on Engjëll's forehead which told a story without language. He decided not to interrupt as he felt the discussion was going in his favor.

"I don't know what to do. What did the others say? They were there too. What the fuck have they told you?" Once again Engjëll was showing his cards. Gojcaj knew that he was making progress and realized that he needed to tread softly. He waited for a while before he made a comment, looking into Engjëll's eyes with a sympathetic pout.

"Let's have some more coffee my friend. Can I send for some food?"

"No, nothing I have no taste for food now. My head is hurting from all of this. I must think about this more. Please, I am tired I don't want to talk now," Engjëll pleaded and Gojcaj thought it best to give his fish some more line and try again later.

"Fine, but the next time I see you, we may not have any chances for you. We are gathering information as we speak. I will make sure you are taken to a safe and isolated place and that no harm will come to you," Gojcaj said.

"The harm has already come to me," Engjëll answered with an even greater look of desperation than before.

Del Greco thought the time was right for him to see Ilir Marku and inform him that his son may not have been killed as he was told. The detective knew that he was treading on thin ice without a confession and with only skimpy facts and a gut feeling. Del Greco did not let Detective Gojcaj know his intentions to see Mr. Marku. How could he? His relationship with the head of the Albanian mob could never be exposed to anyone, especially a young gung-ho detective that was looking to make Sergeant. Del Greco took the ride to Scarsdale not even certain that Ilir Marku would see him. He was met at the door of the Marku home by Pashko Luli .

"I've come to see Mr. Marku and discuss a few things about his son's case with him," Del Greco said a bit awkwardly.

"Are you still chasing your tail Carlo? The case is open and shut. Lekë was killed by that Italian. There is no case in our mind. If you have come here because the Micelis have asked you to use your influence, that is a mistake. That would be an insult," the *Kumar,* Luli warned.

"What are you talking about? No Miceli has spoken to me about this. How can you think of such a thing?" Del Greco was taken aback by the accusation.

"Your services were well paid for by this family. Perhaps others have paid you as well."

"That is uncalled for Mr. Luli. I have been a faithful friend to this man and his family and my loyalty has never been questioned. I resent what you have said." Del Greco was annoyed but did not show his emotion.

"Forgive me Carlo. You are a good man. These times are difficult and we are all strained. I have no right to greet you like this at the Marku home. Please come in and accept my apology." Pashko was sincere in his apology although his thoughts were still untrusting. Ilir Marku came out of his study to see who came to visit.

"My friend Carlo, welcome to my home. Please come in and join me for *Kafe Turke*. Unless you prefer tea or something stronger."

"Thank you Ilir. The coffee is good," Del Greco said with a slight bow of thanks as they walked into the study.

"So what brings you here Carlo? I hope you have located the murderers for us. I am waiting for this news too long." Marku cut to the chase which was out of character for him when a guest entered his home. He was anxious for justice.

"Well, not exactly. We have been investigating the crime scene thoroughly and there are some parts of the story that have not yet been pieced together. I am not one hundred percent certain that the Santoro boy did the shooting. We are still doing everything we can to determine his whereabouts but there are some troubling aspects to the case that I want to discuss with you," Del Greco said as the women of the house scampered to get the coffee served quickly.

"Carlo, come with me. I want to show you something," Ilir said and motioned for Pashko to stay in the study.

They walked through the large house in silence, Del Greco soaking in the opulence of the place. It seemed more like a museum to him than a place where someone would live. He thought to himself that the bad guys lived a lot better than him or any cop he knew. They came to a room with two large oak doors. Ilir gently opened the doors and walked in ahead of the detective. The room was darkened and resembled a hospital room on one side. There was a comfortable sitting room directly across from a large bed where Valbona Marku lay staring up at the ceiling. Two nurses in white uniforms and three short, darkly clothed women with head scarves were attending to the young woman. Del Greco could see the state that Ilir Marku's daughter-in-law had remained since the night his son and grandson had died. Without a word, Ilir motioned Del Greco to the door and they walked back to his study.

Ilir sat in his chair and coffee was served in the customary fashion. He finally spoke.

"You were saying Carlo, about the case?"

The detective was shaken at the sight of the young woman still in a state of shock after so many days.

"I cannot know how you are suffering. This is such a tragedy that I have no word to express my sympathy to you." The detective sipped his coffee when he was motioned to do so by his host. Then Ilir Marku and Pashko Luli followed, sipping from their own cups.

Del Greco continued, "I do not believe that this Joseph Santoro killed your son. The forensic data is not conclusive. The angle of the bullet entry, the shells that were left behind and other things indicate that your son was either shot from behind or from the side at close range. Santoro was, by all accounts, standing in front of Lekë and did not fire a gun. His accomplices were armed, as were the men standing with your son."

"My nephew saw the shots fired at my son. He held his cousin when he died. That is all the proof that I need Carlo. The Italians have visited me with the same story. This is nonsense. If you will not find my son's murderer and his friends you know that I will and the result will be the same. We will have our revenge Carlo, of that you can rest assured. You have been a good friend to me but I am sorry to say that our friendship is being tested now." Ilir was unmoved.

"Give me some more time please. I am questioning the two men who were with your nephew. There is something that one of them wants to say but he is frightened. I am willing to bet my badge on this. Some more time and we will have proof that Santoro is not the killer, I am certain about this Ilir," Del Greco said pleading for what he thought was right.

"You play your game Carlo. I cannot tell you how to do your job but I can tell you that you are chasing after nothing. In the meantime I will do what needs to be done...without you." Ilir's eyes betrayed his stoic demeanor. They were filled with absolute rage.

"The hit that happened on Morris Park Avenue. This could start a very ugly war. There is no reason to escalate-" Ilir abruptly interrupted Detective Del Greco's trial balloon.

"Carlo, I appreciate your coming to my home. I hope that your family is well and we can one day resume our association." The meeting was over, there was no changing the course of the *Gjakmarrja* against the Santoro family. Del Greco knew that he could not hold the Albanians much longer.

24

"Hi pop it's me. We left upstate and I'm in Yonkers at a friend's place. It's cool. Talk to you soon." Joey Jr. left this message on Joey Clams' voice mail, defying his father's instructions to stay put upstate. What was new? Joey Jr. never listened to any advice his father gave him so why would he start now when his life was on the line? While Gino was getting ready to attend the wake of Carmine Miceli Sr., Clams played the message to him with a look of absolute disgust on his face.

"Can you believe this fucking kid Gino?" Joey asked.

"Joey, he's not a kid anymore. He's making this thing a lot harder than it needs to be," Gino said while making his tie. Gino ran back to his home in New Jersey to get some suits and fresh clothes for the wake and funeral. He returned to the Bronx hideout with some fresh towels and groceries for the guys.

"He sounded stoned. I don't know if he's just a mental case or if it's the drugs Gino."

"Yonkers? Why doesn't he just rent an apartment on Pelham Parkway from the Markus? It has to be the drugs Joey," Gino replied, trying the best he could to be kind.

"This way he and his fucked up friends can go to some titty bar and drown their sorrows in silicone. What a fucking asshole. I should just pack my shit and go back to North Carolina and wait for the phone call that he is dead," Joey Clams said out of total frustration.

"Calm down, you're not leaving me here to deal with these crazy bastards. Careful using the cell phone. Try him from a phone booth if you can find one. Pay phones are a rarity anymore. Maybe at the post office on Tremont? In the meantime I have to go downtown and I won't be back until late. Carmine Jr. is hosting a dinner for 'certain people' in his father's honor and he invited me. I can't refuse."

"Let C.C. drive you so he can watch your back. The place will be crawling with Albanians," Joey said, knowing that he could not go near the wake or funeral. The Albanians were notorious for making a statement at a wedding, wake, or funeral.

"I'm safe. It's not me that they want. I just have to be careful not to be followed back here. I'll drive through the Monroe Projects. I can lose anyone there. The place may even scare the living shit out of them." Gino laughed at his off the cuff joke. Joey didn't.

Frank E. Campbell Funeral Home on Madison and 81st Street has buried a lot of New York's famous since they started in 1898. Both saints and sinners were all treated equally and sent off in class from the four-story brownstone in this tiny neighborhood. Carmine Miceli Sr. had made his own arrangements that included a one day wake and a mass to be held at Campbell's rather than risk the carnival atmosphere that the media would make of his funeral. Carmine was always concerned for his family and how he would protect them from the life he led. His apprehension would follow him beyond his death. He knew that the Cardinal was print hungry and needed to show the lemmings that he would not allow the gangster to be buried from one of his churches and into consecrated ground. That was reserved for his pedophile priests and other circus acts that the church permitted. If Carmine Miceli Sr. were a gangster like the

Kennedys, his funeral would be held at St. Patrick's Cathedral and the Cardinal would officiate, but he was far from that. Carmine Sr. made certain that a friendly priest would say mass for him, ask God to forgive his sins, sprinkle holy water on his coffin and say a few words at a non-Catholic cemetery in New Jersey where he would be interred above ground as his family did in Sicily. Gino arrived at one o'clock in the afternoon for the two to five o'clock wake. Carmine Jr. asked that he arrive early so that the family would have some quiet time with Carmine Sr. He also wanted to have a word with Gino.

"He did it his way Gino. When Sinatra did that song all I could think about was my father," Carmine Jr. said as he and Gino knelt before the Don in his mahogany and bronze casket.

"One of a kind Carmine. They don't build them like him anymore. He was a special guy," Gino said quietly.

"Gino, let's take a walk for a minute before my mother and all the people get here. I want to say a few things to you," Carmine Jr. said leading Gino by his elbow toward the door. They went into a vacant salon next to the main room. Carmine Jr. closed the door behind them.

"Gino, I don't have to tell you what you meant to my father. You know he loved you, as I do. He was devoted to you and your family like no other. You are blood, no, better than blood if there is such a thing," Carmine Jr. said holding up a hand to stop a teary eyed Gino from responding. He continued.

"The night before he died he called me and asked me to go to his house to talk. It was as if he knew he was going Gino. He told me how much he loved me, how proud he was of me, how badly he felt for the life he chose for me, how he missed his parents and friends and how he was ready to go. I'm getting goose bumps just telling you this. He also wanted to warn me about the future. You know, watch this guy, don't trust that guy, and watch the taxes, all the things that he always told me to be careful with. Then he went into this Albanian thing. His true feelings came out that night. How he really felt about the future of our thing. He brought up an expression he learned from his days as a boy in Sicily, you know the old *paisani* would have these sayings they all followed. This one is special. *Cu fa assai e nun ci abbada, spenni assai e 'un cogghi biada.* If you put a lot into something, but don't maintain it, you will not have enough of a harvest to re-seed. Do you know what he was saying Gino?"

"I'm not sure Carmine. This goes against what your father said about getting involved with this mess." Gino furrowed his brow, trying to understand what Carmine was getting at.

"If we don't take care of our business it will be gone, taken from us. That's what he was saying to me. He told me that night to be strong and fight for what I thought was right. To protect ourselves and what was ours. Fuck these Albanian bastards and their rules. Our rules are just as old, probably older and just as powerful. There is no way they are doing anything to anyone that is ours. They took a taste of our business, we let them get away with it. Fine, everyone has to eat, it's a big world. Now, they want vengeance without proof. Ain't happening on my watch Gino, I will not mortgage our family's future to anyone. In the next few days I am letting the other families know my intentions. If they agree, great, we have partners. If they disagree we will handle this on our own."

"What can I do to help you Carmine?" Gino asked.

"Are you kidding? My father would come back from the dead and give me one *tumpuluni* in the mouth," Carmine said and laughed out loud. "Let's go, my mom and family will be here any minute. This is gonna be a rough couple of days."

The major players of every organized crime family in the United States and Sicily paid their respects to Don Carmine Miceli Sr. in some way. The carnival atmosphere on Madison Avenue was exactly what the Don had predicted. Media trucks, newspaper reporters, F.B.I. personnel,

Organized Crime Taskforce agents from New York City and New York State, mob guys looking to be seen, and the old timers looking to get into the building without being seen, friends, family, everyone from his favorite restaurant owners to celebrities he had known, doctors, lawyers, and just the average Joe looking to get a glimpse of the last of the real mobsters. Most would be turned away by Carmine Sr.'s trusted advisors who knew who to let through the doors and who to politely refuse. Mass cards and flowers were sent to the side door on 81ˢᵗ Street, where those old time Mafioso were allowed to enter. Police barricades were set up on both sides of Madison Avenue with what seemed like a platoon of blue uniformed police to keep the crowd under control and the traffic moving.

It was indeed a circus as the Don had predicted but he had thought a few moves ahead. Among his final instructions to Frank E. Campbell Funeral and Cremation Services, Inc. was to have his body removed in the very early morning hours of the day of his burial, and staged for internment at the cemetery. The casket holding the *capo di tutti capi*, the boss of all bosses, would be waiting for his family and close friends for their final goodbyes. His family would leave from their homes leaving the media in a lurch.

Gino disliked crowds but made the best of it for the sake of the Miceli family and out of respect for his late Uncle Carmine. Carmine Jr. asked him to stand next to him on the side of the coffin as is the duty of the Sicilian men of the family. This is a place of honor that Gino was hoping would not come for many years. He remembered by name all of the friends and distant relatives that he met through the years at weddings, communions, baptisms and funerals. This was a gift that Gino had since he was a young boy and Carmine Sr. put it to good use. Whenever Sr. would greet someone with "Gino, look who came," Gino got his cue to make a sincere pronouncement. "Oh, it's so nice of you to come, Congressman so-and-so, or *Zia* Philomena, all the way from Connecticut, or

Cousin Ralphie, it's been too long."

There were many people who needed no refreshing announcement, among them Micky Roach, dear friend of the Miceli family. The last time Gino saw Micky was at the Fish Farm when the old guy and his two young and imported Sicilian hit men were asked to help out. Whenever the Micelis needed that extra special muscle, Micky was called on. He was semi-retired now and living the life in Miami Beach. Tanned and rested, Micky looked ten years younger than that night in East Hampton when they were all almost killed by that wacko Colombian Lucho Gonzales.

"Carmine, thank you for calling me and asking me to come pay my respects. My loyalty is to you as it was to your father," the killer whispered to Carmine Jr.

"Micky, My father is smiling that you are here. I need to speak with you later. I'm making a table at Patsy's uptown, I'd like you to come be with me. We have a problem up in the Bronx that may need your attention," Carmine Jr. said so that Gino could hear.

"*Certo* Carmine, of course," Micky said with a look in his eye that said 'I live for this.'

25

The greeting line was exhausting to the family. One day was insufficient for the number of people that wanted or needed or were expected to pay their respects. The seven to nine o'clock viewing was expanded to ten o'clock. Among the last to arrive and the most shocking of all visitors was Ilir Marku who arrived at Campbell's alone. He walked up to the casket, extended his arm touching the hands of his dead friend. He mumbled something that could not be heard and wiped away tears from his eyes. He stood in silence for a few moments, lost in his thoughts and to compose himself. He made his way to Carmine Jr. and Gino.

"Don Miceli, I hope that God brings you only happiness from this day forward. Your father was my friend, a great man who we all will miss. From my heart I say these words." Ilir put his right hand over his heart as is the Albanian tradition.

"Mr. Marku, thank you for coming, I know this time must be very difficult for you. Will you join me and my family for dinner tonight?" Carmine Jr. asked knowing what the answer would be.

"This is the time for your family, I appreciate your kind invitation but as you know I am in mourning. I would be delighted to dine with you at some future time." Ilir Marku bowed slightly and made his way to shake Gino's hand. To Gino's surprise he greeted him with a handshake and a kiss on both cheeks, a sign of respect and friendship. Ilir exited as quietly and elegantly as he arrived.

Ilir Marku arrived back at his home shortly before eleven o'clock in the evening, exhausted from the events of the day and looking forward to a good night's sleep. He was not able to sleep since the worst night in his family history, going back as long as memory and oral narration served. Before he went to his bedroom, he poured himself a double shot of cognac and made his way to Valbona's quarters to see if there was any change in her condition. As he approached the room he heard a man's voice softly singing an Albanian song that he had heard from his own mother many times.

Ilir slowly opened the heavy oak doors to the room and saw a young man sitting in a chair at the side of Valbona's bed with Shpresa and Rick Metalia standing next to him. Valbona was still in a catatonic state although she seemed to have a slight smile on her face. The two nurses and two other women stood on the other side of the bed hoping for what seemed to be the impossible. Ilir entered the room quietly, sipping his nightcap. Shpresa noticed that he was in the room and beamed her beautiful smile. The young man finished the lovely song and Shpresa put her hand softly on his shoulder and acknowledged that Ilir Marku was present. Ever the gracious host, Ilir put his drink on a table and greeted Shpresa and Rick with a warm Albanian welcome.

"What a beautiful voice young man." Ilir put out his hand to greet the stranger in his home. Rick made the introduction.

"Mr. Marku, this is our dear friend Adem who has come to sing our songs to Valbona. Adem, please meet Ilir Marku."

"Mr. Marku, I am happy to meet you. Your home is very beautiful," Adem said while shaking Ilir's hand firmly.

"Adem returned from Tropoja just today Mr. Marku. He is a professional singer and actor and has been home for a few months. Rick and I asked him to sing the familiar songs hoping to stir Val's memory," Shpresa explained.

"Adem I am very grateful for you to bring your obvious talent to my home and help us. Please everyone, to my study for coffee and drinks."

They could not say no to this gracious invitation. They followed Ilir through the cavernous home to the room with the magnificent mural of Skanderbeg. Over the years Rick and Shpresa had been to the Marku home, but they were still in awe of the painting. Adem stopped mid-stride taking in the beauty of the room.

"Adem, come sit next to me. My home is yours." Ilir Marku noticed the young man's wonder at the Skanderbeg.

"It seems alive Mr. Marku. What a magnificent work of art," Adem stated.

"You appreciate art Adem?" Ilir asked while the women prepared *Kafe Turke* and tea.

"Yes sir, I studied fine arts here at Fordham University, and at the Academy of Music and Arts in Albania."

"Of course, in Tirana, a fine school. I read that they recently changed the school's name to University of Arts." Ilir showed he was up on current events in the homeland.

"Yes, I still call it the Academy. That's what it was called when I attended."

"Your parents must be very proud of your wonderful accomplishments," Ilir said while studying the young man's face.

"My mother wanted me to be a doctor. I swear she was Jewish," Adem said laughing.

"So why not listen to her?"

"She had enough to do to help me with Fordham. She is alone and it was a struggle. Besides, I prefer singing and acting to the life of a doctor."

Ilir could see that Adem was a man of conviction, highly intelligent, and sophisticated.

"Mr. Marku, I think that Adem will have a shot at a new movie that they are filming here in New York. The casting starts next week. A tenant of mine is the producer so Adem has an audition," Rick added with excitement.

"Good, good luck to you young man. I must ask you a question. Have we ever met before tonight? You look familiar to me," Ilir asked politely.

"Certainly I would have remembered that honor Mr. Marku but sadly we have never met. I guess I have that all too familiar Albanian face," Adem said, making a twisted face for a laugh.

"Stop it Adem, you are so modest. You are the most handsome man in all Tropoja...except of course for my husband," Shpresa said blushing after she passed the compliment. They chatted for over an hour about Albanian television and movies, the latest news about politics in Tirana, and of course how things were in their hometown Tropoja. The hour was late and the young people could see that Ilir was tiring.

"Mr. Marku, with your permission I would like to sing one more song to Valbona before I leave," Adem asked.

"Under one condition: that you promise to come back again and sing for her," Ilir smiled.

"That is my plan. I will come back as often as you allow and sing to her until she wakes," Adem replied as Shpresa gasped and held back tears after her friend's words.

"Good then. May I listen to your good night song?" Ilir didn't have to ask.

Led by Ilir, they returned to the medically supervised suite. Adem walked over to Valbona's bed and gently took one of her hands in his and softly sang. Rick and Shpresa were in tears as were the nurses and attending Albanian women. Adem's rendition of the song was from his heart and soul. He kissed Valbona's hand and turned to say goodnight to Ilir Marku but he was gone. The young friends saw themselves out and headed for Shpresa's car to make the ride back to the Metalia home in Eastchester. As they were getting in the car they were being watched by Ilir Marku from behind sheer drapes in his study. He was on the telephone.

"Pashko, there is someone I need for you to check out."

26

In the early hours of the next morning, after Carmine Miceli Jr. met with the members of the other families to toast his late father and present his plans to move on the Albanians, Micky Roach had moved into action after receiving his marching orders.

Carmine's arguments were compelling although no one really cared about the Santoro kid or what the Albanians wanted to do to him. Their beef had been building for years as they saw their good earners in construction, gambling, prostitution, dope, and now unions, turning to shit one by one. They were contending with the black mob, the Russians, the Chinese and others while the federal and city governments were nailing them for farting in their cars. The capos were whining like a bunch of girl scouts who didn't get enough Thin Mints in their shipment. It was the worst case of persecution complex since that Al Sharpton paraded that Tawana Brawley girl around.

All Carmine wanted was for the bosses of the other four families to buy into his plan and lend a hand if he needed them. To his great surprise and amazement every family was willing to go all in to make a statement and a stand to keep their businesses operating and flourishing once again.

"We was here first, forget the Irish, they don't count, these fucks need to be clipped so they know we ain't layin' down no more, and the rest of these hard-ons will take notice mark my words, you watch," were

---

the final and deciding words by the head of the Lucchese family. Everyone else also voted to stand by Carmine Jr. The old man was right and so was the timing.

Micky Roach and two young Sicilian imports pulled a newly stolen SUV a block away from the *Djelt E Shqipes* social club on Arthur Avenue in the Bronx. They were backed up by another car with a local soldier at the wheel and one in the front passenger seat that would block any pain-in-the-ass cops or others from getting to the getaway car. In just a few hours the butchers, the bakers, and the mozzarella makers would be opening their stores as their great-grandparents, grandparents and parents had done before them to do business in "Little Italy." Some called it "The Belmont Section," some referred to it as "Fordham" but most of the people who had once lived there simply called it "the neighborhood."

The club was used as an after-hours place for Albanian members, all men, to play cards, drink and watch movies and soccer matches until dawn. This morning there were eight men in various stages of inebriation all reeking of smoke, all of whom were members of Ilir Marku's crew. They had no idea the shit storm that was about to befall their little home away from home.

Micky Roach knew these streets like the back of his hands and knew how to get in, get the job done and get out fast. He also used modern technology that the *paisani* from the hills of western Sicily who taught him his trade as a human exterminator never dreamed about. The 46th Precinct House on Ryer Avenue was a good sixteen blocks away and only two squad cars patrolled the nearby area at that time in the morning. Mostly the cops would park somewhere and wait for a call rather than ride around the deserted streets. Micky saw to it that a call for a domestic dispute, one of the cops' worst nightmares, was made at the correct moment in time on Daly Avenue and at the same instant a fire was set outside the Bronx Zoo parking entrance on Southern Boulevard. Those calls and the aid of a police scanner gave Micky and the *Siciliani* about four minutes to get out of the neighborhood after anyone placed a call for police. The 911 switchboard was about to light up like a Christmas tree in Little Italy.

Micky drove up slowly to the front of the social club and remained in the driver's seat of the SUV. He was armed with a Colt .45 semi-automatic that he was confident he would not be using. The two "zips," as Italian imports are sometimes referred to, Gennaro Bruno and Giancarlo Dolce, were both armed with Protecta, 12 gauge semi-automatics with rapid fire capacity that held twelve rounds each. Twenty-four shotgun shells to take out eight men in small quarters, with an element of surprise for good measure. These guns, known as South African Street Sweepers, were one of the most deadly and effective firearms at close range and make a mess out of the human body. The barrel on these guns was just twelve inches so they were easily concealable in the jackets that the hit-men were wearing.

They entered the front of the *Djelt E Shqipes*, the guns quickly brought to their chest level and away from their bodies as the recoil could nearly break a rib or easily separate a shoulder. They opened fire and swept the bullets from right to left and left to right as planned. In twenty seconds every man in the place was dead or dying. All that could be heard was the Albanian movie on the ceiling-hung television and distant cries of babies in the surrounding building who were startled from their sleep by the tremendous noise that the shells made. A moan or two came from the floor of the social club but that was incidental. The empty guns were dropped in the club. Bruno threw an open deck of *Modiano Siciliane, Le Carte Da Gioco* playing cards, scattering them throughout the room and on top of the bodies and blood soaked floor. The Miceli family was not out for a friendly game of *Scopa*, or sweep as it translates in English. The South African guns proved that this game was for keeps.

Bruno and Dolce jumped into the car. Dolce, nervous from the mass murder, was nearly jumping out of his skin.

"*Vada velocemente...molto velocemente.*" Go fast...very fast, Dolce said in Italian. Micky Roach looked through the rear view mirror for a few seconds.

"*Piano piano acusi nesuno sape che non amo a mazzato na stanze pieno di oume. Stronzo!*" Micky said in Sicilian just to keep it real. The rough translation: "Slowly, Slowly, so we don't look like we just killed a room full of men. Asshole!" He drove down Arthur Avenue, went straight passing St. Barnabas Hospital along the old rock wall, past the parking lot and made his way slowly down to Webster Avenue. The piercing sound of police sirens could be heard in the distance with one patrol car passing them at high speed as they waited at a light like good obedient motorists. If it were up to Dolce, the entire NYPD would be chasing them like they were the Bonnie and Clyde gang down the Grand Concourse. Micky made his way to the Cross Bronx Expressway, drove at the speed limit to Castle Hill Avenue, weaved his way around and under the Bruckner Boulevard elevated highway and made a right on Brush Street. There, a black Lincoln with livery license plates was waiting for them with a handpicked driver from the Miceli crew. Micky, Bruno, and Dolce exited the getaway car, the two zips leaving their jackets and shoes behind, and got into the "cab." They looked like any three pals going home from a long night out. As the car started to pull away, Micky calmly removed a small box from his jacket pocket, pressed a button and the SUV went up in flames. In forty minutes it would be a twisted, melted mess of steel. At that hour in the morning, on that street, the fire department wouldn't be called until the vehicle was unrecognizable.

Micky didn't go to sleep that night. They were burying his Don at ten o'clock that morning. He wouldn't miss that goodbye for anything.

27

Joey Jr. and his shithead sidekicks Dennis and Jimmy were making all the wrong moves just as predicted. Their remote hideout in upstate Orange County was too boring, too noisy, too quiet, not enough action, too far from their friends, all the right reasons for these three idiots to put themselves in harm's way. They were behaving like spoiled children as they had done their whole lives so why would anyone think they would act differently when the whole Albanian world was looking to make sausages out of them. Of all places they picked in the New York Metropolitan area Yonkers was perhaps the worst if they wanted to be inconspicuous. Yonkers has one of the highest concentrations of Albanians that live in the region outside of the Bronx. Just north over the Bronx border, Yonkers was a perfect place where Albanians could buy a home, be close to their businesses in the boroughs, raise kids and send them to decent schools and pretend to live in the suburbs of Westchester County. It was also an affordable stop-over point before they fulfilled their dreams of owning a large home in Armonk, Scarsdale, Valhalla, Bedford and a dozen more appealing zip codes. This kind of life was a signal of success to the rest of the Albanian community. You made it in America if you moved your family to the safety and splendor of the suburbs. No one was asking how you did it, with whom you did it, or the sordid details of success. You made it and that was all that mattered. That kind of pride was not unique to the Albanians, after all the Germans, Irish, Italians, and Jews to name a few, measured their success in terms of where they lived and how they could provide for their growing families.

Yonkers was a way-station to fulfill the American dream.

No matter where they would go within a very wide vicinity of the Bronx, Joey Jr. and his pals would be spotted and the word would get to Ilir Marku within minutes. The best thing for any Albanian to do was get on the right side of the tough guys because one never knew when one would need them. Blowing a whistle on the scumbag murderers would pay handsomely and not with one penny changing hands. It would show loyalty to the community, it would enhance the person's *besa*, be good for business and make the caller a protected species. Everyone was on the lookout but it was like trying for the winning scratch off lottery ticket. No one would expect these guys to be anywhere near New York by now so life just went on as usual. Only pure idiots would stay around town with the Albanian mob looking for them, and of all places in Yonkers, New York.

Joey Jr. and his crew of fellow addicts acted without any sense of self preservation. Clearly their ability to reason was diminished by the use of multiple drugs. That kind of convoluted thinking was more dangerous than uncut heroin and more lethal than any of the three young men could even imagine. Upon their arrival in Yonkers the clock began ticking. It was simply a matter of time, not if but when they would be found and slaughtered in the most unpleasant fashion.

2 8

Shpresa spent as much of her spare time as possible with Valbona. She visited Valbona's bedside daily holding one sided conversations as if her BFF was responding to her words. Balancing her business in the city, her home, Rick and her already demanding life was taking its toll on her but she could think of nothing else but Valbona and what, if any, future she would have. She decided to take a full day off from work and everything else and spend it with her friend. She needed to do this as much for herself as for Valbona.

"Screw everything Rick. All I have on my mind is Val. I'm ready to lie down next to her and cry my eyes out so I'm just going to be with her all day today and maybe even tomorrow. I'm sorry but my heart is breaking a little bit each day. I'm starting to feel sick physically and I am so obsessed with her condition that I'm good for nothing, not business, not you, my family...nothing," Shpresa said to her husband.

"Shpres, you know what? I understand why you feel this way but I can't see you get sick and crawl up in a ball either. I think maybe you should see somebody and talk this out. Not for me or our business or any other bullshit but for you. Suppose Valbona doesn't come out of it. What then? You spend the rest of your life in misery?" Rick said.

"Baby, she will come out of it. I know she will and I have to help her and be there for her. It never entered my mind that she will remain this zombie forever. I will not accept that. I know she hears me I can feel it,"

Shpresa said to her husband gripping her two hands into fists.

"Okay, then I'm going with you today, tomorrow and the next day. If you feel this way then I will be with you all the way. You're my wife, I need to support you as you have supported me all these years. I'll call the office and say we are away for a few days. They can handle things."

"You are soooo sweet Baby. One favor I want to ask...please ask Adem to come too. I think his singing and the Albanian conversation will help her, I really do," Shpresa said.

"Shpres, I will do anything for you. But if this doesn't work you will need to seek some professional help and get your life, our life back. What happened to Val is a real tragedy. I cannot allow that tragedy to kill you too. I don't mean that you will be dead. This can kill your spirit. I can't have that Shpresa," Rick said with total love and caring for his wife.

Rick drove up to the Marku estate and could see from a block away that something had changed. In front of the home there were several cars with men standing around them and scattered around the expansive and impressive front yard. As they made their way toward the driveway one of Ilir Marku's bodyguards approached the vehicle and recognized its occupants. Rick stopped the car and asked in Albanian if everything was all right. The burly bodyguard looked inside the vehicle and waved him into the driveway without responding. Shpresa looked at her husband and rolled her eyes. Adem did not yet understand what was going on. Ilir Marku came out of the house to greet the unexpected but welcomed guests. He shook the hands of both men and kissed their cheeks and embraced Shpresa.

"From my heart I welcome you all to my home. Please come in," Ilir said. The head of the Albanian mob was always the perfect gentleman and he was sincere in his words to these fine young people.

"Mr. Marku, we came to visit and to comfort Valbona but if this is a bad time..." Shpresa said motioning to the men around the house.

"My dear Shpresa, there is never a bad time for guests to enter my home. My men are here to make sure that nothing happens to me because of the horrible things that are happening around us. This is not for you to worry about. So Rick how is your business doing? I hear good things," Ilir answered the question and changed the subject.

"Thank you sir. Yes things are good. We are all working hard and I have picked up some good properties to manage recently," Rick said.

"I am happy. We will talk soon as I have an opportunity that you may be interested in. With your permission I will call your office for an appointment," Ilir said.

"An appointment? Mr. Marku, you never need an app—"

"Rick, your time is valuable and I will act accordingly," Ilir said, interrupting Rick and then continued. "So good to see you again Adem. Have you come to bless us with your talent again young man?"

"Mr. Marku, I could think of no better way to spend my time than to be with my friends and help with Valbona," Adem replied, his right hand over his heart.

"Good, good but first some coffee with me and then we can spend time with Valbona," Ilir said extending his arm toward the Skanderbeg room.

Pashko Luli had completed his preliminary inquiries of Adem and as Ilir's *kumar* and *probatin* had dutifully reported the information the day before. Ilir was told that Adem was the child of an Albanian woman with no husband. He was born in Albania and visited the states very often when he was a child. Adem's mother settled in an apartment in Yonkers and raised him alone sending him to the best schools, hiring the tutors, music teachers and whatever it took to mold her son into a good man. She had always worked two jobs and arranged for Adem to spend his summers with her family in a small town just outside of Tirana. While he was in school Adem worked hard on his studies and always worked to help his mother of whom he was very devoted. No police record, no trouble in the States or Albania, didn't hang around the wise guys, no current girlfriend in Albania, not even a traffic ticket. He was also devoted to the arts and his profession, slowly building a celebrity status in and around Tirana. Pashko could find nothing so far that pointed to danger for the Marku family. He certainly was not here on a *gjakmarrja*, but Pashko would continue to gather more information from his sources just in case there was something in his background that could cause danger to the clan.

Coffee and cookies were served by the women of the Marku household and the conversation between Ilir and his three young guests was warm and friendly and centered mostly around Valbona and her unchanged condition.

"Valbona was the light of my son's life, as he was of mine. So long as she is alive our family will take care of her in any way we can. I pray that she comes back to us and begins to live her life. Up to now we see no sign of hope," Ilir said.

"Mr. Marku, if I may...

I have known Valbona my whole life and we are best friends. I know that I can reach her; I can feel it in my bones and in my blood. With your permission and with all respect to your home we would like to try a more powerful approach to reach her. I would like to spend more time with her and Rick and Adem have agreed to help me." Shpresa was asking Ilir for his approval to bring Valbona out of her catatonic state and not giving him any details.

"Well, let me see. The doctors have been no help with this situation. The elder women are drawing weary and their prayers are unanswered. I do not understand how the mind works in a situation like this. I am not sure if your method can do any more harm to her and I truly believe that you all have her best interest in your hearts. I trust you and I agree with your plan, whatever it is. If there is anything in my power that I can do to help you, please do not be bashful to ask me," Ilir said to them looking in all of their eyes.

"Sir, we will do our best to reach into Valbona's heart and soul and bring her back. Shpresa feels strongly that Val is hearing us and we are prepared to do what it takes to get her to respond. Thank you for having this confidence in us," Adem said.

"Adem, what I know about you, what I sense about you is that you are very bright and very good and you will do your best. I will remain here at home to assist you in any way that I can. Thank you from my heart. My house is yours," Ilir said while staring into Adem's eyes.

Shpresa, Rick, and Adem left Ilir alone in his study to begin their work with high hopes knowing that their task was daunting and their "cure" was strictly experimental. They entered the darkened suite where Valbona was sleeping in a comatose state. Shpresa politely asked the three Albanian women and the duty nurse to leave them alone for a while with Valbona and opened the drapes as they left. The light poured into the room drenching Valbona and the medical equipment with the warmth and radiance of the sun. Rick raised the head of the bed so that Valbona was sitting upright. Shpresa opened her purse and removed several Rick Springfield CDs that she and Val listened to for endless hours back when they were younger and as recently as a month before the tragedy that put her in this bed. Shpresa put one of the CDs into the laptop that was used by the visiting doctors and the duty nurses to track Valbona's vital signs. She began combing Val's beautiful light brown hair while she, her husband, and Adem began speaking in Albanian and English like they had planned. They started talking about music and how they were not at all fans of rap just as if they were all gathered as friends in their own living room. They decided to stop calling for Valbona to come back, stop telling her that everything would be all right and all of the other pleadings that were being made for this beautiful young woman to return to life. That clearly wasn't working and it was starting to sound more and more like the wailings at a *hater*. They wanted to leave the old fashioned customs for their proper time and place; this was certainly not what they believe Valbona needed. Their method to cure Valbona was to have her hear that life was continuing around her. Life was still worth living in spite of the horrors that could happen to anyone.

Hour after hour went by and the conversation carried on normally. Laughing, singing along with the music, changing Valbona's position, talking about how things were now in Albania, cursing, arguing, as Rick and Shpresa were known to do on a variety of subjects, and of course, they had to eat. Shpresa went out of the house to her car and returned with two large bags filled with food for a picnic which she laid out on plates from Ilir's kitchen and placed them at the foot of Valbona's bed. Shpresa made a special trip the day before to the Mergimtari Grocery on 187th Street in the Bronx and picked up a few things for an Albanian buffet. Adem, Rick and Shpresa snacked on yellow fefferoni from Macedonia which, very much like eating peanuts, once you start you can't stop, with these long tangy peppers in white vinegar. Dried smoked meats, Albanian bread, and of course a large square of feta cheese were laid out on the bed. Ilir looked in the room when he heard the clanging of plates and cutlery and in an instant he knew what his three guests were doing. They were bringing Valbona back to her familiar world simply by behaving normally. He went to the bar in his study and brought a quart of Jack Daniels and three glasses back to Valbona's room, placed the liquor and glasses on the bed and left without saying a word. He approved of their method. Rick poured the booze neat into the three goblets and they said an Albanian toast.

"This feta cheese is the best ever," Shpresa said while taking a chunk of the creamy white cheese on a small piece of bread.

"It's good but I like the Bulgarian feta better," Rick said knowing it would start his wife off on a rage about feta cheese.

"You are really crazy Rick. Your family likes that Bulgarian stuff, but this French feta rules. Yours is like that yellow American cheese next to this," Shpresa said laughing but ready for a feta war.

"My ass, what do you think Adem?" Rick asked Adem to be the final judge on the issue and he wasn't biting.

"As long as it's not Greek feta they are both fine with me," Adem said with a hearty laugh.

"Coward," Rick said.

"Are you kidding, French feta is creamy and solid and the taste is way better than any others," Shpresa said not willing to capitulate.

"That's because your mother is from Belgium and she loves the French...what does she know? The French suck anyway," Rick replied

"Shpresa is right the French feta is so better." Valbona was awake.

Shpresa gasped and nearly choked on her last bite. Tears welled up in her beautiful big green eyes and a few ran down her face. Their plan worked. She knew in her soul that her friend Val would come around.

"Val? Oh my God. Are you back?" Shpresa said, not prepared and not knowing what to say or do.

"Can you close the drapes just a little, I'm blind from all this light," Valbona said shading her eyes, looking around the room.

"Valbona, it's nice that you joined us for our picnic," Rick said, also not knowing what to say but always saying something very cool.

"Valbona...Val...this ...ah...this is Adem do you remember him?"

Shpresa asked.

"Of course I do, he is your friend on Albanian television and he was singing to me. Such a beautiful voice," Valbona said looking from Adem to Rick to Shpresa.

"What can I do for you, are you hungry? Want some water?" Shpresa said not knowing if she should hug her friend, feed her, call the nurse, or call Ilir. She was walking in a circle with both her heart and soul soaring.

"No, but if you get another glass I would like to have a little taste of Old Man Jack." Valbona was back.

29

"I can tell you on my honor and on the souls of seven generations of my family that I did not kill Lekë Marku," Engjëll said to Detective Gojcaj and a special investigator from the U.S. Marshals Office. Engjëll had been moved to a safe house in the Riverdale section of the Bronx along the Hudson River. A brilliant maneuver by Detective Del Greco, who called in the U.S. Marshal Service for the Southern District. They would see to the detainee's physical protection and assist in any way possible with the investigation. Del Greco asked the special unit to take over the protection of the Albanian detainee primarily to signal to the Marku family that the interrogation was no longer fully under his control. At the same time, his asking the federal government to get into the case eliminated any possible question as to his relationship with the mob family. Del Greco was covering his bases and going for broke to get information or a confession from Engjëll, the weakling of the two Albanians who were at the murder scene of Lekë Marku.

"Engjëll, I have to be honest with you. My partner is with Gjergj as we speak filling out the necessary paperwork to release him from custody. He has told us certain things to lead us to believe that you were the shooter. I guess he is looking for leniency from the district attorney as a material witness. After his testimony, he will be free to return to Albania and you will be indicted for capital murder. They may even allow him to stay in the United States on a special Visa for his co-operation. He played his cards very well Engjëll, very well indeed." Gojcaj was going along with a plan that was sure to make Engjëll flip out and spill his guts if there was anything to spill.

"So you are telling me that my friend from childhood has said that I was the one who shot Marku? This is what you are saying to me?" Engjëll said looking straight into Detective Gojcaj's face.

"When it comes to freedom, to life, there are no friends in this world Engjëll. Stop with this myth of *besa* and wise up. Your 'friend' saw that it was him or you and he chose freedom over principal. It happens every day," Gojcaj said.

"Not in Albania," Engjëll shot back.

"And there is a Santa Clause in Albania too. Are you a man or a child that you believe in fairytales? You are facing life in prison my friend. He walks out and you go away, probably die in jail quickly from some Marku soldier looking to make his family comfortable."

"I am no rat you *qyqan*. I am not afraid to die," Engjëll said, referring to Gojcaj as a kind of wimp.

"Suit yourself. When they release Gjergj after he signs a statement swearing that you murdered Lekë Marku, these nice men from the United States Marshal Service will bring you to jail and you will await indictment for murder. You may not make it to court when Ilir Marku or his sidekick Pashko Luli or that lunatic Ukë Marku find out that it was you who spilled their family's blood. This will surely be the shortest *gjakmarrja* in Albanian history." Gojcaj closed the notepad that he had on the table in front of him, slowly and deliberately put his pen into the inside of his jacket pocket and started to stand up.

"Wait. Sit down. Please sit down. I want to say what happened on that fucking roof. A cigarette please?" Engjëll asked, his face now ashen and his resolve evaporated. Gojcaj tossed a pack of Marlboros with the matches attached to the box top across the table and opened his book.

A tape recording and video of the interview had been running all the while, all part of the safe house strategy set up by the Marshals.

"I had no beef with Lekë or the Marku family. I knew that they were a powerful family, running a lot of things here in New York. They came from my home town in Albania and were famous for their courage in clan wars for over a hundred years. When they came here we all knew that they would be on top. We were all proud of their success. One day Gjergj introduced me to his friend Ukë Marku who came to Albania for a funeral. He told us of the possibility to make big money in the states and to maybe have our own clan here, maybe not New York but somewhere. We would have to work for him for a while and show that we have balls and do whatever he asked us to do but he would take care of us big time. He wanted to break away from his clan, the Markus, and be his own man. We met a few times in the week that he was in Albania and he arranged for us to come to New York to work for him. The trip was paid for, we had a place to live for free, he set us up with women at a men's club in Manhattan and we each had five thousand dollars to spend in our pockets. I thought I had died and went to heaven for sure." Engjëll took a long drag on his cigarette, holding the smoke for a few seconds and exhaling evenly through his nose.

"At first we did a few easy jobs for him, mostly running drugs into Harlem and collecting money. Once we had to beat the shit out of one of his pizza shop managers who was caught skimming off the top. Ukë demanded that both arms and both legs be broken on this poor bastard. That was easy stuff. The guy cried like a baby when we pulled him by his hair from his office in the store into the basement. He pissed himself too. I felt bad for him but it was just a job. We were getting paid one thousand dollars a week for being tough guys. My uncle has been here fourteen years and he makes six hundred dollars a week breaking his ass painting apartments in slum buildings. He paints for twelve hours a day. What the fuck, we were making easy money. Then one day Ukë wants to meet us in Manhattan at the V.I.P. Club. We go. We each get a girl for a few hours while we wait for Ukë, an American college girl, beautiful. Bottles of Hennessey, food, whatever we wanted on Ukë. He comes and looks very serious telling us how his cousin Lekë is fucking up the whole family business. How the boss, Ilir Marku, is fed up with him and knows he is no good but will not make Ukë a boss because Lekë is his only son. He tells us the Italians will take back what it took the Albanians years to build and that the *zezaks*, the blacks, are controlling more and more of our business because of Lekë. Ukë wants us to go with him to this drug buy in the Bronx and protect him while he ices his cousin and then he will be in a position to take over the family. We would each get ten thousand dollars, and all we had to do is kill an Italian kid that was buying some shit from Lekë. Ukë would do his cousin and it would look like they had a shootout and the Guinea was the killer. Of course we had to swear an oath to Ukë and we would be rewarded with big jobs in his organization. Just like the Guineas, they call them made-men you know, like real Mafioso. Who gives a shit about some punk Italian kid? I would do him just for the chance to be part of Ukë's clan. Ukë's plan was to hit his cousin, make it look like a drug deal gone bad. When the shooting started I missed that kid with almost a full clip and I saw Gjergj dive behind this fan thing on the roof. He looked scared with all the shooting and then the Italian kid and his boys ran so fast it was too late to make a move. I did not shoot at Lekë. That was not my job. I could barely see him but I know that he was supposed to be hit by Ukë. That is the truth. I did not shoot Lekë, please believe me. My life is worth shit now. Less than shit. I am dead no matter what happens." Engjëll finished, lowered his head into his chest and began to cry softly, wiping the tears from his eyes with the sleeves of his jail issued jumpsuit.

"You are telling me that Ukë planned the hit, planned to kill his own cousin, in an Albanian family, so he could run things? Come on Engjëll who is going to believe that story? This does not happen in an Albanian family, especially in a family like the Markus," Gojcaj said.

"Ok cop, now who is believing in fairytales? I have told you what I know, I am now *i pa besa*. I am shit, dead to the world, so go and fuck your grandmother while your mother watches," Engjëll said without even looking at Gojcaj. *I pa besa*, without *besa*, without honor, is as good as a plague for an Albanian.

"I'm sorry Engjëll. I do believe what you are saying but are you sure you did not see Ukë kill his cousin? This is very important."

"I can tell you he was supposed to kill him, he planned to kill him, he wanted to kill him, he probably killed him, yes. I cannot tell you that I saw him kill him. That whole act that he did when he was hit was complete bullshit. I was stunned at his bullshit. He wanted him fucking dead and then he carried on like a woman. I felt like shooting him right there where he sat," Engjëll said, his green eyes filled with anger.

"Is there anything else you want to tell me about that night Engjëll?" Gojcaj asked.

"That cousin Zef, the superintendent, I don't think he knew anything about Ukë's plan to kill Marku. He was not part of the plan and he looked like he was in shock when Marku dropped. And one more thing. Ukë told us not to worry because your partner the Guinea cop was on the Marku payroll and he would fix the reports and make them right. Not to worry, he said. We were going to be bosses and rich one day he said. Men of total respect. Look at me now Gojcaj, I am a dead man," Engjëll said. He was finished with his whimpering and now seemed resigned to his fate.

"Tell me more about the cop that was on the Marku payroll, what else did he say about that?" the U.S. Marshal Special Investigator, also fluent in Albanian asked.

"Wait a second, how could you give any credence to Ukë's remarks about my partner? Del Greco is a true cop. One hundred percent straight as an arrow. Let's not go there pal. Ukë is a piece of shit gangster," Detective Gojcaj jumped in to preserve his partner's reputation, again showing how much he believed in fairytales.

"Take it easy Detective, we can discuss this another time," the Marshal ended his query for the moment.

"Anything else Engjëll?" Gojcaj asked.

"No, nothing that I can think of. What will happen to me now? What will happen to my family in Albania?" Engjëll asked imagining the possible horrors.

"We can talk about that another time. Right now I have some paperwork for you to read and sign. You will stay here for a few days under the watchful eyes of the United States Federal Government. You are safe Engjëll. Relax, I will do the best that I can for you," Gojcaj replied. His mind was still on the accusation that fell upon his partner and mentor Detective Lieutenant Carlo Del Greco, who was just about to take his pension. Or, if what was said was true, more than likely he would walk away with a jail sentence and not one red cent of tax payer pension money. The game of pension roulette had started long ago for Del Greco.

3 0

G ino, in Albanian we have a proverb: *Per nji, pleshte djeget jargani.* Sometimes for one flea, you have to burn the whole blanket," Shpresa said to Gino.

"Okay, so what does this mean? Is that a solution to the bed bug problem plaguing New York?" Gino said laughing.

The two old friends decided to meet to discuss the events surrounding the murder of Lekë and the resulting blood feud. Shpresa selected a restaurant that was out of the way and not Albanian owned, which is no easy task in the New York metropolitan area. Her solution was a Sushi restaurant called Yama on East 19th Street and Irving Place in Manhattan where they were unlikely to be seen together. A tiny place in the bottom of a townhouse with no real windows to see into, Yama had arguably the best sushi in New York City. The lunch time crowd was always busy and the owner held a table for Shpresa, who was a frequent take-out customer.

It was difficult not to notice such a beautiful young woman and a nice looking older gentleman and not be curious. Gino was very familiar with the scene and how most people were using their imagination to determine if Shpresa was a business associate, his wife, his girlfriend, his *commade,* or his daughter. They walked arm in arm into the restaurant as two friends would do in Europe. No matter what it looked like to the rest of the world Gino and Shpresa loved each other in their own way and screw the rest of the world and what it looked like. Shpresa's theory about Sushi and the Albanians and not being seen together at this critical time was to protect Gino more than anything. Her supposition was wrong.

"You need to understand the way these men think Gino. They want to get Joey's son. To get to him they will get to his father, his brother, you or anyone that they believe is in their way. You are not real blood but they don't care. If they can smoke the kid out they will get anyone that they can. After what happened on Arthur Avenue you are in danger Gino. No bullshit, real danger. Are you paying attention to me or looking at that blonde's ass at the sushi bar?" Shpresa went from being deadly serious to laughing out loud at Gino's expression when she caught him checking out a hottie.

"Yes, I hear you Shpres, you think she's a lesbian and totally uninterested in an old man like me," Gino said.

"Ginooooo, you are a wild man. Focus for a minute. I'm not kidding with you. This is real Albanian mountain stuff. They play for keeps Gino. You are in danger and you need to be very cautious until this thing is settled," Shpresa said.

"Settled how? They are not interested in hearing the facts. This kid did not kill the guy. I don't know who did but it wasn't Joey Santoro Jr. Your people want blood and that's it." Gino knew he used the wrong choice of words.

"Oh so now it's my people versus your people? Come on Gino," Shpresa said.

"Shpres I'm sorry. I apologize. That was just a wrong choice of words. These guys just don't want to hear that maybe this kid is innocent. I understand the *vendetta* thing better than most people and you know that. Call it *vendetta*, or *gjakmarrja*, or blood feud; I know the root of this behavior and what makes up the need to get even. It's in my blood too but this time it's so wrong. The kid is not the best kid we know, we agree on that, he has drug problems but he is no way a killer. That's all I'm saying honey."

"Gino, they have an eyewitness from the family. Their case is open and shut. Joey Jr. will die because of this, maybe not this week or this year or this decade but he will meet a violent end, trust me on this. My biggest fear is that you will be caught in the crossfire. I can't deal with that Gino," Shpresa said and her eyes began tearing up.

"If you start crying Shpresa, the people here will think I took your allowance away or that we're having a lovers' quarrel," Gino said.

"Gino you jerk, can't you ever be serious, this is not funny," Shpresa said but began laughing at the look on Gino's face.

"I hear what you are saying Shpres but I'm in this thing. What can I do? Run and hide? This is going to get a hell of a lot worse before it gets better. Every time Carmine Jr. hits them, they hit him back and on and on and on. When *vendetta* and *gjakmarrja* meet the result has to be bad on so many levels."

The conversation went on for almost three hours and solved little except that Gino gave Shpresa his promise not to take unnecessary risks with his life and expose himself to the Albanian mob. Little did they know that a busboy in the restaurant, one Sevdet Sheji who lived in the Bronx, recognized Shpresa and overheard some of the conversation that she and Gino were having. The industrious Sheji made the appropriate call to the appropriate party and soon after, some Marku soldiers were dispatched to Yama with orders to lay back and tail Gino before reporting back to Ukë Marku. Sevdet Sheji was told to report to a certain restaurant on City Island, in the Bronx the next day to begin his training as a waiter. In the Albanian world, rewards are just as certain as punishment.

3 1

Gino removed the orange parking summons from the windshield of his car and, unlike most people, did not check the time and the penalty amount to add more misery to the experience. He had a lot more on his mind than the sixty-five dollar fine, or the fifty-dollar one he knew he got going through a light on the West Side Highway going to meet Shpresa. That one was done by camera which usually really pissed him off as the light goes from green to red in a millisecond. Gino was more intent on getting back to the Bronx and making plans for Joey Clams to get him into another safe house outside of New York.

Gino drove north on the FDR and passed the Ed Koch Bridge to make his way to the Bruckner Expressway and the Bronx. Only a couple of years ago that bridge was named the Queensboro Bridge and he used it often to visit his old girlfriend, Lisa Devlin, who nearly cost him and his friends their lives out at the Fish Farm in the Hamptons.

"Holy shit," Gino said out loud to himself getting chills as he passed the bridge, his mind flashing to that time of his life. He thought of Lisa and the carousel that he had jumped onto and how lucky he was to barely get off with his skin intact. It was two years ago, or a hundred as far as he was concerned. He realized that the situation he was in with his friend Clams was no less dangerous than fighting Lucho Gonzales, the crazed Columbian pervert.

He shook his head and started thinking about something else. That something else was a meeting he asked to have tomorrow with Carmine Jr. Gino wanted in. In the mob that he kept away from his whole life. He knew that Carmine Jr. looked up to him and valued his advice. Why not stay close and help Carmine make the right choices, help watch his back as no one else would?

Gino's mind began racing and so was his car. He didn't realize that he was doing ninety-five on the Bruckner and was unaware of the car tailing him at two hundred yards. Gino never thought that anyone would be following him from a tiny sushi bar in Gramercy Park to the Bronx with four Albanian goons, one of them being the wild man Ukë Marku, out for blood.

Gino parked his Cadillac a block away from the Ohm Avenue house where Joey Clams and C.C. were playing *Briscola*, the Italian card game with Babbu. They were all waiting for Gino to get back from his "secret meeting" and decide what to do for supper and discuss their next move. Babbu's stomach was already growling.

Ukë and the three soldiers were close enough to see the house that Gino entered yet, far enough away not to be spotted. Gino wasn't even thinking of a tail on him and was so distracted by everything that was on his mind that the Albanians could have almost parked right behind him and he would have missed them.

"Did you check your route and drive around Pelham Bay Park like I told you?" Joey Clams asked at the door when Gino entered the small red brick house.

"Yeah, don't worry Joey nobody followed me. There are a billion people in this city, do you think I'm gonna be followed?" Gino said and in effect brushed off his pal.

Joey didn't like the answer but he let it go, looking between the Venetian blinds on the living room window to check outside. He saw nothing out of the ordinary but was not getting a warm and fuzzy feeling from Gino's attitude toward their security.

"Ohhh, I'm friggin' starvin' like a *morte de fame*, let's get some food or go out and eat or something," Babbu said and folded his hand and stood up from the table.

"Hey Pete you just can't fold in *Briscola* because you're hungry. Play the cards," C. C. said a bit pissed off.

"I ain't playin' those cards for two reasons Charlie. First off, they suck and second, I'm fuckin' ready to eat my sneaker, okay?" Babbu would not be denied his rightful spot at the food trough.

"Joey, should we take a quick ride to Angelina's up in Tuckahoe? I know the owners, great food. It's fifteen minutes by car from here and I think we will be pretty safe there. It's a family spot," Gino said.

"It was a family place where Michael Corleone shot that Irish prick cop and Sollozzo, remember?" Joey said half kidding.

"Yeah, you're right but that was a movie a long time ago. Let's go. We'll be fine. Tomorrow we have to blow this place anyway. We can talk over supper," Gino said.

The four men started gathering their wallets and keys, Joey Clams and C.C. putting their pistols into waist band and ankle holsters. They both carried two automatic Glock .45 and two Beretta M80s as backup. Suddenly Babbu stopped dead in his tracks.

"Wait a second. I got a question. They call it sauce or gravy?" Babbu asked.

"What are you talking about? Whose they?" C.C. asked

"This Angelina's place. They call is sauce or gravy? 'Cause if they call it gravy I ain't goin," Babbu said. Gino, Joey Clams and C.C. broke out laughing.

"Sauce you moron, let's go," Clams said laughing and pushing Babbu toward the door.

"Ohhh, one more question I gotta ask yous. They have spaghetti number eight? I only eat spaghetti number eight ya know?" Babbu asked.

The friends all broke out in laughter again. The funniest thing about the question was that Babbu was serious.

"Yes Pete, they have eight, eleven, nine, sixty-four, all the numbers that you need, *a fa in goule,* let's go," Gino said.

The four men walked toward Gino's car down Ohm Avenue still laughing at Babbu's food jokes which they were not really sure if what he was saying were jokes or in reality true Babbuisms. As they approached the car Joey Clams noticed two men walking in their direction on the opposite side of the otherwise empty sidewalks. They had that unmistakable sinister look of trouble, and they looked Slavic or Albanian. One of the two gave two too many glances in their direction and that was all Joey needed to go into action. He pushed the smaller Gino toward a parked car and removed his Glock in the same motion.

"C.C. nine o'clock," Joey said sending his Vietnam buddy into defense mode. C.C. drew his gun quickly and came up a moment too late.

The two Albanian hit-men opened fire with no fear in their eyes as they began walking across the quiet street in the direction of their intended victims. Gino fell behind the side of a car, smelling the familiar scent of dog shit in the street and not quite sure what was happening. C.C. was hit once on his left side and managed to drop one Albanian with a head shot before the pain doubled him over and he hit the concrete pavement hard. The Albanian's brains, blood and bones splattered all over the windshield of a parked car as his body fell back onto the front hood of the vehicle. Joey Clams was circling the car parked behind the one that was protecting Gino and had his sights on the second Albanian shooter, who was in the middle of the street firing wildly. Babbu was hit twice a second or two before Clams sent the Albanian to his maker, dropping him with four well placed body shots.

The car that followed Gino back from his lunch with Shpresa roared down the street with a Marku soldier firing his automatic handgun at Clams from the driver's side back seat, missing him and breaking the windows in one of the look-alike houses along Ohm Avenue. The driver was Ukë Marku, who looked to Joey like a wild animal, his nostrils flaring, eyes bulging and tongue licking his sallow lips.

The two Albanians were stone dead, and C.C. was sitting up on the sidewalk. He removed the golf shirt that he was wearing and held it against his wound with his left arm, still holding the Glock in his right hand. Babbu was bleeding heavily from a stomach wound and lying still on the small front lawn of one of the homes. He was not responding to Gino and Joey's voices and his color had drained from his face. He was in shock from the wounds but still alive. In the near distance police sirens' were heard getting closer by the second.

"Fuck the cops. Let's get them to Jacobi. I'll drive. Get the car, fast Gino," Joey Clams said as calmly as someone asking for a match to light his cigarette. Joey had ice in his veins. The years of training in the Army and the tours in Vietnam, with the death and carnage that he saw, covered his spirit with an impenetrable callous.

Gino ran the block and pulled the car alongside the two dead Albanians. The police were just a couple of blocks away; the sirens' piercing sounds were almost blood curdling. The hair on Gino's neck was standing on end as Joey carried his blood soaked and unconscious cousin Babbu to the car. Gino jumped out of the car and opened the door so Joey could lay Babbu onto the back seat just before he darted over to help C.C. off the blood stained concrete sidewalk. C.C. was able to get into the passenger seat and Gino was in the back trying to prevent Babbu from bleeding out.

Jacobi Hospital has one of the best trauma centers in New York and everybody who has lived in the Bronx for the past fifty years knows that. A city-owned hospital, this is the place where NYPD brings their wounded police officers. The emergency room is alerted by the police department's Bronx Boro Command when a cop is shot. The trauma team at Jacobi Hospital follows a strict protocol when an officer is hit, no matter how minor or how grave. A six to ten physician surgical team, along with a dozen highly skilled nurses, is paged through the sprawling complex on Pelham Parkway South, and they all converge on a special unit within the ER. Jacobi is within walking distance from where Lekë Marku was killed on the rooftop of his family owned apartment building. This irony did not pass Joey Clams and Gino as their minds retraced the events that brought them to yet another disaster in their lives.

There would be no triage and trauma team waiting for C.C. and Babbu, but the care would be as good as a civilian could get. The police would be notified within minutes of the arrival of two men with gunshot wounds and an enormous amount of pressure would fall upon Gino and Joey Clams to explain why their friends were shot and why two men lay dead on quiet Ohm Avenue.

Joey made the five mile drive in about eight minutes, racing down the Hutchinson River Parkway and then to Pelham Parkway like low flying aircraft. Red lights, yield signs, one way streets and stop signs were not on his agenda. He knew the only chance to keep Babbu alive was to move quickly and get him in front of the doctors. Joey knew that C.C. would survive so when they arrived at Jacobi, C.C. would take second place.

"Fuck...fuck, he's bleeding bad Joey," Gino said with more panic in his voice than Joey or C.C. ever heard.

"Talk to me Gino. Is he breathing?" Joey asked.

"Christ…I can't even tell. He's very still and his eyes are open, God damn these motherfuckers."

"Gino, stay calm. Open his mouth and breathe into it. Squeeze his nose shut and give him some air and then you can tell if he's breathing or not. Just keep giving him some air," C.C. said. C.C. was unable to turn around and help as his own wound was seriously painful.

Gino held his cousin's head in his lap and although his pot belly made it difficult to do what C.C. said, he managed to put some puffs into Babbu who coughed up some blood but was breathing.

Joey went up the wrong side of Pelham Parkway South, into traffic with one hand on the steering wheel and one on the car's horn and an impassive look on his face as if this was a routine day on his job. He was moving so fast that he banged the bottom of the car on the pavement when he entered the ER entrance at the hospital. The sound of the car hitting the ground sounded like a small explosion inside the hospital, the roar of the engine and the blaring of the car horn was enough to send a few orderlies and nurses to see what the commotion was all about. Joey slammed the car into park as it came to an ear piercing halt.

"I got two down with gunshots. One abdomen, not conscious, back seat, one front seat, side wound. Move it!" Joey yelled his instructions so that they could be heard on the third floor of the building.

Gino was in shock. He felt as if everything was going in slow motion. His stomach was sick from the eight minute ride and there was blood all over him. He wasn't even sure where he was. After the ER personnel took Babbu on a gurney, two nurses grabbed Gino and asked him if he was shot and where. He looked at them blankly and did not respond. They brought a gurney for C.C. whom they rushed into the ER behind Babbu and brought another one for Gino.

"He's fine, I got him, just in shock. Look after the other two," Joey said taking Gino by the arm leading him inside.

"Sir, you can't keep your car parked there, it's an active ambulance entrance," said a rent-a-cop dressed all in blue with a silly fake cop hat tilted to one side.

Joey looked at the poor guy like he was going to rip out his larynx and introduce it to him.

"Sorry sir, but I could lose my job and they will tow you," the Barnie Fife look-alike said.

Joey tossed Gino's car keys to the guy.

"Here, keep the job and the fucking car. Get the tranny looked at."

3 2

The medical trauma team hovered over Babbu in the emergency room and did their routine gunshot wound evaluation. Aside from policemen that are shot while on duty Jacoby Hospital sees a good amount of gunshot victims. Not many days go by that a victim of a shooting is not treated here. Jacoby gunshot survival rates rank among the highest of New York City hospitals, and for good reason—the trauma team is well schooled on knowing what needs to be done to get the victim stabilized and into surgery quickly to give the wounded patient a chance to live. Babbu was in the best hands to save a life.

There are a few critical details to consider during treatment for surviving the kind of wound that Babbu sustained. The size of the bullet and the place that he was hit is obviously critical. The amount of time it took to get Babbu to Jacoby and the amount of blood loss before he arrived at the hospital are also important in order to keep him from being prematurely interred at St. Raymond Cemetery.

Joey Clams followed his instincts and got him to the hospital quicker than any City of New York Emergency Services ambulance would have. Gino did his best to keep pressure on the wound but was by no stretch of the imagination a qualified EMT. The rest, as some people would believe, was in the hands of God. Gino and Joey were not among those who would begin to pray to anyone to save anyone.

C.C. was also being attended to but it seemed that the bullet that hit him passed through his ample love handles. C.C. was in no danger and was sent to have an MRI to make sure that there was no additional damage or bullet fragments that would cause any serious hazard to him. Lots of pain would be handled by lots of pain medication.

Babbu was moved quickly into the operating room as Gino and Joey Clams waited in the ER waiting room, which was full of people with injuries and illnesses from a cut finger and a broken ankle to asthma and AIDS related sickness. This was no fun place to be on its best day. Joey sat quietly in a row of chairs as far away from the crowded room as possible, getting up every few minutes to go out onto Pelham Parkway for a cigarette. Gino nosed around for bits of information from any nurse, doctor or orderly that would make eye contact with him.

When two plain-clothes detectives and a uniformed officer from the 49th Precinct arrived to follow up on the gunshot victim report, Gino and Joey Clams stood out like sore thumbs. Two white guys, who were not sick, not hurt and looked like a mess, were real easy to spot. Gino had Babbu's blood all over his clothes and he was an obvious person of interest for the investigating trio. The policemen approached Gino while Joey hung back to see the lay of the land and listen to how Gino was going to handle them. This was not one of those times when Clams would be kicking anyone's ass or firing shots and giving out orders to save his buddy's ass.

"Excuse me sir. That's an awful lot of blood all over you," the tall, Irish looking detective asked Gino.

"My cousin was shot on Ohm Avenue tonight," Gino said.

"Shot by whom?" the shorter of the Irish-looking cops asked.

"No idea officer," Gino replied.

"Were you there when your cousin was shot sir?" Tall Irish asked.

"Yes I was." Gino was calm looking from one cop to the other with his dark eyed glare.

"Name?" Short Irish asked.

"My cousin's name or my name officer?"

"Let's start with your name and date of birth." Tall Irish took out his memo pad.

"Luigino Ranno. December 21, 1950," Gino replied.

"Mind spelling that?" short Irish asked.

"Yes officer I do mind spelling it but I don't mind giving you my card to cut to the chase and not make this an all night affair." Gino was about to lose his cool as he had this thing about the Irish to begin with and he was still reeling from Babbu being shot. He handed Short Irish his business card.

"Take it easy buddy, we are just trying to find out how your cousin got shot and who shot him," Tall Irish said calmly. Joey Clams rolled his eyes expecting that Gino would be arrested at any second. Gino's blood pressure went from stroke level down to just high.

"Sorry guys. It's not every day my cousin is shot in front of me and almost dies in my arms. I apologize," Gino said, but his demeanor showed no sign of regret.

"Your cousin's name please?" Short Irish asked.

"Peter, Peter Ranno. I don't know his date of birth or address, sorry," Gino said.

"Who shot him Mr. Ranno?" Tall Irish asked. He had taken Gino's card from Short Irish.

"I have no idea detective. We were walking on the street to go to my car and these guys went riding by and shot at us. It all happened so quickly. They were white guys is all I could tell," Gino answered.

"We? Who is we Mr. Ranno?" Short Irish asked.

"My friend Charlie who is here in the ER and the guy behind you. There were four of us. We were going to my car," Gino repeated.

"Yes you said that. Where were you coming from?" Tall Irish asked.

"We rented a house on that street from a friend of ours," Gino said.

"Do you know why anyone would want to shoot at four guys walking on a quiet street Mr. Ranno?" Short Irish asked.

"No sir, I have no idea why anyone would have wanted to shoot at us." Gino looked right into the shorter detective's eyes. The cops all knew there was more to the story and that Gino was not going to give any information that would help them. They knew that they were getting nowhere with Gino.

"Look Mr. Ranno. There are two DOAs on that street where your cousin was shot. Did you happen to see who shot those two?" Tall Irish asked.

"No sir. All I know is that my cousin and my friend were shot. Now if you want to ask me a million questions lets go down to the station house. I will call my lawyers and we can start this dance. My cousin and my friend were shot. I shot no one. I'm here to see that my cousin is cared for. I would appreciate it if you would extend some courtesy at this difficult time," Gino said slowly and lowly.

"We're gonna be here for a while Mr. Ranno. We're gonna ask your friend here a few questions and both victims when they are able and then ask for you to come to the house with us. If I were you I would call my lawyer now to save some time," Tall Irish said politely yet firmly.

"Thank you. I appreciate it. See you later," Gino said

The cops asked Joey to step into a room to ask him a few questions and he looked at Gino with a blank stare that said he was not going to say anything. Gino went back to doing his information gathering from the hospital staff. He found one pretty nurse in her early forties having a quick coffee break, and she seemed like a supervisor. She indeed was head of the ER and offered Gino a cup of coffee.

"You look like you need this more than I do," the nurse said, handing Gino the Styrofoam cup of steaming black coffee.

"Thanks. I do really need something but I think vodka or tequila is indicated," Gino said smiling at the younger woman.

"Can't help you there but we all get together after our shift at Frankie and Johnny's. They have plenty of what ails ya at the bar. You been there?" the nurse asked.

"Yes, a few times. Great place. I'm Gino."

"Cathy. You look like you were in a war. You okay?" Cathy asked.

"Not really. My cousin and my buddy are here. Both shot tonight," Gino said searching Cathy's face for a clue about Babbu's condition.

"Yes I know. One is in the OR now. The other will be stitched up and sent home. How'd it happen?" Cathy asked.

"Walking along and wham. Drive by. This city is full of crazies," Gino lied.

"You're telling me! What I see can't fit into five books. One more year and I take my son and I up to Pearl River for us," she said.

"Good idea Cathy. Can I ask for a favor? Can you find out how my cousin is doing? He's the one hit badly. Stomach," Gino said putting on the charm.

"Give me a minute. Be right back," Cathy replied.

Cathy walked briskly and officiously through the ER toward a set of double doors that had a large sign announcing "HOSPITAL STAFF ONLY BEYOND THIS POINT." Gino checked her out as she walked away. She was wearing green scrubs that did not hide a great body. Gino had a thing for cute women with freckles and a great ass and Cathy fit the bill. She was Irish as Patty's Pig and Gino didn't have a problem with Irish women at all. Just the men, who he thought were basically all full of shit like the Kennedys.

Gino sipped his coffee and kept his eye on the double doors waiting for Cathy to return. He glanced from station to station noticing how behind every set of sliding curtains the human condition went from dreadful to shocking. Anyone who wanted to work here was very special or very fucked up in Gino's mind. Along with the fast pace of the doctors and nurses, the sounds of people moaning, groaning, hollering, speaking in Spanish, Haitian Creole, Russian and Ebonics made Gino start to get that panicked feeling that he dreaded.

The double doors hissed open and Cathy walked toward Gino more slowly than when she left. She motioned to him with her eyes and head to meet her in a lounge near the nurses' station. Gino placed his coffee cup on top of a cluttered counter and took off in her direction. He was on her heels as she entered the stark room.

"Look, I don't know you but you seem like a nice guy. I can get my ass chewed out for giving you any information," Cathy said to Gino.

"I appreciate it Cathy. I heard nothing from you I promise," Gino said his right hand over his heart.

"He's your cousin you said?" Cathy asked.

"Yes. How's he doing?"

"Gino...he didn't make it. They're filling out the paperwork and will talk to the police in a little while. I'm so sorry. I'm sure they did the best they could," Cathy said a bit sympathetic yet a bit clinical.

"He's dead?" Gino asked.

"I'm sorry, yes he's dead."

Gino's eyes showed enough rage to unsettle the hardened nurse who led him by the hand to a chair in the room.

"Here sit down and take a few deep breaths. I got to go. I'm so sorry," Cathy said with as much pretend sympathy as she could muster.

"Thanks kiddo. You are very kind Cathy. Thank you," Gino said. He sat in the chair for at least five minutes thinking of Babbu and his life and who in the family he should call and what he was going to say. Gino started to rub his forehead with his left hand until the friction started to burn his skin.

"How the fuck did this happen?" he said aloud to no one.

33

Ilir Marku was sitting in his back yard with Shpresa, Valbona, and Adem enjoying quiet time with three young people that he found solace just being around. Since his only son Lekë was killed there was no happiness in Ilir's eyes. His spirit had been crushed beyond repair. He now lived only for vengeance and the thought of retiring and going back to Albania was now foremost on his mind. Sipping iced tea and munching on olives and imported French feta cheese, with a man-made babbling brook, feeding black squirrels nuts from his hand, and smelling the aroma of honeysuckle and lilacs temporarily made his life bearable or perhaps simply put, less miserable. In his heart and in his mind he not only blamed the Santoro boy for Lekë's death but himself for encouraging his son to join his life of crime. If he had only pushed his boy to law school, legitimate business, some life that was less treacherous, perhaps he would be enjoying him and his baby grandson today. Instead his heart was full of bitterness and regret as he was now looking forward to his own death rather than suffering the mental torture he would be forced to live with until that day came.

"Adem, are you planning another trip back to Albania or are you staying here for a while?" Ilir asked.

"I think I want to stay here for a while." Adem glanced at Valbona for a millisecond. Shpresa, like all women with intuition and radar, caught the look and her mind began to race. Ilir did not notice the possible interest that Adem may or may not have had in Valbona.

"What work will you do Adem?" Ilir asked

"Something in the art or music world I suppose, but I will probably wind up working in a restaurant," Adem said and laughed. Valbona and Shpresa laughed along with him although Valbona's laugh was stifled.

"Not a problem Adem, the Albanians own almost every Italian restaurant in the United States. If it weren't for Italian restaurants we would all be building supers and in construction," Shpresa said and the laughing continued. Ilir did not join in the laughter as work for a man was a serious subject to him. His temperament brought a more serious cloud over the exuberant Shpresa and she knew that she had overstepped her boundaries.

"No restaurants for you Adem. That is a hard way to make easy money and the business is full of bad habits. Let's discuss your field. I'm certain we can help you follow your heart my friend," the Albanian boss said.

"I'm so sorry everyone, I have to get downtown to my office. Rick is closing on a new client and I really need to be there. Adem, I can drop you off on my way," Shpresa announced.

"Shpresa dearest Adem can stay a while if he wishes. We can arrange to get him wherever he wants to go," Ilir said looking only at Adem for his reaction.

"That would be great. I brought along some photographs from home to show," Adem said with a big smile, which also caught Shpresa's already alerted radar.

"Pictures from Albania? I would love to see them," Valbona said.

Shpresa was soaring inside, her thoughts racing. Can you imagine, could this be real? Is he interested? Is it much too soon? Fuck that, who said there is a calendar on a heart?

"It's settled. We will look at the photographs from Albania, Shpresa will go to her husband and then return with him later to join us for a roast lamb on the spit," Ilir pronounced.

With that, a very solemn looking Pashko Luli entered the backyard through the rear of the house. With him were two bodyguards who were unsmiling and unshaven. Luli said something to them and pointed to either side of the property where they dutifully took up sentinel posts. Clearly there was trouble in the Marku world from the look on the three men's faces.

Shpresa said her goodbyes and exited as fast as possible. She knew that if she stayed to learn what was going on it would be awkward and embarrassing to Ilir. She moved quickly around the large house to the circular driveway where her car was parked. Her mind was racing and her heart was beating so quickly that she needed to pause to catch her breath once she got behind the wheel.

"Ilir, a word please," Luli asked.

"Of course. Adem, show your wonderful photographs to my dear Valbona. Let her see Albania through your eyes. I will ask the women of the house to look after your refreshments and food," Ilir said before he and Luli made their way to his study. The bodyguards remained at their posts, their eyes scanning the adjoining properties for signs of trouble.

"I must report unfortunate news. Evidently Ukë attacked the father of Joey Santoro. Ukë discovered that he was staying in the Bronx and he moved too quickly. Likely he is trying to impress you but his move did not have a good result." Luli paused to wait for questions. There were none as Ilir remained quiet.

"They opened up on Mr. Santoro and Carmine Miceli's friend Gino and two other men. Santoro and Gino were uninjured, thankfully. One of the other men was wounded, one was killed. He is cousin to Gino.

Two of Ukë's men were killed. The police are all over this as they believe we are at war with the Miceli family. The heat is on all over town Ilir. Once again Ukë moves without discussing his plans with us. He is acting poorly and with bad judgment Ilir and he must be reined in right now. I am concerned how the Micelis will respond. No one is safe."

"Where is Ukë?" Ilir asked

"He is not answering his phones. No one has seen him in any of his stores. My answer to you is I do not know. I am sorry." Luli held his right hand to his heart and bowed his head to his boss slightly.

"Please find him and bring him to a safe place. Call me when you have him. Luli do not show him that you are angry or upset. We must have a serious discussion with my *nipash*. I will make some inquiries myself. It is time that I get back to business and grieve for my son in a different way." Ilir Marku gave the instructions to his *kryetar* and expected that they would be followed to the letter.

In the mountains of Albania, there is a rare social custom that can still be found to this day. There are still living relics in the women who were made widows from blood feuds or wars. These women had the social right to become Sworn Virgins. From the day that they decided to act as the man of their family, they wore men's clothing, wore their hair short and spoke as men do and even carried weapons to protect their family and property. They did men's work and represented their family and clans as if they were indeed a man. They swore a vow of celibacy from that day forward until their deaths.

This transformation was very much a part of the ruthless eye for an eye justice that formed *gjakmarrja* as a way of life. Where men are sometimes agreeable to forgive, Albanian women, unwavering in their contempt toward their enemy, are generally unwilling to stop a blood feud for a lost son, husband, or brother. A modern woman whether born in Albania or the United States need not swear to become a Sworn Virgin upon the murder of her spouse or other male loved one, nor does she have to excuse the murderer of her relative. Deep in their blood and etched into their souls Albanian women have a strength of purpose for survival.

Although Valbona Marku was not yet discussing, nor for that matter accepting, the horrible tragedy that took her young husband and unborn son, she was not by any stretch of the imagination going to become a Sworn Virgin or a ward of the Marku family. Her independent spirit would move her in the direction that she always dreamed about. Valbona wanted children, a few of them, to raise in the traditions and customs of her Albanian heritage of which she was extraordinarily proud. All that Valbona needed at the moment was peace and quiet and some time to sort out what had happened to her and how she would plan her future. She loved Lekë with all of her heart and never questioned what he did to make a living for his family. She would not make that mistake twice.

Adem was well aware that Valbona was raised by an authoritarian father who was so severe in his rules of behavior that it was a wonder why his American born daughters didn't flee from his house. Shpresa's dad was no less fanatical in his control of her life until she was married. Shpresa exposed both her and Valbona's difficult, yet accepted early lives with Adem who naturally understood how things were among the Albanians. Not having a sister, or a father for that matter, made his frame of reference limited and left to his imagination. He was not sure if his inner feelings for Valbona were because of her great looks, her soft yet determined personality or simply out of sympathy for what she had been through. Adem was notorious for being a champion for women who needed to be saved from any number of life's horrors and he had promised himself that the next woman he fell for wouldn't have the baggage that he seemed to gravitate toward. In his self analysis he blamed his

"Florence Nightingale Syndrome," as he termed it, to his own mother's lifetime situation. Raising a son alone was no walk in the park for Adem's mother and all his life he felt obligated to help her and make her proud of him. Adem was not the least bit concerned about his rushing things or making his intentions known in the immediate future. He knew full well that his feelings would be held to himself as Valbona needed time to fully come back to reality and accept what had happened to her. If his feelings for Valbona developed into something greater than they were at the moment, Adem also knew that time and the Albanian traditions would be the great regulator of any relationship that was smoldering. He also knew that Valbona likely had no feelings toward him as at the moment she was capable of only feeling a deep rooted pain in her soul. If there were to be any courting of Valbona a vast amount of patience would be required. What Shpresa had sensed was indeed real even though the ember was not burning brightly.

34

Instead of reporting to the police as they asked, Gino called Carmine Miceli Jr. from his cell phone to report the circumstances that led to the death of his cousin Babbu. There was no way Gino was going anywhere near the Four-Nine Precinct house without a lawyer and without some protection. The area was full of Albanians and Gino wasn't sure if he was marked for death as well as Joey Clams. He also felt as if he needed to protect Joey, from himself as much as from the Albanians. Joey had that not very pleasant, thousand yard Vietnam stare that he was now famous for and he seemed to be in a dangerous mental zone. Gino remembered that the nuns would say 'an idle mind is the devil's workshop.' Joey's mind was way beyond any silly religious theory. For him, there was no difference between the jungles of Laos, Cambodia, Vietnam and the streets surrounding Arthur Avenue in the Bronx.

"Gino, they picked the battleground, now it's all about body count. Fuck them and that mountain revenge bullshit," Joey said without even looking at Gino for a second.

"Calm down pal. Carmine wants to see us as soon as we can get there. He's gonna have his lawyer Greg Onorato there. He's the best in the business, so we can get a story straight for the cops. While I'm there I need a few words with the kid in private. I've had enough of this shit too. Enough is enough but I don't want to see you make a move that will get you killed. These are treacherous killers Joey," Gino said.

"Don't worry about me. I know you know the owner of that funeral home where all the Albanians get laid out. Farenga Brothers right? Call the guy and tell him to buy a summer house in the Hamptons or some place in Florida because I'm gonna make the streets look like the fucking Tet Offensive. If they think they lost a lot of men in Kosovo just wait. I don't give a fuck no more." Joey's head was getting red, his eyes bulging as he rubbed his hands together. Gino thought Joey was about to snap.

"Okay look, your son is safe and you will be too. Let's get into the car and go downtown and sort things out. We have a lot ahead of us Joey."

Carmine had already made a move. Before Gino called, Carmine knew about the attack on Gino and his crew and about Babbu's death. Carmine was about to call in Gino, anyway to keep him safe from the action that Micky Roach was about to bring down on the Marku family. Carmine gave Micky the order to make things happen in a big way. Quickly, visibly and deadly. Micky knew that Carmine had the rest of the New York mob behind him and covering his back, so in effect he knew that for the first time in a very long time, the strength of the five families was with him. That gave the aging hit man lots of wind in his sails. Micky, taught well by his father and grandfather in Sicily, was the Miceli's muscle for good reason. He knew his business and had absolutely no blood in his veins when it came to violence. Micky had pre-planned his attack long before it was needed so that he would be able to strike at a moment's notice. As any good military tactician, Micky knew from experience that planning and surprise were among his biggest advantages. When he hit his target they would least expect it and they would be absolutely stunned. A three pronged attack was planned to simultaneously hit the Albanians and send the war into the next deadly level of *vendetta* and *gjakmarrja*.

Gabriel Luzzi, a full time waiter and journeyman assassin for Micky Roach, was a tall, Hollywood handsome thirty-five year old with a simpatico face and a clean-cut appearance. Sicilian born but raised in the Bronx, Gabriel fit the description that Micky had cast him for. If his task was pulled off correctly, there would be no witnesses to recognize and finger him. If he failed, he would be dead without a doubt. Micky knew that Luzzi would make his bones on this particular day and get his button more for bravery than for obedience and loyalty. Micky was sending the young man into the mouth of the lion. In this case it was more like sending him into the talons of the eagle.

Pietro Salerno, born and raised in Lercara Friddi, Sicily and grandson of Micky Roach's first cousin, had the perfect look for Micky's second hit. Short, stocky, and with a dark complexion, Pietro could pass for coming from any number of Central or South American countries. Pietro had started working for Micky doing odds and ends in his extermination business. Killing roaches, rats, fleas, bed-bugs, termites and the like wasn't that much of a step up from the menial labor he did in Sicily but the ancillary benefits of learning the human extermination business from the master kept the young Pietro interested. His immediate reward was a pocket full of money, a trip back to Sicily to see his mama and his choice of greater opportunity there or a return trip to take over the extermination of vermin business for Micky. He was getting much too old to go down basement stairs to kill insects and four legged hairy things.

Peter Joseph McKenna was the third hit man chosen by the master. P.J. was much different looking than anyone Micky Roach had ever used. Born in Dublin, Ireland, and raised in upper Manhattan, P.J.'s family was one of the last of the Irish holdouts to leave the Inwood section, giving him a street attitude and the gift of fluent Dominican Spanish. Tall with sandy blonde hair and powder blue eyes, P.J. learned his trade from the Westies, the Irish mob from Hell's Kitchen, and specifically from Sean Gibney, a demolitions expert trained by the Army Corps of Engineers in Vietnam. P.J. was on his own after this job and he could do whatever the fuck he wanted with the twenty thousand dollars that Micky gave him.

The UPS Distribution Center on Conner Street in the Bronx is like most of the UPS hubs around the country. The workers move at a frenetic pace to get the packages sorted, out on the trucks, and delivered to the customer on time and without damages, loss claims, or injuries to their employees. They have turned package delivery into a veritable science with amazing grace. The stress on the UPS employees, who are timed on virtually everything they do, is like a daily Marine Corps drill. The UPS driver is rated by a GPS system and electronic tracking devices can tell their distribution managers the location of the truck, the speed at which the truck is moving, if the truck is idling, and if the driver is sitting in his seat when he should be humping bundles or envelopes. If a driver farts in his truck, they can tell you what he had for lunch. If there is a need to check on the status of the vehicle or history of the driver's day, it's simply a click of a button.

Gabriel Luzzi and two handpicked Miceli crew members watched as the UPS trucks left the barn and headed for their destinations in the Bronx and southern Westchester County. Their two day surveillance of the truck routing was all they needed to pick out the perfect driver and the perfect location to begin the first component of their job. Truck 908 was routed to the Throgs Neck Projects, a low-income public housing development with thirty-three buildings covering hundreds of acres. It was a perfect setup for what Luzzi needed as the Projects have natural boundaries and escape routes in case things went bad. St. Raymond Cemetery, the Cross Bronx Expressway, Tremont Avenue, and the Throgs Neck Bridge were seconds away from the place where they expected to seize the truck. They could quickly take the truck itself or the car that they parked further down along Randall Avenue if the play was a bust and take any route they needed to avoid any interloper. To rob a UPS truck doesn't take a whole lot of brains, however to hijack one of the big brown square vehicles, kidnap the driver and take it 3.61 miles and eight minutes away from its route takes precise timing and steady nerves. They would ignore the GPS system but stay within the speed limits to the truck's final destination.

Luzzi and his crew of two moved with surgical precision, having timed every step down to a thirty second tolerance. The driver was built similar to Luzzi and his identification photo was close enough for a quick glance match. Once the move was made each of the three men had their routine down cold.

The unsuspecting driver pulled truck 908 alongside the parked cars on Randall Avenue. The second he opened the truck's inner door where the packages are housed, all three men were on him. They quickly and efficiently smashed him in the head with a blackjack just enough to daze the poor guy. The two Miceli goons covered his eyes with a ski cap and masking tape while the burley Luzzi started undressing himself. When the driver's uniform was on Luzzi, he jumped into the driver's seat and took off toward the intended destination. One Miceli soldier stayed in the rear of the truck to make certain that the driver was not going to be a stupid hero while the second soldier went for the car to meet up with the hijacked truck. A second car with two other Miceli men sat two blocks from the real estate office of Ilir Marku on Eastchester Road waiting for their associates to arrive. Their role was simple. They were in the plan as a backup to the first car in case anything went wrong, and to be a blocking car to stop any pain in the ass cop or Marku from catching Gabriel Luzzi and his two partners when their job was completed.

Luzzi rolled the truck on the west side of Eastchester Road and across the street from the Albanian boss' office. He checked his watch and mentally noted that it took him twelve minutes instead of the planned eight. No big deal he thought. If Ilir Marku was there the plan would be immediately abandoned as his security was comprised of all top people and hardened veterans of the war in Kosovo. It was evident that he wasn't in his office as the three or four cars that traveled with him of late were absent. In fact it looked as if the office was empty from Luzzi's vantage point. He took the electronic signature pad and placed it

LOUIS ROMANO

on top of a box that was almost entirely covered with masking tape. The box had a false bottom, brought onto the truck by Luzzi, and contained a fully loaded Uzi SMG, sub-machine-gun, the grand-daddy of all Uzis with a firing rate of 600 rounds per minute. His Beretta handgun in his rear waist band was a toy compared to the SMG.

A Miceli soldier gave the UPS driver another whack in the head for good measure and quickly sent him to the Sandman for a few minutes. Everyone and everything was moving as planned.

Luzzi approached the exterior of the two story office building whistling and chewing gum. He blew a bubble for special effect and stayed in UPS driver character in case the cameras mounted on the walls were actually working and being watched by anyone inside the office. He amazed himself at his composure. So much was at stake for him on this job but yet his planning was thorough and his confidence was soaring. He tried the door. Locked. He rang the bell.

"Yes?" a male voice answered. Someone was in the office. It didn't matter who. All they wanted was a kill.

"Hi, UPS," Luzzi said while craning his neck to look at a woman who came out of the restaurant next door to the office.

"Okay, just leave the package in front."

"No can do sir. It's signature needed. A package from Albania it seems by the return address."

"Where is the regular guy?"

"Sorry sir, they just give me the route sheet and I make the stops. I'm normally just doing Einstein all day," Luzzi said referring to the Albert Einstein Medical Center across the street.

"Okay, hold on."

The door buzzed and the lock disengaged. Luzzi was inside. There were four men inside the office. Two were standing in front of a man sitting at a large desk on the telephone and one reading a newspaper. A flat screen television showing a soccer game was on with the sound muted.

"Who's winning?" Luzzi asked as he let the electronic signature device slip off the box and crash to the floor. All four men looked at the ground to see if the thing shattered. In that time Luzzi made his bones without a moment of hesitation. He pulled the Uzi from the false bottom of the box and came up firing. The noise of the SMG was deafening and the bullets tore through each man killing them instantly. The office walls were blood and gore and gun powder. The man on the telephone was thrown in his chair against the wall and held onto the receiver in a death grip. Luzzi, as all good hit men know, quickly wiped the gun of any fingerprints, dropped the Uzi to the ground, picked up the electronic signature device and walked out of the office, whistling and chewing his gum. Instead of another ride in the brown truck, he calmly got into a car with the two Miceli soldiers and they left like they were going to the Bronx Zoo to see the exhibits.

Luzzi and his crew did a perfect job almost in perfect time and made the perfect getaway. Only thing was, Luzzi didn't know how perfect. The man sitting in the chair taking on the telephone was Ilir Marku's *kreytar,* the underboss Pashko Luli.

35

The simultaneous hits were completed as planned. P.J. McKenna was driven to the corner of Westchester Avenue and Castle Hill Avenue. His target was La Bella Roma Pizzeria around the corner on Castle Hill. This was one of Ukë Marku's joints and protected by the cops in the Four-Three Precinct. They got free food and once in a while a blow job from one of Ukë's sluts in return for looking the other way when gambling and drugs were selling better than the homemade *burek* which was popular in the mostly Hispanic neighborhood. Ukë introduced pulled pork *burek* which became a big hit there. Any respectable Albanian wouldn't touch it and not for religious reasons. Pork *burek* to them was like eating chunky peanut butter and mayonnaise. It's just not done.

McKenna walked into the pizzeria with a knapsack on his arm. He sat down at a small table and called out to the counter guy.

"A slice of that Sicilian not too hot. Corner piece. Coke."

The counter guy, who looked Dominican, held his cell phone in the crook of his neck while he filled the order. Other than P.J. McKenna the narrow store was empty. McKenna opened the bag that he had put on the chair next to him and fiddled with something. The counter guy was evidently talking sweet nothings to his *mami chula*. The pizza came out of the oven and the Dominican placed it on a piece of aluminum foil and onto a paper dish and then onto the counter. The coke was already waiting for his only customer.

"Three seventy-five my friend," the Dominican man said. McKenna left his chair and walked over to the counter without a bit of concern on his face.

"Buddy, hang up the phone for a minute, I want to do you a tremendous favor. The best tip you will ever get in your whole entire life," McKenna said with a wide smile.

"*Mami* let me call you back okay?" the Dominican man said to his sweetheart, or maybe someone else's sweetheart.

"Wassup my man?"

McKenna started taking the pizza and the coke off the counter.

"Listen to me okay. You're a nice guy. I like you. Forget my face or you're a dead man. Follow me out of the store. Lock the front door. I'm going left you're going right. Don't look back. In just about two minutes that bag on the chair over there is gonna make this place into toothpicks. Do you understand me? Thanks for the pizza and coke," McKenna said in a conspirator's whisper. The counter man did exactly what he was told and sure enough, within a couple of minutes every store on both sides of Castle Hill Avenue, for a block in either direction, lost their windows. Even the ones behind the pull down metal gates shattered from the concussion of McKenna's bomb. La Bella Roma was gutted. Ukë had one less store and one more headache.

Pietro Salerno, the home boy from Lercara Friddi, did his job quickly and efficiently. It wasn't a particularly difficult job; all he had to do was visit a particular restaurant on City Island in the Bronx.

City Island has one way in and one way out over a small bridge that stretches over the Long Island Sound and Eastchester Bay. The Island is about a mile and a half long and has more bars and restaurants than the four thousand inhabitants need. City Island Avenue, the main street that dissects the island, has over thirty restaurants that are packed with people all summer long. Having New York City busses driving up and down the main drag and the throngs of Latinos that visit to catch a breath of fresh salt air gives the place a little honky-tonk flavor. None of the restaurants are great but some are very good as for instance Portofino, the restaurant that Lekë and Valbona had planned to eat on that fateful night.

Niki Balaj was Lekë's cousin and the restaurant business was not nearly his only source of income. Much of the Albanian mob's heroin trade passed through Niki's hands before it was delivered into the distribution channels throughout the east coast. City Island has great access by small pleasure boats and the dock at Portofino was what enticed Niki to buy the place. The perfect setup. The smack arrived by boat and by food delivery trucks that looked as if they were doing normal everyday restaurant business and it left the same way. Balaj ran the place without incident for three years and was protected by the Miceli family from any overly aggressive drug dealers who thought they had a better recipe for fried calamari and dime bags.

The Micelis were steady customers of both the restaurant and the drug trade. Carmine Miceli Jr. always had thought Niki was a bit too cocky and a bit too greedy and blamed him for much of the family's business losses in the Bronx. His feeling was more gut than fact so Carmine Jr. waited until the right time to take the appropriate action. Carmine knew that Balaj was somehow related to the Marku family so he gave specific orders to Micky Roach. The new Don wanted a signal to be sent that had his signature all over it.

Salerno was dropped off in a stolen Ford Taurus a block away from Portofino Ristorante by two Miceli soldiers familiar with City Island and the Bronx. Their rapid exit was far more important than their arrival. They planned to leave the island as the contraband did so they docked a boat owned by a friend, a Brooklyn wise guy, down near the end of the island. After the "piece of work" was finished, if there was anyone going after them, the natural place to go was over the bridge and onto a long road that led into the mainland of the Bronx. Their escape route off City Island was to go the opposite direction of the bridge. They would drive Salerno to the dock, abandon the hot car, and ferry past Hart Island to Sands Point, Long Island, where a car would be waiting to take the crew to a safe location. If needed, they could lam it for a few days on Long Island at a number of Mafia safe houses.

Pietro walked into Portofino and saw Niki on his cell phone. Niki was taking in the sun on the wood deck behind the restaurant just in front of the dock. Salerno walked to Niki calmly and stood as erect as his short, stout body would allow. Niki was talking to someone who owed him money.

"Listen my friend, there is an old Albanian adage. *Shoku shok, por kosi esht me pare.* I know you don't speak Albanian you dumb fuck so I'm gonna translate it for you. Friends are friends but the yogurt is for cash only. Get the point?" Niki waited for an answer on the other side of the receiver.

"Okay. By next Friday or it will be a problem," Niki said and clicked off his cell phone.

"Delivery is around the side buddy," Niki said barely looking at the Sicilian hit man as he started to dial another number on his phone.

Pop-pop-pop. The bullets turned Niki's head into minestrone soup all over the glass table top and exterior rear window of the restaurant. Pietro took a deck of Sicilian playing cards and scattered them on Niki's body and the blood soaked table.

In two hours young Pietro Salerno would be hanging out by a pool in a Long Island mini-mansion with a gorgeous American gal at his side and on his dick, awaiting instructions as to when he would return to *Sicilia.* He made his bones in New York.

Detective Carlo Del Greco wasn't sure how he would handle the information that he obtained from Engjëll. He approved the release of Gjergj and put ten bucks into a house pool that said he would come up dead within a week. Carlo had the under with two days. Jimmy Gojcaj took the over and bet he would last the week.

Del Greco's nerves were on edge with all of the hits that were taking place in the Bronx. He knew that sooner or later all roads would lead back to him and his dealings with the Marku family. He realized that his next move had to be the right move for him or he could very well wind up dead or in jail. At his age he was exhausted from the stress and the hours he was putting in. The timing of this whole Marku murder and the *vendetta-gjakmarrja* was as if someone had put the *malocchio*, the evil eye, on him and it was working quite well. Del Greco never believed in that Italian folklore crap before. He heard it as a child from his grandparents and parents and now it was starting to seep into the 'there must be something to this' thoughts in his repressed psyche.

With the information about Pashko Luli's killing at the office on Eastchester Road, Del Greco could only bring Engjëll's confession to the big man himself, Ilir Marku. He knew that he had to be wary of an I-told-you-so attitude for fear of losing the last bit of friendship he was hoping he still had with the Don.

The Marku estate in Scarsdale now took on the look of a fortress with cars blocking the front of the home and driveway and a small army of Albanian men standing guard. Cigarette smoke billowed everywhere as the guards milled around with a conspirator's look about them. The town of Scarsdale didn't send a patrol car to the estate in spite of several calls they received from concerned neighbors about the strange activity.

Detective Del Greco's car pulled onto the street and was stopped by three of the bodyguards who immediately recognized him. In spite of their acknowledgement he was told that he could not enter the estate grounds with his vehicle and he would be escorted by two men into the home. The guards spoke in Albanian to each other, deciding whether or not to ask Del Greco for his service revolver. They decided it would be an insult and the two men who would be escorting him could drop him in an instant if he scratched his nose, never mind reached for his gun. No one could be trusted after the hit at the realty office and these guys were trigger happy at the very least.

Del Greco entered the Skanderbeg room and was greeted warmly by Ilir Marku. What he was not prepared for was the presence of four other men, one of them being Ukë Marku.

"My friend Carlo. It is good to see you. Please, take coffee with me," Ilir said, ignoring any introduction. Del Greco could feel Ukë's cold stare making the hair on his arms and neck stand.

"Thank you Mr. Marku, it is always a great pleasure to see you," the detective said nervously. Marku sensed that there was a stiff formality with the Lieutenant.

"So tell me Carlo, your family is well?"

"Yes indeed. And I am getting ready to retire very soon. To live the good life."

"Nonsense my friend. You can never retire. What will you do with yourself?"

"I was thinking about playing some golf, fishing, getting back into shape." Del Greco patted his pot belly.

"So when you have done all those things for three months you will then be bored. Men like you don't retire. Work less, do some other form of work perhaps but never retire. Retirement approximates death," Ilir said, his voice becoming somber at the last three words.

"We shall see my friend, I trust your judgment on many things and my good sense tells me that you are right. Mr. Marku, can I have a word with you in private?" Del Greco asked, finding the strength that he needed to get to his business.

"Ordinarily I would say yes my friend, but this meeting is a difficult one. I suppose you know about the problems we are having on the street. I cannot have my people being killed this way without answering in a like fashion, Carlo. Can you wait for a few days and we will meet again?" Ilir motioned to the door as a polite way for him to escort the Lieutenant out.

"Mr. Marku, I am sorry but this cannot wait. It is official business. I am here as a friend but also as a...," he trailed off, unable to say the word but Ilir finished the sentence.

"Police officer. Why do you find that hard to say Carlo? Are you embarrassed by your role? Please, give me a few minutes with my meeting and I will see you."

Ilir spoke in Albanian to the guards that were standing so close to Detective Del Greco that he could smell their cheap cologne. Del Greco was then brought to a room with a view of the back gardens. He could see the men standing guard along the perimeter of the estate all holding shotguns or other firearms. For a moment Carlo didn't think he was in Scarsdale but felt as if he was in the mountains of Albania or Sicily or some other foreign place that he could not fathom.

36

"*A*xhë, let me show you what I can do. I will make those mafia boys wish they were never born," Ukë Marku said to his Uncle Ilir.

"Ukë, you have done enough to get us in too deep in this fight. You are better to show me that you can work as a team than attack without direction," Ilir said.

"*Axhë*, the Feds are all over them. Every day we hear they are falling apart. They have no *besa*, no honor at all. We must take our place at the table now when they are weakened. Give me the chance to make us great, to make you great. Make me your new *kryetar* and I will make you proud."

"You will do nothing without my order *Nipash*. Your ambition is without boundaries. Peace is better than war with the Italians. We have lived together with them for many years. Many of us lived in Italy to save ourselves and the Italians treated us as brothers so why make them our enemy? Our business here is good, we don't need to be, as you call it, great. You have much to learn *Oj Nipash*. The position of *kryetar* is not given by blood but is earned by action. Right now, tend to your stores and I will call for you when other work is needed." "You are sending me away *Axhë*, throwing me out?" Ukë asked

"No. You will be called upon when I need you. For now you need time to tend to your business while I deal with the Italians. You need time to cool off young *nipash*." Ilir was emphatic. He rose and kissed

Ukë on both cheeks before leaving the room with the other men of his council. Ukë could feel the blood rushing to his head, the saliva in his mouth suddenly was gone and he felt as if he would vomit. He left the house in a blind rage.

Ilir entered the room where Detective Del Greco was waiting with the two Marku bodyguards. Del Greco was standing by the window staring into space and wondering how things got so screwed up so quickly. The plans he had made for himself were pretty solid he thought, but now with this mess going on anything could happen to destroy his dream of living as a gentlemen. His pension and the money he made on the side would be enough fuck-you money for a life of luxury.

Ilir cleared his throat to announce his presence. His council waited outside the room for him.

"Mr. Marku, I was day dreaming."

"And now suddenly I am Mr. Marku. No longer Ilir your friend, Carlo?"

"No...no, no, it's not that...not at all, it's just that in front of your men I did not want to show familiarity," Del Greco said.

"Yes, my mother often told me that familiarity breeds contempt. Do you agree Carlo?"

"Ilir, what I have to tell you may change the direction in which your family is going. I wish the news I am about to bring to you was better for you. It hurts me to say what I need to say." Del Greco's voice cracked.

"Carlo, Carlo...the news of my son being killed, his boy, my dearest friend Pashko, the men around me who have been killed, I am well beyond being hurt by news. Forgive me, say what is on your mind Detective Del Greco."

Del Greco found the unusual salutation to be unsettling.

"I have reason to believe that Ukë Marku, your nephew, was the one who killed your son. The information that I have obtained from the crime scene and from an eye-witness discloses a plot that Ukë had made to gain power in your family. One of the two Albanians at the scene, who were brought in by your nephew, said they were promised high positions for their help in carrying out the hit. The forensic evidence is not one hundred percent but it points to your son being killed at close range. Ukë was next to him when he was shot from behind." Del Greco paused for a moment before continuing.

"All of this death and the killings to come were because of one of the oldest sins. Greed. Bottom line, the Santoro kid is innocent in your son's killing. I am issuing an arrest warrant for Ukë Marku when I return to my office. I wanted to speak with you first out of respect, in spite of the confused feelings you may have about me," Del Greco said as a warm feeling of satisfaction enveloped him. He made no apology for the news.

"Do you know what you are saying to me Carlo?"

"Yes sir, I am fully aware of what I am saying and know beyond doubt that what I am telling you is the truth...on my life Ilir."

Ilir Marku steadied himself on a sofa and lowered his large frame into a winged chair. His complexion went from sallow to white. His eyes blinked slowly and purposely every five seconds as if he could not comprehend what he had just been told.

"My son and grandson are dead. My *nipash*, my nephew is a murderer, he murdered his own cousin, his own blood; my best friend in life was killed. Other men around me have been slaughtered. Are we cursed? Did our family draw blood without cause? Have we been unjust? Did we break our *besa*? Why has God abandoned us? I am shamed by this and my life is now over Carlo. I don't know how to carry on from here. For what purpose will I continue? No son to leave my world to, now not even a nephew. My life has been a failure. I have no reason to live."

Del Greco had no words of encouragement for Marku who was dark with depression.

"You are certain of this Carlo?" Ilir asked after a long silence hoping that there would be some reprieve, some hope from his pain.

"Without any doubt. The pieces all fit together perfectly and we have a confession," Del Greco said.

"Can I see the two men who were with Ukë that night?"

"One is in Federal custody, likely to go into a protection program. The other will be released today."

"I will do what needs to be done to make certain you have not made an error. Then I will ask for you to help me with some things my good friend."

"Ilir, I will do whatever you ask from my heart." Del Greco was choking back tears for his long time financial backer. He knew the chickens may soon come home to roost for him.

37

After the hit on the Marku real estate office the Bronx was ready to explode into an all out war between the Italian and Albanian mobs. Carmine had the full backing of the rest of the New York mob families but the Albanians were strong and fearless.

Arthur Avenue, where both ethnic groups worked together in harmony for decades, was virtually shut down. No one knew when or where the next attack would occur and everyone was lying low so as not to get caught in the cross fire. The butchers were sitting around looking at each other, Mike Greco at Mike's deli was pacing back and forth behind his counter, the vegetable guy had no one to scream at, the eating area was completely empty. The only activity was the Dominican cigar rollers who seemed to never stop making their hand rolled tobacco tubes.

Outside on the streets there were no double parked cars, and for that matter not even parked cars, or the usual drivers circling the blocks looking for a spot. The restaurants were empty, and many of the shops and delicatessens closed early. The two fish markets were looking to sell their fish at huge discounts to restaurants outside the neighborhood rather than take a total loss. Morris Park, where the first two hits occurred, was no busier. Once the New York Post and the Daily News headlines read 'BRONX MOB WAR' and 'THE BRONX NO THONKS' no one with half a brain was looking for veal scaloppini or manicotti for dinner.

A massive police presence included the huge Mobile Command

Center from Bronx Borough Command and several NYPD EMS units that were parked on 187th Street and Arthur Avenue, in plain sight of anyone who had violence on their mind. The S.W.A.T. team was also on the scene, with cops in black helmets and automatic weapons walking around window shopping. A few took photos of their buddies in front of Vincent's Meat Market with the hanging lambs and goats in the windows as their background. The life that so many people made for themselves and their families, a good life spawned from hard work and dedication looked to be coming to an end in this enclave of Italian and Albanian people.

Neither the Miceli family nor the Marku family wanted to be the first to ask for this war to stop. The Markus had their tradition of *gjak-marrja* and *besa* to deal with and the Micelis, not trapped by any sense of vendetta, were not about to show weakness to their latest business rivals. The war in the streets was going to be a long and bloody mess that no one really wanted. The two sides were trapped by their own mentality, their own pride. Call it what you will but this war was not unlike any other in the history of mankind. There was no logical reason for it. Men have behaved this way since Cain killed Abel and that is how it will always be until something or someone with sense comes along to change things. There was a guy who tried it and they put him on a cross. Things were not looking good for the time being and a second coming was not scheduled any time soon

Shpresa was in her office at home trying to salvage some part of her business that she had been neglecting since the night of Lekë's murder. It was bad enough that the recession was killing the apartment rental business and the competition for listings was like hand-to-hand combat but she was totally unfocused on her job. Her cell phone vibrated and showed 'Unknown Number' before the first ring.

"Hello this is Hope, how can I help you?" she asked in a business voice, using the English translation of her name.

"Hello, is this Shpresa Metalia?" an older woman with a slight accent asked.

"Yes, it's Shpresa, who is this?" she answered with a smile hoping it was a potential client.

"Shpresa, you don't know me but I know very much about you. My name is Tenuta. Tenuta Gashi and I think it is most important that we meet."

Gino was not letting Joey Clams out of his sight for a second. The apartment hideaway in the Bronx was done with so Gino, Clams and C.C. checked into the Roosevelt Hotel on Madison Ave. Gino got a large suite for cheap, the friends and family rate. The manager was a friend of the Ranno and Miceli family from the old days and was happy to oblige. Gino's plan was to find another safe house but this room would have to do for the time being. He had more important things to do. Gino jumped into a cab on Madison and 45th Street and went to see Carmine Miceli Jr. The five minute ride was enough to make Gino half car sick so he told the driver to stop at 72nd Street and he walked the rest of the way to clear his head and get the taste of bile out of his throat. All the while he mumbled to himself about the horrible and smelly cab drivers that now plagued his city. When he arrived at the Miceli townhouse he had half expected four or five familiar faces to be guarding the front door on 79th Street. Instead he found a police car with two women police sitting inside drinking Starbucks coffee. These two lady cops were all that was needed to protect the home of Carmine Miceli Jr., who made his father's office his own.

Gino rang the doorbell and was buzzed inside where two of the largest men he had ever seen greeted him. They escorted him to the familiar office, the aroma of fresh espresso and anisette cookies filled the place.

"Gino, *meenkia*, you need to get some sleep. Are you okay?" Carmine Jr. greeted him with the usual hugs and kisses.

"Carmine...what sleep? How can a person get sleep with these crazy people trying to kill you and your friends all day and night?" Gino asked with a slight grin.

"Like a baby I sleep. These fucks have to worry about our crazy bastards killing them day and night. Here, have some coffee. Let me get you something to eat, you look like you lost some weight."

"Coffee okay, food will make me sick. I just got car sick coming here."

"From a kid Gino. I remember when we were kids that the old men had to stop a few times on the way to Peach Lake so you could toss your cookies," Carmine laughed.

"In my case they were cannolis, not cookies, and yes, till this day I get car sick, can you believe it?"

"What's on your mind cuz?"

"I know you've been wanting to talk to me but I've been a little preoccupied with this Albanian situation. It's getting hotter by the minute. They took out Joey Dark Glasses last night in Brooklyn. You remember him, he was in my wedding party, Joey Piccirilli. All hell is about to break loose.

"Carmine, I know that your father always wanted me to stay clear of this thing. My mother, rest in peace, would roll over in her grave if she knew what I came here for. I'm going to cut to the chase. I want in. I want to help you with the business. I don't need money. I don't need power. What I need is to help you for everything your family has done for mine back to Sicily. You can use my business advice, my contacts in the legitimate world, my street savvy, in short you need me Carmine and I will do whatever I can to help you. From the bottom of my heart," Gino said without taking his eyes off Carmine's face, looking for a sign of approval or disapproval. Carmine was blank and gave no hint to his feelings. Gino thought to himself how Carmine's father taught him well.

"Gino, this is something that I need to think about. I am honored by your offer, but I need to mull it over."

"I know I have no experience in really rough stuff but I have a sense for the business. It's in my blood Carmine and you know that. All I can ask is for you to consider my request. No one would watch your back as close as I would."

Carmine didn't bite.

"You feeling any better? Your color has come back. You looked like friggin' Dracula when you walked in here Gino. Go get some rest. Tell my guy downstairs where you are staying so I can reach out for you. Right now I need to get to Brooklyn and see what's happening across that very wide river." Carmine embraced Gino and was off like a shot.

Gino walked the thirty-four blocks back to the Roosevelt Hotel

Engjëll remained in Federal protective custody and his and his family's future back in Albania was not looking promising. Gjergj was released by the Bronx District Attorney's office after Detective Del Greco reported that he was at a dead end with the witness. Del Greco knew that he was releasing the Albanian to his death. The Lieutenant knew that he had to do this for his benefactor and learn to deal with the stain on his conscience. He notified his contact with the Marku family a few hours before Gjergj's release and Ilir wasted no time in making his move.

Two Marku soldiers were dispatched to pick up Gjergj and bring him to the late Niki Balaj's restaurant on City Island for a nice dinner. Niki's death didn't stop anything as business was business. The restaurant, the drug trafficking were all open for business. All that was needed was a good scrubbing of the back deck and windows, which needed it anyway. Niki's brother Jack jumped right in to handle things for the resilient Marku family. A little thing like death wasn't going to stop the cash flowing from this asset. At the same time, Ilir reached out for his nephew Ukë to meet him at his home in Scarsdale to have dinner with him to discuss the future of the family business. Ukë was nearly orgasmic. His time had come he thought. The old man was getting tired and needed him to run things. It was just a matter of time before he was on top and would show the world who he really was. Ukë got to the Marku estate and was greeted not by his Uncle Ilir but by three of the bodyguards.

"Mr. Marku, your uncle has entrusted me to take you to your cousin's restaurant and meet him there. He did not want to go together for security purposes, you understand. I am to be the lead personal body for you in the future. Please let me have your car keys. You will not be driving again sir."

"Yes of course. Let's not keep my uncle waiting, understand?" Ukë barked out his first command as the new *kryetar*, the new underboss of the Marku family, soon to be the Boss himself and all the while thinking, *my time has finally come.*

They arrived at the restaurant within ten minutes. Ukë nearly jumped out of the back seat of the car, his bodyguards close behind. He was greeted at the door by his cousin Jack and a few other bodyguards. His cousin kissed him hello and offered a curious wink that Ukë knew was a congratulatory gesture. He was soon to be *kryetar* and everyone in the family, everyone in this world would show him the respect that he earned and deserved. Jack escorted the group, led by the nearly hyperventilating Ukë, down a flight of stairs to a private banquet room that was in use tonight solely for the Marku family business. When they arrived, Ukë was not surprised to see his uncle Ilir at the main table but was very surprised to see the Albanian national Gjergj, who swore his allegiance and *besa* to him, sitting to the side. Ukë's stomach came alive with butterflies. Ukë fought the temptation to flee and hide from what he was about to hear. He stopped himself from running but made a turn to quietly and quickly excuse himself from the room. This move was anticipated by his bodyguards who turned him back toward the table to face his uncle.

"*Nipash,* I am so glad that you could come here to learn what happens to those who try to do bad things to the Marku family. Watch and learn *mi Nipash.*"

Ilir turned his attention to the trembling Gjergj who sat in a chair next to Ilir Marku's table, flanked by two enormous and hard faced men.

"You have made a bad mistake thinking that you could come to this country and walk away with money and position. Blood money. Money that was easy to be made and that would make your life and the life of your family in Albania easy. For one second did you pause to think that perhaps you would be sitting in this chair tonight waiting for justice to be served upon you? Did you wonder what would be done to you if your plans, or the plans, of others did not work?" Ilir glanced at Ukë and stared coldly at him but did not wait for an answer from the soon to be dead Gjergj.

"We come from the same town, we know your family for many years. They are good people. Hard working people, people who believe that *besa* is a real and honorable thing that we live by. Because of the way that they have lived for generations I will give my promise that they will not be harmed in any way because of the actions of their foolish and greedy Gjergj. They are innocent of my son's death and have no blood on their hands. Face death bravely."

Ilir Marku starred into Gjergj eyes as one of the burley men choked the life from him with a wire garrote. Blood spurted from Gjergj's neck and his eyes bulged from their sockets. He never made a sound.

Gjergj's death took only a few violent minutes. Ilir took his attention to his wobbly nephew, who had tears streaming down his agonized and twisted face.

"Now take his head from his shoulders and drop it in a garbage dump far from here. Then remove his hands. They will be sent to his family in Albania. The rest take to the ocean for the fish to feast upon," Ilir said to his henchmen while looking with no feeling toward his nephew.

"Uncle...I..."

"No words from you Ukë. I do not want to hear your voice. I wanted you and my son to run this business one day. Your father and I knew that you had ambition and that you were impatient but we would never dream of what you have done to our family. You have cursed us for seven generations. My brother rolls in his grave for your acts of murder against your own blood. I was the one who named you after my father's brother who died fighting the Turks. I watched as you fathers *kumar* held you as a baby and gave you your first haircut. We saw that your business was lucrative and that you were given the proper respect in our world. Your cousin loved you and you repaid him by shooting him in the back of the head like a coward. This poor moron that we just sent to hell is another victim of your appetite for power. So how should we kill you? The same way you killed my son, with a single bullet to the brain? Strangle you? Drown you? Torture you and then hang you? All of that is simple and easy. There is not a man here tonight that would not gladly snuff the light from your eyes as you have taken the light from my life. No Ukë, I will not waste one bullet from my gun on you. Your blood will not shame me or any of the men in this room because it is rancid. You have desecrated our blood in front of the whole world and every mountain and valley will know of what you have done. No Albanian will look in your direction as you now walk the earth alone. If your father were alive I know he would beg someone to shoot you dead here and now because you are indeed dead already. Your soul is dead." Ilir paused for a moment to collect his thoughts.

"Now take him to the place where he killed my son. Take all of his money and all of his property. I will take over his business and give them to someone more suitable. Give everything else he owns away to the less fortunate of our clansman. Then leave him to walk the earth alone."

Ilir got up from his chair and left the room with a forlorn look that his nephew indeed had killed his son Lekë and his yet unborn grandson the family was without a rightful blood heir. His time was short as he knew that his mind could not live with what had happened to his clan. Ilir was certain that if his mind was not strong his body would react and he would soon be dead. The old timers would say that he died from a broken heart and in this case the cliché was true. He had no fear at all about his future. He knew that he needed to make amends with and recompense the Miceli family. He asked his friend Hamdi to reach out for Gino Ranno to make a meeting. Ilir was so used to having his underboss do all of the set up work that he didn't know the correct mob protocol and was concerned to offend anyone. He knew full well that he had to go with his hat in his hand to Carmine Miceli Jr. and that position made him sick to his stomach.

Hamdi was amazed when he called Gino's phone that Gino answered on the first ring. Gino was still holed up at the Roosevelt Hotel waiting for the next wave of violence to subside and the second he saw Hamdi's name come up on his cell phone he knew there was something important that needed his attention. Whether he knew it or not Gino was already taking on the role of the Miceli family *consigliere*.

"Gino my dear friend it is time that we meet," Hamdi said forgoing the usual query about Gino's health and family.

"Hamdi, it's good to hear your voice. What is on your mind my friend?"

"I have been asked to talk with you by someone very important. There is not much that I would like to say on the telephone Gino."

"I understand. Where would you like to meet?"

"I will come to you Gino. Tell me where. You will be safe."

"Hamdi, if I cannot trust you, if your *besa* means nothing then my world is over and I no longer want to live on this earth. Let's meet at the Club Macanudo on 61st and Madison. I can walk there in thirty minutes," Gino said, not wanting to bring Hamdi to the Roosevelt just in case Hamdi was followed, and not wanting to get back into another taxi for a long time.

"Gino, how many times have I asked you to quit those cigars? Okay I will be there. I am coming alone." Hamdi said

"So am I."

Shpresa waited for Tenuta Gashi at the bar at The City Crab on Park Avenue South, a corner restaurant a few blocks from her and Rick's office. She waited ten minutes and needed to tell three different men that she wasn't interested in a drink or chatting or anything else. Underneath the soft and pretty exterior was a true daughter of the eagle. 'Don't mess with me and I will not sink my talons into your eyeballs' was her fallback position.

"Are you Shpresa? Shpresa Metalia?" a beautiful, well dressed woman of about sixty with flaming red hair and green eyes asked. It was certainly Tenuta Gashi. She had that classic Albanian look of high cheekbones and beautiful skin, dressed in a colorful and very tasteful below-the-knee dress.

"Yes...yes I am. You must be Tenuta."

"Thank you for seeing me. I am sorry to be so mysterious but what I have to tell you is of the utmost importance. I know that you are close to Valbona and to Mr. Marku. I have no one else to tell." Tenuta seemed as if she was going to cry.

"Please, let's get away from this horrid bar and get a table. The bar is no place for two ladies," Shpresa said relieving some tension.

The two women stayed at The City Crab for more than two hours. Shpresa kept ordering coffee after coffee and kept tipping the waitress rather than getting thrown out during the busy lunch rush. She couldn't help but think how much Tenuta reminded her of her own mother as she listened to the woman's amazing life and compelling story that left her virtually speechless.

Gino walked briskly straight up Madison Avenue checking out all the nice looking women along the way. He loved to count in his head the number of women that he would not mind rolling around with. He was still fifteen years old in his behavior but he knew damned well that at his age he would stop lusting after just one...if that. It was a fun fantasy and generally he got to twenty-five after three blocks. The game was harmless and kept his mind off the pain in his left knee and lower back. *Some stud*, he thought as he checked out the ass on a tourist who was walking with her boyfriend just in front of him. Luckily she stopped to window shop at the Salvatore Ferragamo store, saving Gino's life as he was sure to be hit by a bus or one of the taxis that he so loathed. Gino was very easily distracted, but no matter what was going on or how stressed he was, there was always time to look at women. The walk from the Roosevelt Hotel to the Macanudo Club took just about fifteen minutes and garnered 102 women that Gino would have liked to screw. He thought he was better off counting the ones that he wouldn't touch and made a mental note to do that on the walk back.

Today, however, was serious business and Gino waited at a table for Hamdi with a freshly lit H. Upman Bankers Series Churchill cigar. The Macanudo club is one of the last remnants of restaurants that are permitted to serve food and cigars in New York City. The Club has that masculine woody and dark look that appeals to men as well as many women. Gino had been going there for years but kept a low profile. He never owned a humidor wall box with his name on it, always stayed away from the bar where the men would brag about their money deals, cars and lady conquests. Gino didn't have a need to expose his resume, his money and especially his penis size, which he always thought was the real problem with men like this. No one at the club knew his name and that is exactly how he wanted it, except for the bartender/waitress/cigar girl that had one of the best asses in North America. He looked and flirted now because all that had to stop when Hamdi arrived.

Within ten minutes Hamdi walked in looking as if he were about to make a fruit delivery. Never one to dress fancy or spend money freely on wasteful things like cigars or tailored clothing, Hamdi was not at all comfortable in places like this. He tolerated it because he knew that Gino enjoyed the occasional smoke.

Gino rose as Hamdi approached the table.

"Hamdi, so good to see you my dear friend."

"Gino, how are you. Everything is good? Your family?"

"Well I haven't seen the family much lately Hamdi but I'm told by my wife that all is well. And yours?"

"Everyone is good thank God. Your business affairs are good?"

"Yes thank you. The money keeps coming in and I don't lift anything too heavy so yes indeed, thank God."

"Gino I have to talk about some serious issues with you if you permit me to get to business please," Hamdi said as if embarrassed by the quick segue.

"By all means Hamdi, what's on your mind?"

"This terrible business of fighting between my friends, my Albanian friends and your friends, the Italians, needs to come to an end. My dear friend has asked for me to speak with you. You know Gino, I am from the old school and I dislike using names in such matters. My dear friend would like to meet with your friend and settle the matter appropriately. The time for violence has come to an end."

"Hamdi, this is not an easy thing to do. What about the vengeance that you have against us? Do you just turn it off like a faucet?" Gino was confused but needed to probe a bit.

The *gjakmarrja* has ended. There is no need for this as there was no blood taken by anyone that you know; that young man is indeed innocent. We know who did the killing and justice is being served in our way, in our tradition. I am sincere in what I say to you Gino."

"Never doubted your word for one moment Hamdi. I will need further proof of what you are saying before a meeting can be set but I will bring this news to my friend and try to get all fighting to stop. This is like a chain reaction you know. Shooting back and forth, bombing back and forth, and there is never a real winner."

"The only proof I can offer to you is that we know that the killer was a family member and not the one that was accused. What more can I show you?"

"Okay, I understand but a lot of damage has been done on both sides Hamdi, I will do my best."

"I will explain something to you Gino and do not take offense to this please. The Albanians do not fear your Italian friends. They only fear other Albanians. This is not a good thing for anyone. If there is no respect and no fear the blood will run for a long time, and really over nothing but people seeking power and more power," Hamdi said.

"I understand fully. There will be only losers in this battle for king of the hill," Gino said with sincerity in his voice.

"Gino, make the meeting happen. For everyone's sake."

"I will see what I can do tonight, and get back to you as soon as possible."

Hamdi stood up and kissed Gino on both cheeks and embraced him for longer than normal. His face was ashen. Gino knew that many lives depended upon his quick action, and the manner in which he made his presentation to Carmine Jr. was vital.

Gino ignored his taxi phobia and car sickness and hailed a cab on Madison Avenue to save time. He kept his head out of the window for the eighteen blocks after giving the driver a ten dollar bill and asking him not to jerk the car too much. The cab moved quickly up the avenue past the most expensive stores in the world and came to a smooth stop on 79th Street and Madison. Gino wasn't green and felt fine. He threw another twenty at the driver who was praising Allah for the windfall.

Gino entered the Miceli townhouse hoping that Carmine Miceli Jr. was home. He was and Gino took a deep breath before he entered the office of the new Don.

3 8

Detective Del Greco had put the finishing touches on his retirement papers and sat in his office staring at the documents almost in disbelief. He wasn't ready to retire but knew he was playing pension roulette. He was in deep thought reviewing the many years of service in the department and where he would go from here. If the Feds decided to dig deeper into the Marku connection to him he was toast. No pension, possible jail time and, most of all, the dishonor of being labeled a bad cop. He knew he had to make the move and get himself as far away from this mess and the Albanian-Italian street war that was escalating by the minute. He knew Ilir Marku was on thin ice after seeing him but was not at all concerned that the old man would flip and tell anyone, least of all the United States Federal Government, what sins he had committed as a public servant. But what if Marku was no longer in power? That was a gamble he was not willing to even consider. It was time to go.

He would present his papers today to the Bronx Borough Commander, effective immediately and recommend a promotion for his protégé Gojcaj who he knew was a good, clean, cop. At least he felt this would be the right thing to do for the department and his own legacy. He knew in his heart that he did a good job for the NYPD but didn't at all believe his own bullshit. What he did over the years with the Marku family was criminal. He did what he did not only for monetary gain but also for the rush of power mixed with danger. Now at his age with all the cards on the table he was afraid that the all-in bet was too rich for his blood.

A knock on his door startled him causing him to almost bounce out of his chair. It was Gojcaj.

"Hey boss, you okay?" the young cop asked.

"Yeah. Yeah, just daydreaming. Come in I have something I want to talk about," Del Greco said as he tried to focus on the here and now.

"They just got another wise-guy. This one was a doozie. Shot him just after he dropped his kids off at school. Not our problem. They hit him in front of Our Lady of Fatima in Yonkers. One of Miceli's lieutenants. This thing is going viral boss," Gojcaj said with a sense of relief that the murder didn't occur in the Bronx.

"Jimmy, sit down please we need to talk."

Gojcaj could tell Del Greco was troubled and that this talk would be trouble. His first thought was that he would be transferred to some God awful house where he would hate his life for a very long time.

"First of all, if Yonkers asks for help or advice make sure you help them in any way possible, understood?"

Gojcaj nodded in agreement but was nonplussed by the comment.

"Jimmy, I'm done. I'm putting my papers in today and will shove off as soon as I can. I'm recommending that you take my place. It's the right move for me and a great step up for you. You deserve it more than anyone in the Department and I still have juice with Borough Command. Congratulations, I'm happy for you, kid."

"Boss, what the hell is up? I thought you wanted a few more years. I think I need more time with you. I'm not ready," Gojcaj said almost pleading.

"You were ready a year ago. Stop putting yourself down and grab hold of the job. As for me, ya gotta know when to fold 'em Jimmy. Look at Ted Williams. His last at bat was a homer. I want to go out like him, on top instead of drooling on myself and pissing my pants. The Marku case was enough for me. That was my last home run. We have done some good things together kiddo and I hope that I've helped you more than hurt you," Del Greco said with a bit too much quiver in his voice.

"I don't know what to say boss. You've been like a father to me since I came on the job. You always taught me to do the right thing and be the best that I could be. Tough, you bet your ass, but this ain't working the toll booths at the Whitestone Bridge. Boss, I can't tell you what you have meant to me and my family. I really don't know what my life will be with you retired. I was putting it off in my mind and now here it is. Fuck!"

"Yea, the right thing to do alright. That's the ticket. Keep your head down and do the job. Always do your best. If only I would have listened to my own advice," Del Greco spoke his thoughts out loud and wished that he hadn't.

"What are you saying Carlo? Are you in some kind of trouble?"

"Don't mind me Jimmy, just an old man with some regrets is all."

"Look, I'm not prying but I did notice that you were taking the Marku thing a bit too personal. That was one of the first lessons you taught me. It's a job you said, don't get too close."

"Tell you the truth, that's why I think my fastball is gone kid. That's why I have to go to the Dominican and live a different kind of life," Del Greco said.

"But your worst pitch is still better than anyone else in the department."

"Appreciate that. You just be you and do your time. Get the pension as early as you can and move on. This job changes you into something that you may not want to be Jimmy. Here is my last bit of advice to you. Buy a building, get into the real estate game and have something else to back you up. You have a great head on your shoulders. Don't finish up as a security guy at some college or hospital. Be your own man. Pass something on to those kids of yours and give them some options."

"I'm always here for you, boss. If you ever want to talk you know I'm a good listener." Gojcaj knew that there was more to his mentor leaving the job so suddenly but didn't want to press the matter. After all he was a detective and could easily smell that there was something behind Del Greco's decision.

"Thanks kid. Now let me get this fucking paperwork to the man so you can plan a party. Don't forget to get the paperwork from the DA so we can bring that prick Ukë Marku in for murder. I'd like to wrap that up tomorrow and ride off into the sunset. And Jimmy, one more thing. My place is yours. You better come down and see me."

39

Ilir Marku was sitting in the dark in his study at the Scarsdale estate. His eyes were sunken deep into his skull and were rimmed with large dark circles. The house was still under heavy guard but Shpresa was able to gain entry into the house without any questions. She first went to Valbona to check on her and found her friend was also forlorn and down in spirit. This house seemed cursed to Shpresa but she knew in her heart that her mission could only make things better. She could not imagine that anything save more death could make things worse for Valbona and Ilir.

Shpresa went to the Marku estate to check in on Valbona but her underlying reason was to see Ilir. Her stomach was doing flips from the butterflies. She had rehearsed her words over and over in her mind and in front of the small mirror in the small bathroom in her office.

Shpresa was not at all a perfectionist but she knew that her discussion with Ilir Marku needed to be absolutely on the mark. Not only did she need to guard against insulting him, there was this whole Albanian culture thing that she needed to dance around. What to say and more important what not to say was what she had been practicing until she was almost stammering.

When Shpresa got past the small army of body guards around the house she went right to Valbona's suite only to be greeted by Adem and her 'BFF,' and the three old Albanian maids listening to beautiful Albanian folk music. Evidently Adem brought a CD along as an excuse to see Valbona.

"Soooo, you guys have a party and no one invites me I see," Shpresa joked. Her broad and beautiful smile lightened the room. Even the babushka women couldn't help but show their gold teeth.

"Shpres, Adem brought this music for us to listen to. It brings me back to when our families got together and we were forced to listen to it instead of to our one true love Rick Springfield," Valbona said smiling, her eyes showing a hint of sparkle like she had before that tragic night.

"Did you guys actually like Rick Springfield? AND I WANT TO BE JESSIES GIRL!" Adem sang half mocking but respecting their adolescence at the same time.

"Are you kidding Adem, if he called us tonight we would both be on the next plane to wherever he is," Shpresa said and the two women laughed out loud, Valbona blushing just enough to put some needed color in her face.

"Well, I'll be sure to learn some of his music and do a Rick Springfield medley for you two. If you like it I will get it on Albanian television the next time I'm back. That may get me thrown out of the country but I'm getting kind of homesick lately. I think I'm getting that urge to stay near home and maybe settle down," Adem said and glanced quickly at Valbona then added, "You know, near my mom. She's getting older and I want to be around more."

"So you've sowed your wild oats Adem? Is that what you mean, after all you're almost sixty," Shpresa joked and they all laughed, Adem laughing the loudest.

"Not quite Shpres but I'm ready for the next stage in life. I want to start a family; you know three kids, the house, and the dog," Adem said, instantly wishing he could have pulled the words back into his mouth.

Valbona gasped as if she suddenly remembered what happened to her family, covered her face and started to cry softly into her hands.

"My God Valbona I'm so, so sorry. That was the wrong thing to say, please forgive my stupidity," Adem said with a pained look on his face.

"Adem, go get us something to drink please, she will be fine. Give her a minute," Shpresa said nodding at the door to Adem, who made a quick exit.

"Val, he didn't mean anything. That was just a slip but he is saying how he feels, that's all."

"I know Shpres but it's just so hard to deal with it. I want to just bury the thought of losing them deep into my dreams. I don't know how much I can take," Valbona said as she wiped away her tears and checked her eyes in a mirror that hung in her suite.

"Val, look at me. I hope you see what's going on here?"

"See what Shpresa?"

"Are you blind girl? Adem is crazy about you, can't you see it? Why do you think he comes so much and brings these thoughtful things like the music. Look, he is gorgeous and I see the way he looks at you."

"You're crazy. There is a time and a place you nut. It's too soon for me even to think about that kind of thing. Maybe one day *Marsalla,* but not now. What will they say?"

"Who the fuck are they? They? THEY always have something to say. Look we are not back in the time of Skanderbeg for fuck's sake. I'm not saying you let him jump into your bed but wake up girl. Life is short and then you die. And you are dead for a long time BFF," Shpresa said looking into Valbona's eyes with all the love she had. Just then Rick appeared with Adem who was holding flowers that he picked from the garden.

"I understand that my friend here opened his mouth and inserted his foot. What do you expect from an Albanian?" Rick said.

"I picked these for you Valbona, please forgive me," Adem said softly as if he and Valbona were the only people in the room. The hair on Shpresa's arms stood up.

"Adem, you did nothing wrong. It's me who needs to apologize for being so emotional and making you feel uncomfortable. I need to deal with this better and I promise I will," Valbona said. Even Rick could feel the electricity.

"Hey, I came here to collect my absentee wife and take her to dinner. You guys wanna come?" Rick said.

"Jerk, you know that Mr. Marku will not allow that. Now look who's putting his foot in his mouth. I'd like to put my foot in your ass but then again you may enjoy that too much," Shpresa said causing everyone, including the women on watch, to laugh.

Suddenly Mr. Marku appeared at the door to Valbona's suite. He looked like he aged twenty years but smiled through his pain.

"So, can anyone come to this nice party?" he asked.

"Hello Mr. Marku, we were just acting stupid, perhaps not a party for normal people," Adem said holding his right hand to his heart.

"I'm certain that you can learn to perfect stupidity simply by hanging around me for a while," Ilir said attempting to make a joke but no one laughed.

"Mr. Marku, we are about to leave for dinner but I would like a word with you if you have a moment please," Shpresa said, the butterflies from her stomach now in her throat.

"For you Shpresa, I always have time. Come."

Ilir led the way to his Skanderbeg room. Shpresa waved at Rick who had a puzzled look. What could his wife want to tell the Boss of the New York Albanian mob that was so important? Shpresa hadn't told him what she needed to tell Ilir Marku.

Marku entered the study and asked a household attendant to bring coffee for both he and Shpresa.

"What is on your mind my dear Shpresa?" the Boss asked.

"Mr. Marku, forgive me I am nervous speaking to you but I need to share something with you that is very important and very personal," Shpresa felt her face go red hot.

"Shpresa, just say what you want to say. You are the friend of my *Reja*. I am your friend. Relax and tell me your problem. I am sure I can help you."

"Oh no Mr. Marku, I don't need any help. I need to tell you that there is someone from your past life that would like to see you and it can cause some difficulty to you. Do you remember a woman from when you were young? Her name is Tenuta Gashi." Shpresa swallowed hard at the name.

The fearless boss of the New York Albanian mob looked at Shpresa in disbelief and did not respond at first. A long ten seconds passed before he spoke.

"Yes. Is she in some kind of trouble? Some need?"

"No sir but she needs to see you to tell you a story." Shpresa's rehearsal was working.

"Do you know the story Shpresa?"

"I do."

"So why don't you tell me the story and save the awkward meeting?"

"Mr. Marku, what Tenuta needs to say cannot come from me. I gave my *besa* to her."

"That is enough for me young lady. I will meet with her but it cannot be known. I have my reasons."

"How about at my home tonight? It would be my honor for you to come for a visit," Shpresa said bowing her head.

"Good. Is seven good?"

"Can you make it eight? I know she works and I will pick her up."

"Fine. I am honored to be asked to yours and Rick's home."

At that same moment in time, Gino was meeting the new Don of the New York Mafia, Carmine Miceli Jr. at his office on East 79th Street in Manhattan. Carmine seemed agitated and restless and Gino had, like Shpresa, rehearsed his presentation.

"Gino, this job really sucks. I know that my father, rest in peace, trained me for this life but I needed a few more years at his elbow. There is more politics in this life than Washington D.C. I feel like a juggler in a fucking circus. *Madonna*, what headaches," Carmine Jr. said while taking a Zantac for the acid reflux he was suddenly afflicted with.

"Did you give some thought to my proposal Carmine. You know, about my helping you?" Gino asked.

"I have, yes. My father loved you like you were his own son that you know. Yet he always kept you from joining this life of ours. I don't know what he would feel about this Gino."

"Well I do Carmine. He always said, *Noi non potemo avere perfetta vita senza amici.*"

"Yep, 'we can't have a perfect life without friends.' Where the hell did he get that one?" Carmine asked.

"Actually Carmine, your father took that one from Dante."

"No shit? Dante, of all people."

"Your dad was one of a kind Carmine."

"You're telling me!"

"Well, when I look around there is no one that is more the logical right hand for you, someone you can trust more than me. Yeah, I don't have a button, I made no bones, no history in this business except what's in my blood. Only you can make the decision. Our friendship will not be affected no matter what you decide Carmine, I give you my word," Gino said.

"Let's try it. Worst case scenario I fire you and you can file for unemployment," Carmine Jr. said and they both broke into a hearty laugh.

"Okay, here is my first proposal. I've been contacted by a friend of the Markus. They want a sit down over the Santoro issue. They know that Ukë Marku killed Ilir's son. He's out of the family and soon to be arrested for murder. They want to drop the whole thing and apologize. I say we make them pay restitution and we settle this war but not without a clear agreement that what's ours is ours and that no more of their muscling in on our business affairs will be tolerated. Anything they took has to be given back. It's perfect. They need to save face as men of honor," Gino said as if he was the family *consigliere* for ten years.

Carmine Jr. paused and looked into Gino's eyes.

"You were born for this shit Gino. I'm a genius for bringing you in."

They laughed again and Gino Ranno knew that he was in.

"Okay, set up the meeting Gino. I will talk to the rest of the family heads and let them know our plan. Micky Roach will handle security. And one more thing Gino. Thank you for being here for me."

4 0

Gino had to make his way back to Joey Clams and C.C. but not until he met with Hamdi and set up the meeting of the warring mob families. Business had to come first. Then they would decide when to get Joey Jr. back and get him the help that he needed with his addiction issues. All of the pieces had to fit into place before Gino could do what he needed to do for his best friend Clams and his kid. There was still a lot of ground to cover. Gino knew he had to close the right deal for the Markus to save face and for the Micelis to agree to the truce and long-term peace. It was still a sale that needed to be closed and Gino knew how to close better than anyone. Was there a difference between making a real estate sale or settling a mob war? Gino didn't think so as long as both sides were satisfied with the benefits of a deal.

Before he met with Micky Roach, Gino's first step was to contact Hamdi Nezaj to set the stage for the power meeting with Carmine Jr. Hamdi would see a part of Gino that he had not seen before in their many years as friends. Going up to the Bronx was respectful to Hamdi but the respect game, in Gino's mind, had to take a back seat to positioning. Gino called Hamdi and told him, not asked him, to meet in Manhattan at the Plaza Hotel lobby in two hours. The Plaza was in no way a comfortable meeting place for the ultra conservative and frugal old world Albanian. Hamdi could likely buy two apartment suites at the Plaza for cash but the place was far too ostentatious for him. Gino wanted to keep the other side off balance from the get go. Gino, while not planning to be at all disrespectful or harsh, had no intention of playing the role of an affable smiling face that was his trademark. He knew that Hamdi had to know that his role in the negotiations was no longer as a go between.

Hamdi showed up at the Plaza and met Gino promptly at the appointed time with the usual European greeting. Gino kept a serious demeanor from the start as they sat in a window seat overlooking the hotel's majestic entrance facing Fifth Avenue.

"Hamdi, my friend has asked me to be involved with him throughout the meeting with your friend. I must inform you that there is reluctance on his part to meet while blood is running in the streets. I must request that all retribution on both sides be halted before the meeting is made. I believe that my request is reasonable and in the best interest of a successful outcome." Gino sounded more like an Ambassador than a *consigliere*.

"Gino, I must tell you that my role with the Marku family has changed as yours has. Let's be open with each other. We are both, Hamdi and Gino, no longer the messenger boys. Both sides want to stop this fighting because it is hurting business. Both sides want to maintain their honor and want to enjoy the peace that existed for many years. Now it is our role to see if that is possible or not."

Gino had met his match. He had no idea until that moment that Hamdi was now the new *kryetar*. Of course Ilir Marku needed someone that was a trusted friend to replace Pashko Luli just as Carmine Jr. had. Gino was surprised that he had not figured that out before this meeting and made a mental note to start playing the chess game a bit better.

"It is a wise choice that your friend has made Hamdi," Gino said with a no-tell face.

"As wise as your friend Gino," Hamdi quickly replied.

"This is not the time and place to start our discussions. We have a lot to do in order to set the meeting. I suggest a moratorium on the street and that we consider a meeting time and place. I suggest a safe and neutral location with as few people involved as possible in 48 hours," Gino said.

"Agreed. But we both must understand that there may be an incident that is not approved. There are, after all, many emotions in play now. We cannot be expected to monitor every soldier on the street," Hamdi said with a slight smile.

"Hamdi, there must be no mistake here. The word will go out from my friend and his associates that any violence against the Albanians will not be tolerated and that the penalty will be severe. I expect that same approach on your side."

"That is fair. I will make that work. I think that you and I should meet again to discuss details."

"Yes. How about tomorrow at three o'clock, here."

"Gino, the time is fine but let's make it a neutral place. Do you know the Greek diner just over the RFK Bridge?" Hamdi asked coyly.

"I do. That's fine."

Gino knew that Hamdi understood his positioning and was not having any part of it. This was going to be the toughest sale of his career.

4 1

etective Del Greco got the nod from his superiors at Bronx Borough Command to retire. There really wasn't much they could do
or would do to stop him. He was after all a civil servant and put his time
in for the people of the City of New York. Hate to see you go, you were
the best Carlo, great job great knowing you, you better keep in touch and
all the wonderful platitudes that people who are left behind always say
when someone leaves an organization. Del Greco had one more collar to
make and then he would be available for any court cases when the District Attorney needed him but the reality was, he was finished as a cop
and he was retiring because he screwed himself. He was a great detective
but a crooked cop. He was tainted, and if the Feds went after him the
whole world would know the ugly truth.

No decision would be made for a while on Jimmy Gojcaj's promotion but no one in Command said no. Del Greco was going to do the
right thing for Jimmy and do what he needed to do to see that this guy
was taken care of. Carlo needed to feel better about himself and this was
as good a way to close things out as he could think of at the moment.

Del Greco wanted to orchestrate the arrest of Ukë Marku and today
was as good as any day to get that asshole behind bars. If the judge set a
bail of a measly five-hundred dollars Ukë couldn't post it and nobody in
their right mind would spring him after the word was passed on from
Ilir Marku. Ukë was indeed a man without a country. Finding him was
another story and Del Greco had every confidence that Jimmy Gojcaj

would reach out into the Albanian world and they would get a bead on him in no time. The pieces would all fall into place and Del Greco would ride off into the sunset like Clint Eastwood.

Sure enough, a few calls from Gojcaj that morning and they discovered that Ukë was holed up in an apartment that he owned at the Ansonia Hotel right on Broadway on Manhattan's West Side.

Del Greco made certain that all of the paperwork was in order before leaving with Jimmy Gojcaj to arrest Ukë Marku. As he was leaving the Bronx Homicide office Del Greco's commanding officer walked into his office.

"Carlo what's going on with that Marku homicide? I just got a call from the Commissioner and I have to see him today and meet some Federal agents. Why are the Feds asking for a meeting?"

Del Greco felt his stomach turn over.

"No idea boss. Maybe they want credit for solving the case. You know how those guys are. Always looking to climb up a pay grade."

"Christ Almighty, who needs this shit. Look, come into my office later today. Maybe I'll have an idea what they are snooping around for."

"Okay boss. I'll be back after we bring the perp in," Del Greco said, his mind racing a mile a minute.

No Albanian in his or her right mind would have been seen with Ukë since the word on the street from Ilir Marku marked him bad. To go against the Marku family on this edict was to have the same or worse fate than the one that faced Ukë. The word in the Albanian community in New York City and, for that matter, throughout the world, seems to travel at the speed of light.

Ukë realized he was done. He knew that his life was over and he considered opening the window in his twelfth floor apartment and smashing himself onto the pavement below ending his miserable existence. He thought his luck was so bad that he would survive and be a vegetable in a wheelchair in some horrendous state facility with burns on his ass from not being changed out of his shitty diapers often enough.

His thoughts of suicide were all that he had on his mind since he was dropped off by his uncle's men on Pelham Parkway, the place where he bet it all and shot craps.

In his apartment there were several guns that he decided to use to end his now worthless life. The decision came down to using the .45 Colt Automatic or a nice Walther 9 millimeter. He decided on the Walther, got some paper and started to write a letter to his Uncle Ilir to free his soul of the burden of murdering his cousin and destroying the family legacy. Ukë sat at a table in his kitchen staring between the gun and the paper, almost going into a trance.

The reality was that Ukë didn't have the balls to take his own life.

Ukë poured himself a tumbler of Louis XIV Cognac and waited. He knew they would find him.

Halfway into the second full glass, the doorbell of his apartment rang followed by three pounding knocks on his door.

"Ukë, Ukë Marku this is the NYPD. We have a warrant for your arrest. Please open the door and step away. It's Jimmy Gojcaj, Ukë. Let's do this easy, what do you say?"

Gojcaj, Del Greco, two Midtown North Detectives, and four uniformed cops were in on the arrest along with the building manager who was ordered to wait by the elevator. The uniforms all had their service revolvers drawn. Gojcaj and Del Greco were posted at either side of the door also with guns in their hands when Ukë unlocked it.

"I don't want any trouble Jimmy," Ukë said, his voice muffled by the distance that he put between him and the door.

"Okay Ukë, just stand in the middle of the room with hands behind your head. We want to take you in nice and easy. Everything will be okay Ukë," Gojcaj said knowing that the word okay was not in Ukë Marku's future.

"Just don't shoot me please," Ukë implored.

"No shots Ukë. All we need to do is bring you in," the Albanian cop assured him.

Gojcaj opened the door slightly and peeked in seeing Marku obeying his command. Suddenly Del Greco put his arm between the door and his protégé and pushed his body into the room. For whatever reason, Del Greco wanted to be the first one in.

Ukë Marku pulled his 9 millimeter automatic from behind his head and started shooting, hitting Del Greco three times in his stomach. The senior detective dropped like a stone where he stood.

"Come on, you motherfuckers, do me!" Ukë screamed while firing wildly at the door.

Gojcaj came in low and fired his weapon hitting Ukë at least once wounding him on his right side. Ukë stood for a moment stunned by the searing pain. The rest of the cops did their duty. Ukë took a hail of bullets, the momentum of the shots knocking him a good five feet from where he had stood.

Ukë got his suicide wish, but instead of splattering his body against the street or his brains against the walls it was suicide by cop. Ukë was hit so many times the coroner stopped counting at twenty five. The back of his head was opened like a melon and his internal organs virtually exploded. Both of Ukë's eyes were gone. He would have been better off doing the job himself.

Del Greco was barely alive, shot in the stomach and liver, the expensive carpet on Ukë's floor already soaked with the detective's dark blood. His worries would soon be over.

"Carlo…boss, just hold on partner. Don't move help is coming. Roosevelt is just a few blocks away. Just breathe easy," Gojcaj said to his mentor while he held his wounds with his bare hands in a vain attempt to stop the bleeding.

"Not your fault kid," Del Greco said between pained breaths.

"Quiet, just be quiet, we will argue about why you pushed me aside and was first in tomorrow," Gojcaj said.

"Tomorrow? Not this time Jimmy. I did the right thing Jimmy. In the end, I did the right thing," Del Greco said and went silent.

His pension was now a guaranteed monthly check to his widow for the rest of her life. He would be given a full inspector's funeral, all honors and respect due to a cop killed in the line of duty.

42

Ilir Marku arrived at the home of Shpresa and Rick without the usual security entourage. He was driven in a plain black sedan with only two of his trusted bodyguards. No one knew where he was going or when he would return. His wife had been through enough and he did not want to let her know he was meeting with his old lover. There was nothing good that would have come out of her knowing that he was meeting Tenuta.

Ilir got out of the car. The bodyguards were suspicious of the house and held their guns down behind their thighs, walking closely next to their Boss.

"Boys, it is fine. I trust these people. Just stay by the car please," Ilir commanded. The men reluctantly obeyed, keeping their guns at the ready.

Marku walked past a car in the driveway leading up to the steps and the front door of the Metalia home. He could hear the clicking of the engine as it cooled off. For the first time in a long time there was a flutter of anticipation in his stomach.

He rang the doorbell promptly at eight o'clock with a bottle of rare Raki for the visit and two small bouquets of flowers for Shpresa and Tenuta. Shpresa opened the door immediately, with her beaming wide and white smile greeting him.

"Mr. Marku, welcome, our home is your home," Shpresa said.

"I am honored to enter such a beautiful home that is filled with peace," Ilir said holding out one of the bouquets to Shpresa then putting his right hand to his heart in a sign of sincerity.

"Please Mr. Marku, come in."

Ilir removed his shoes as is customary.

"No need to remove your shoes Mr. Marku," Shpresa said in deference to his position. Ilir ignored her.

"Where is your husband? Where is that good man Rick?" Ilir asked.

"I asked him to visit his brother. There is no need for anyone else to be here."

Shpresa led her esteemed guest to the living room where Tenuta was waiting.

There was no need for an introduction. Tenuta had been sitting on the sofa and rose when her former lover, the only love of her life, entered the room. She was smiling and looked radiant.

"My God! You are still as beautiful as the last time I saw you Tenuta." Ilir handed her the bouquet and bowed his head in deference to her. He felt his legs trembling and he bit the inside of his lip, both things he had not done since childhood.

"Ilir...Ilir I am happy to see you. I'm very happy that you accepted my invitation to talk," Tenuta said, her eyes conveying her adoration.

"I will be in the backyard. I hope the coffee is hot." Shpresa motioned to a sterling silver platter with cups and a carafe of coffee and a few cookies. They didn't seem to hear her or even notice that she was still in the room. The emotion in the room was palpable. Shpresa made a quick exit grabbing a dish towel from the kitchen to wipe the sweat from under her neck and brow. She had to breathe deeply.

"My dear Tenuta. So many years have passed. So much water has flowed under both of our bridges. I have missed you all of those years. I wish things could have been different. I—"

"Ilir, no need to go back. Life took us our separate ways and has been both kind and cruel to us both. You are alive, I am alive and that is enough right now," Tenuta said.

Ilir sat on the sofa and invited Tenuta to join him. They sat on either side, far enough away from each other that they did not invade the appropriate space that was needed to comply with proper decorum.

"I am barely alive Tenuta. My son's death was my death. I have nothing left. There is no reason for me to pretend to be alive as my family tragedy leaves me like a barren field. I am sorry to say this to you but I speak the truth old friend. All I wait for now is for my eyes to close and my body to be put into the ground in Tropoja," Ilir said solemnly, his eyes filling with tears.

"Ilir. I can do or say nothing that will bring your son and grandson back to you. You know that I have always loved you and always will and you know that if I could change things for you I would. Before you put yourself into your grave you need to hear what I want to say to you," Tenuta said looking squarely into Ilir's sad eyes.

Ilir nodded his head slightly in response.

"Ilir…your son is gone but you have another son my dear. Our son. I had your child and never told you. I never wanted to disrupt your family and was satisfied with being the unwed mother. Ilir, Adem is your son, on this I swear on the souls of my ancestors. Your blood and your spirit continue in him." Tenuta's lips were quivering from her words.

Ilir was speechless as his brain processed this information. His mind flashed back to when they said goodbye for the last time as she left for Albania and he for the marriage with someone he didn't love.

43

Gino went to the Roosevelt Hotel first thing in the morning to see Joey Clams and C.C. to give them an update on what was going on both with the Joey Jr. situation and with himself. His plans to see Hamdi had been made for three o'clock that afternoon at a restaurant in Astoria, Queens. *Kakeledis* is a Greek restaurant serving the best fresh fish anywhere in New York City without forcing it's patrons to take a loan from their bank. Although the owner of the place was Albanian he wasn't at all involved with the Marku family. Gino was a semi-regular, dropping in for lunch or dinner at least twice a month. Gino felt at home in this family style restaurant and never remembered seeing any wise-guy Italians or Albanians hanging around the joint.

Kakeledis is closed from three until five-thirty in the afternoon so a mutual advance team representing the Micelis and Markus would spread a few bucks on the owner and a polite word of wisdom to convince him to let the place be used for a special event during that time. Micky Roach was in charge of making sure everything went smoothly.

Gino had no doubt that the meeting would take place as planned and that *Kakeledis* would not be shot up, bombed out, or otherwise destroyed during the sit down. What was going to happen after was something he was not willing to predict. Gino was concerned that the mob war could escalate into a long and bloody mess, something that was far beyond his experience as a street smart business man. Gino knew from his years in the corporate and not so corporate world he lived in to cross one bridge at a time. He also knew that when necessary, blowing up some bridges was okay, unlike what so many people warned him to avoid. Right now he needed to pull off a safe sit-down for Carmine Miceli Jr. and Ilir Marku. They would have their meeting with their respective newly appointed *consiglieres*. The future would be laid out for him this afternoon.

Joey Clams and C.C. met Gino in the restaurant at The Roosevelt Hotel right at eight-thirty as planned. The heat was off but Gino's two pals were not yet brought up to speed. Clams was in no mood for any more waiting or Albanian bullshit. He and C.C. were ready to take on all comers and end the nonsense once and for all. They had no idea what plans were being made and what role Gino was playing in the power struggle.

"You look like shit Gino," Joey Clams said as Gino approached the breakfast table.

"How are you this fine morning Joey? C.C.? That's always a great thing to hear so early in the day," Gino said with a smirk as he sat down and waved the waiter away.

"How are we? Tell him how we are C.C.," Clams said looking out the window onto Madison Avenue.

"We suck that's how we are Gino. What the fuck? We have to hide out like fucking cocksuckers while Joey's kid is in Italy fucking Gabriella or Theresa?" C.C. said with a wild eyed look.

"And let's not forget that these Albanian, dick-faced motherfuckers killed Babbu, Gino. They have to answer for that Gino. I will see that they answer for that, bet the farm my friend because I'm as serious as lung cancer," Clams said and Gino saw his frustration and rage. Rage with Joey Clams was not a good thing. No one was safe when Joey was in that frame of mind.

"Listen, a lot has happened so I need to fill you both in. The Albanians know who did the work. That's been dealt with. Ukë is as dead as can be. The cops did a Santino Corleone on him. Thank God Jr. is off the hook," Gino said then paused to sip some water.

"So it's all over? Another great adventure in the shit storm I've been living?" Joey Clams asked.

"Joey, listen to me nothing is over until you close your eyes. It's just another stage of being all fucked up. Look, there's a meeting this afternoon with Carmine and Marku. Marku needs to eat some shit and Carmine needs to let him lose with honor. I hope that we can make the peace, get what we need back from Marku and get a few bucks for you two and Joey Junior. It may finally help get your son straight Joey," Gino said.

"We? Am I hearing what I think I'm hearing Gino?" Joey Clams asked, holding up his hand to silence C.C. who only heard the word bucks.

"That was the next thing I need to tell you both. I asked Carmine to bring me in. Let me help him with this mess and watch his back for him. He agreed to give it a try," Gino said. Gino seemed a bit embarrassed by the news about his new career.

"So you avoided this life since you were a kid and now, when you are ready to file for social security benefits, you jump in with both feet. This is crazier than that broad you were with and that Fish Farm place where we all almost bought it. Gino, at least the girl had nice tits. What the fuck are you thinking pal?" Joey Clams went from a bad mood to having a low throbbing headache in a minute.

"Hey Clams, speak for yourself. I want to hear more about the money coming our way and I could use some work and I want my landlord's legs broken. Now all I gotta do is call our boy over here and I can get what I need. So Gino, now you're a real live wise guy instead of a pretend gangster," C.C. spouted like a geyser while Joey just gave him the 'you're-an-idiot' look.

"Take it easy with that kind of talk C. Nobody is breaking anybody's legs over here. Look, I'm helping Carmine run his business. That's all. He looks at me like a big brother, like a father. It's not like I'm taking numbers on Arthur Avenue or selling dope to school kids for Christ's sake. I'm advising Carmine on certain issues when he needs a sounding board he can trust. This Albanian thing needs a bit of finesse that Carmine has to learn. I'll try to smooth out this thing and work with him for a while before I hang up the cleats for good," Gino said.

"And what do you think you're gonna tell Ellen? You remember her Gino, your wife? Hi Honey, everything is fine, I'm now a capo in an organized crime family? Let's go tell the kids the good news. Every year or so, you lose your mind Gino. This time you're ready for the wacko ward," Joey said before signaling for the waiter.

"Good, I'm starving. Hash and eggs anyone? Look at the tits on that blonde over there," C.C. said once again illustrating that he never got past tenth grade. Gino gave the waiter the look and he stayed away again.

"Joey, I will admit that there are parts of this thing that I've not thought out. Let's see how things play out today and a few days from now. It's not like I'm in it for a four year term."

"Stupid…it's a life term Gino and you know it. Once you do something you do it all the way. Who knows you better than me? You immerse yourself past your balls and up to your neck. With your brains you will be in every aspect of this thing and risking that nice life that you've made for yourself and your family. And when you say you ain't selling drugs and breaking legs and taking numbers you know you sound like a real asshole because you will be doing all that plus more. Yeah, maybe on a high level but it's all the same to the Feds," Joey said with that vein in his forehead protruding.

"Relax Joey. I'm smart enough to have you two ugly bastards to bail me out right?" Gino said with a laugh.

"Ain't funny Gino. This is the real thing and you know it. We will always be there for each other no matter what. That's all I'm gonna say about this thing," Joey Clams said shutting the door on the conversation.

"Okay, let's talk about getting your boy back here and into a good treatment center. I contacted Hazelden in Minnesota last night. They have a bed waiting for him. We get him back from the old country in a day or two after this heat is gone and he's out there getting better."

"Okay, so I rob which bank Gino? I can't afford that fucking place. Don't you think I would have done that if I had any money? It's like twenty thou a month for fuck's sake."

"More like thirty. Not your concern. I owe you for saving my life. It's on me," Gino said.

"Gino, there was a very wise lady that I knew that used to tell us 'Italian men can't cope with success.' Remember her?" Joey asked.

"Why do you always have to break my balls Joey? Why? Now we can eat. C.C. did I hear you were paying?" Gino said.

"I can't afford a bagel in this friggin' place. Let's eat a huge breakfast and leave one at a time and hang them for the check like in the old days...what do you say?"

44

Everything in life happens for a reason my friend. Your father's sudden death, my son getting himself killed, the sun shining today, the cost of milk for children. Some people say it is the hand of God. I don't believe in such fairy tales Carmine. I don't profess to know what the reasons are but who knows, someday I may."

Ilir Marku sat across from Carmine Miceli Jr. at *Kakeledis* Restaurant and began the meeting by waxing philosophic as old men do. They did the routine of kisses on each cheek and warm hugs that showed mutual respect for each other's position in their respective crime families. Micky Roach had swept the place clean and had an army of nearly three hundred men in and around Astoria just in case. Hamdi Nezaj also had his soldiers at the ready. They numbered seventy of the meanest looking Balkans imaginable. The hoods drove around the streets of Long Island City, Astoria, Corona, and Flushing or waited in every restaurant, funeral home and city park parking lot anticipating a call to rush in like the cavalry. It was like the Cuban Missile crisis in a way. At any time holy hell could have erupted.

Gino Ranno and Hamdi Nezaj greeted each other in the same manner albeit somewhat more reserved than usual. They went from dear friends to competitors overnight and the awkwardness was noticeable to both men.

"Ilir. My father taught me to listen more than I speak. He also told me to respect my elders which I will teach to my children. I want to hear what you have to say today but I too don't believe in fairy tales. What we agree on or disagree on here is our work not God's," Carmine Jr. said.

"Yes. Let me start by again telling you how much I respected your great father and how that respect now transfers to you, his son. What happened to my son and grandson was unfortunate. What happened to our friendship and the casualties we both suffered in battle was just as unfortunate. I have come here to apologize for the harm that I caused to you and your people and take responsibility for the evil work of a Marku family member. I ask you to forgive me and to set ourselves straight again." Ilir held his right hand to his heart.

"Your words are genuine and sincere Ilir. We can accept your apology but more is needed as damages were done to my family and other families not at this table. We are representing all factions of our association and any agreement we make will be acceptable within certain guidelines that have been requested. Please know that we need to be realistic about the cost of these damages. An apology is fully accepted but now we need to discuss real life. Strictly dollars and cents. I know I can be too direct at times but that is my style so understand that no insult is intended." Carmine Jr. put the cards, although not all of them, on the table.

Hamdi spoke for the first time.

"We agree Carmine. If we are looking to be friends for the future then the tax for a mistake in judgment should be realistic. Is it a cash settlement you have in mind?" Hamdi was sending out a trial balloon. Gino knew the negotiations were now underway, full speed ahead.

Gino now spoke.

"When Carmine speaks of dollars and cents it is not simply a cash deal, although some cash will be required to show good faith and settle expenses."

"What are you suggesting?" Ilir Marku addressed both men rather than insult either.

"I must be honest gentlemen. For years our business has suffered as some of your, shall we say, over-enthusiastic people took bits of our core business from us. My father and the heads of the other families either allowed the loss or pushed back, depending on how much we were willing to share. My feeling has always been that we gave up too much and that a meeting like this should have taken place years ago. We sniffed around each other like two dogs and then marked our territories. In my view the time has come for you to show respect rather than just talk about respect," Carmine Jr. said, straddling the line of honor.

"We are prepared to offer thirty million dollars in full restitution for this misunderstanding," Ilir responded. Hamdi nearly cringed as the offer was premature.

"Mr. Marku. That offer can only be viewed as a down payment for what the families require at this point. We were expecting a larger sum over a period of time as well as a rollback of some business ventures that were once ours."

"So what are you saying Gino?" Hamdi asked.

"We are prepared to accept five million dollars a month. One million dollars per family for the first two years. Payable directly to the Micelis who will distribute accordingly."

"That is crazy money. That is one hundred and twenty million dollars over two years. What do you mean for the first two years?" Hamdi asked with a wide eyed, shocked look.

"Then one million dollars per month to the Miceli family for three years. A payback for our losses over a five year period is a bargain," Gino said.

"An expensive bargain Gino, don't you think? As opposed to?" Ilir Marku said without batting an eye.

"Alternatively we can take your very generous offer of thirty million in cash and you give back what was taken from us over the past thirty years. The numbers, loans, unions and the street powder that we know comes in heavy to you from Detroit and Canada. Mr. Marku, you know the numbers better than anyone. This is a bargain you can afford and keep your power," Gino said pointedly.

"Will I insult you if I say no?" Ilir said.

"Yes, you would, unless you have a better offer to put on the table. And one more thing that Gino failed to mention Ilir. No more taking over our positions anywhere in New York City. No pushing out any of our people without a sit-down and an offer to buy, just as when you purchase a piece of property," Carmine said.

"That does not mean we are for sale. That means we are business men looking to get along with our friends," Gino added.

"Gino, you know I never make a decision quickly. I would like to discuss this with Mr. Marku for a few days and get back to you with our decision and an offer that we can live with," Hamdi said.

"I did not expect a done deal today gentlemen. I do expect something however. I would like to have your offer within forty-eight hours. I would also expect that there be no fighting until we agree on a settlement," Gino said.

"Carmine, Gino, my dear friend Hamdi. We must agree upon one thing tonight. The Greeks cannot make good wine but we must toast with it for lack of anything better in this place. I offer a toast to our friendship and to agree on the forty-eight hour peace. We will be back to you within that time," Ilir said and signaled to the waiter for service. They spoke about old times, politics, sports and food like old friends do until six-thirty.

Both sides ordered their lieutenants and soldiers to stand down and await further instructions. They were informed about the moratorium that was controlled by the harshest penalty. The next two days would determine the course of organized crime in New York City and the rest of the underground throughout the world. The web of crime was woven tightly.

Ilir Marku never mentioned a word about his visit from Tenuta and the new found heir to his family and crime empire.

45

Carmine said nothing for the five minutes that it took to leave Astoria and get over the Robert F. Kennedy Bridge. It seemed that he was waiting to get back into Manhattan to say what was on his mind.

"You did good Gino. I'm proud of you. These people are no push-overs. They want what we have and they want to hold onto their piece of the pie."

"There is plenty of pie to go around Carmine but we need to see that they don't eat all of it. They ran a little crazy over the years and it's not gonna be easy to keep them on a diet," Gino said ignoring the compliment from the Don.

"So what's their next move, *consigliere*? Will they buy or will they die?" Carmine said half joking.

"No clue. Hamdi always plays things very close to the vest and squeezes his cards very tightly. We need to be patient and play it out to our best advantage. It's a bit touchy with Marku because he's old school and we need to guard against insulting him."

"Yeah but I will only allow him to play that card to a point. I have the other families ready to rumble with these people. It's not what I really want but it may be what we need to settle things to our advantage. In the meantime we need to meet Micky Roach and get him ready just in case," Carmine said.

"Not so sure Carmine. Like you said the Albanians are no push-overs. They are only afraid of each other. I've been studying some of their history. Their opponent may think that they have won but history tells another story. They never really surrender."

"Sound familiar?"

"Sounds like Sicilians to me," Gino said.

"You got that right my friend. Very much like the Sicilians. Every-body took a piece of us until we said enough."

"Exactly like Sicilians. So, we need to think how we would feel if we were put into the same position. That's the secret to coming out whole with the Albanians." Gino looked across the river as they began to exit onto 71st Street on the FDR. His wheels were turning. He realized at that moment that he was born for this business.

46

Ilir and Tenuta had agreed to tell Adem who his father was together when they met at the Metalia home. They wanted to be able to face him together and answer any questions that he might have. It was decided that Shpresa would ask Adem to make a visit to Valbona with her that evening and Tenuta would be brought to the estate shortly after they arrived. Ilir was contemplating his next move with Gino and the Micelis but he could not concentrate on business with the task of officially announcing the news to Adem. There was plenty of time for that. He had already made up his mind and would see Hamdi later that evening. Ilir's heart was soaring at the thought that he had a son, an heir to his fortune and a continuation of his bloodline. The news was a gift, a last chance to see a grandson and at the same time news that would break the heart of his loyal and faithful wife.

Ilir needed to tell his wife the news before he met with Adem. An hour before Adem and Shpresa arrived at the Marku home, Ilir told her the news in the privacy of their bedroom. Mrs. Marku took this news as she had taken everything in her life, with stoic acceptance. She believed Ilir and was relieved that her husband had not soiled their wedding vows. She accepted the fact that Adem was created before they had been married. One thing struck Ilir like a bolt of lightning. His wife was not at all shocked by the news; in fact, her face seemed to hint that she knew about Tenuta and her child. It seemed that there were not many hidden secrets among the Albanian women. Ilir thought it best not to press his wife on the matter but he had questions that he wanted to ask. Why didn't she tell him that he had another son years ago? Why didn't she tell him there was an heir when Lekë was killed? Ilir knew that these would be her secrets forever.

Shpresa passed the security detail as if they were not even there. They were now part of the landscape and she and Adem barely noticed them. They noticed her of course and as men do, they made a few remarks about her figure. No harm done.

Adem seemed excited to see Valbona and brought some flowers and a Hall and Oates Greatest Hits CD. He wanted to show her that he was more about all music instead of only Albanian music. This was Adem's subtle way of letting Valbona know about himself without looking like he was laying out his résumé.

Shpresa and Adem were told by a woman who answered the door that Valbona was sitting in the yard and not having a great day. Adem was steps ahead of Shpresa as they made their way to the rear of the estate. Adem opened the French doors leading to the gardens and Valbona greeted him with a beautiful smile even though it was obvious by her eyes and make-up that she had been crying. Shpresa stayed behind Adem to let things happen naturally.

"Valbona, you okay?" Adem asked.

"I'm fine Adem, just a bit blue I guess. My mind is playing tricks on me, that's all," Valbona said dabbing at her eyes with a tissue.

"Shall we stay, or do you need time to yourself?" Adem said while motioning to the door.

"Are you kidding? I couldn't wait to see you. I mean, I'm happy you are here," Valbona's face reddened at her faux pas.

"Hi Val. I'm here too!" Shpresa said with her signature hearty laugh.

"I'm happy to see you too but you didn't bring me nice flowers like Adem." Valbona was now laughing.

"Girl I will bring you flowers only when you cook me a meal which will be never," Shpresa said and they all laughed.

"I got this CD for you also. Shpresa said you guys liked Hall and Oates back in the day. Me too. I thought we can listen to them a bit tonight," Adem said, his eyes never leaving Valbona's face.

"That would be great. I could use some cheering up and a drink or two. Some Captain and Coke would be good. My father-in-law will think I'm drinking iced tea if he drops by. By the way Shpresa, is that proper? Do I still refer to him as my father-in-law?"

"Are you crazy?! Always! I'm afraid we need to take you back to the hospital for tests," Shpresa said in a joking tone but with a serious look on her face.

"Relax, just saying," Valbona said, dismissing the weird question.

"Okay, is there Captain in the bar?" Adem asked as he wanted to please Valbona's every wish.

"Yes, you go get the bottle and I will ask the ladies to bring the coke and ice."

Adem was no sooner back in the house when Shpresa went at Valbona with a flurry of questions.

"Val have you lost your mind? What kind of question is that to ask? You forgot who we are? You forgot your place in this family? I can't believe you Val."

"Relax Shpres. I just wanted to see the reaction, that's all."

"Do your testing when we go to the mall but not here you fruit cup," Shpresa said.

"Is this half gallon of Captain going to be enough?" Adem came back into the garden with a bottle of Captain Jack Rum.

"Plenty, but let's not get started so fast. Adem, Mr. Marku wants to see you," Shpresa said. She felt the blood rush to her head and her face get warm.

"He does? What's up?" Adem asked looking from Valbona to Shpresa. Valbona had no clue and Shpresa didn't know where to put her eyes.

"He's in his study. Go and we will start this bottle. You can catch up Adem," Shpresa said.

Ilir was in his study looking up at the giant mural of Skanderbeg when Adem entered the room. He was dressed in a magnificent blue pin-striped Brioni suit with all the proper finishings. He turned to greet Adem with a radiant smile that Adem had not yet seen on the man who had so many terrible things happen recently.

"Adem, I am happy to see you. Please sit. Coffee? A drink?" Ilir asked.

"Thank you sir. Whatever you are having is fine," Adem replied.

"Then Louie the fourteenth it is," Ilir said as he took a glass from the table and poured a healthy double shot.

"We have a special guest coming in a few minutes and we can talk in the meantime," Ilir said.

"Special guest? May I ask?"

"You may ask. I will not tell. I will save it as a surprise."

"Okay. So how have you been Mr. Marku?"

"Considering events of the recent past and a possibly difficult future, I feel very well. Almost as if my blood has been made younger,

Adem. Life takes us down strange and unfamiliar paths and we some-times are lost for a while. I am now hoping to find my bearings," Ilir said. Adem was not following the mysterious analogy.

"So I guess a person is never too old to find himself?" Adem asked trying to discover the Boss' meaning.

"On the contrary. Sometimes age is what it takes to know what you were put here for."

The door to the study opened slowly and Hamdi Nezaj appeared, leaving the door open.

"My dearest friend. Thank you," Ilir said and stood.

Hamdi said nothing but simply put his hand over his heart and backed out of the room. The doorway remained empty for what seemed like a minute but was in real time less than ten seconds. Tenuta appeared in a long and colorful traditional Albanian gown. She, like Ilir, was also beaming.

"Mom, what are you doing here?" Adem asked and looked quickly at Ilir for a clue.

Tenuta walked slowly toward her son, took his hand and led him to a divan.

"Please sit down Adem," Tenuta said. She sat next to Adem still holding his hand in hers.

"Mom, what's going on? Why are you here? I don't get the connec-tion."

"Adem, perhaps you will allow me to explain," Ilir began.

"Ilir, please permit me," Tenuta said quickly.

"Of course."

"Adem, before you were born things were a bit different than they are today. My parents were very strict and the old world customs controlled our lives on a daily basis. I am not saying that that was a bad thing. I wish the young people today followed our laws and understood why they were made. I was a young girl and full of life. I fell in love with a man that was promised to another woman. He was also deeply in love with me. Our marriage could not be, according to our customs, and that man lived by his family's promise. We parted ways and I returned to Albania, to the safety of my family. I was broken hearted as you can imagine. I was also pregnant with you. Rather than disgrace my family, I married an older man in our town man who secretly agreed to raise you as his son. He was killed in a *gjakmarrja* and never even saw you but my honor was upheld. My family never knew the real story. As far as they were concerned the man I married was the father of my baby. I never married again and raised you as a single parent. I did the best that I could and you were the best son to me, of that I am forever grateful and blessed." Tenuta took a moment to compose herself.

"Mom, why are you here and why are you telling me this now?" Adem asked not putting the pieces together.

"Adem, my son. Ilir Marku was that man that I fell in love with. He is your father." Tenuta took both of Adem's hands in hers.

Adem did not grasp her words immediately and seemed to be waiting for more to come.

"My only wish is that I would have known about you at that time Adem. I loved your mother with all my heart. I would have provided for you both."

"Provided? With all due respect Mr. Marku, we provided for one another just fine. I needed a father not an envelope every month," Adem said.

"Perhaps I chose the wrong word. I am sorry. If I knew about you I would have broken my family's promise and married the love of my life. I say this on my honor Adem," Ilir said with tears in his eyes.

"You know what? I believe you. I'm in a state of shock but I do believe you Mr. Marku. This must have been very hard for you to hear this news but I have to ask my mother some questions," Adem said and turned to Tenuta.

"Please do not hate me son," Tenuta said tearfully.

"Are you kidding? How can I hate the person who was there for me as a mother and a father and worked herself like a mule for my comforts? There is nothing but love in my heart and in my soul for you, Mom. I have so many questions I don't know where to begin," Adem said rubbing his face with his and his mother's hands.

"Say whatever you feel my son," Ilir said using the word son to Adem for the first time.

"Wow, that sounds a bit strange. I guess it will take me some time to adjust to that. But Mom...why now? Why did you wait to tell me this now and to tell Mr. Marku this news?"

"Why? Because I still love him and he is hurting from the loss of Lekë. Ilir needed to know that he had another son. If that terrible tragedy didn't happen I would have taken this secret to my grave. No one, not him, not you would have heard these words come from my mouth. I told your father this because I still love him. More than I love myself," Tenuta said holding her head up with pride.

"And his wife?" Adem asked.

"Adem! I said I still love him but I can never be with him. He is a married man and that I hold sacred. His wife is a good woman and he made his choice before you were born. This is our way Adem. There is no other way for us."

"Then I love him too," Adem stood, kissed his mother and went to embrace the Albanian Boss.

"Sir, thank you for giving life to me and for loving the greatest woman on this earth," Adem said holding Ilir's arms.

"Adem, can you call me something other than sir, or Mr. Marku? Ilir is acceptable."

"*Babe*, I am happy to be your son. I hope that God gives you a long life so that we can enjoy each other," Adem said smiling broadly, calling him Dad in Albanian.

Ilir Marku embraced his only living son and out of character, cried into his shoulder like a baby.

4 7

The emotions ran heavy for a while. The father and his new found son were talking about everything that came to their minds. Adem wanted to know about the elder in his Marku family and Ilir happily obliged with an impromptu family tree.

In the gardens Valbona was getting anxious.

"What the hell is going on Shpres? What could Mr. Marku want with Adem for so long? Is it about me? Do you know something, you bitch?"

"Look who's the bitch. Two drinks and you want to start a bar fight," Shpresa said and they both laughed like they did in the tenth grade.

"Seriously Shpresa. You do know what they are talking about don't you?" Valbona asked.

"I do Val. Listen, it's not about you. It's about something that they will have to tell you. Please don't press me on this because I can't say."

"Jesus Christ, my best friend and she can't break a secret. This must be big, yes?"

"Big, yes!" Shpresa said and the doors to the garden opened and Adem appeared alone.

"So did you save me a shot of Captain?" Adem said.

"I'll give you a shot. Right in the face, Adem. What was all that about with Mr. Marku?" Valbona asked.

"Well, he said if I told you he would have to kill Shpresa. Now is your chance to get rid of her once and for all," Adem joked.

"Bye Shpresa, it was real. Now tell me Adem...tell me!"

"Nice, she throws me under the bus for some news. Great friend I have here. Seriously Adem, do you want me to leave?" Shpresa asked.

"No. Please stay. This is for both of you to hear from me."

"Spill the beans Adem. You are going to work for the family right?" Valbona blurted out one of her manufactured scenarios.

"Absolutely not Val. In a few minutes I want you to meet my mother. She is here, inside with Mr. Marku. Tonight she told me that Ilir Marku is my father. She left for Albania pregnant with me and he married his wife. She kept that a secret until now."

"Shut the fuck up." Valbona blurted it out and not in a bad way, but simply her reaction to the news.

"No way. This is for real or a joke Adem? Don't play like this." Valbona said.

"No it's true Val. I set the meeting in my house so Tenuta...I mean Adem's mom could tell Mr. Marku."

"I don't know what to say Adem," Valbona said.

"Say nothing until you hear what else I want to tell you. Shpresa, would you mind going in to say hello to my mother?" Adem asked.

Shpresa said nothing and moved like an Olympic track star for the doors to the house.

Valbona's eyes looked like two brown saucers. Her mouth was

slightly open as she wondered what else could be expected from Adem.

"Valbona, I know that you are not ready to think about yourself and your future. You've been through hell and it's a miracle that you are doing so well. From the moment I first saw you I wanted to help in any way I could. I've put off plans in Albania to stay close by in case you needed my support. I never felt that my concern for you would turn into love. Valbona, I love you and I want to ask your father-in-law if I may court you with all respect and honor, as is the custom of our people. I will not ask him unless you approve."

"Are you saying what I think your saying Adem? What do you mean by court me?" Valbona said sweetly.

"See you, date you, be with you and hopefully, when you are ready again...to marry you," Adem said reaching for her hand.

"Adem, I am very fond of you but you know our culture, you know our people and our ways. Aside from that I am still so hurt and confused about how my life has turned out so far. There is nothing I can think about right now. I may never be the same person as I was. Adem, you are a great guy, maybe you should not come around and go about your life," Valbona said.

"How about if I just take my chances?"

"Adem, you are so sweet but I can make no promises to you. I may need too much time to repair myself from what has happened. I may never get over losing my Lekë and my son. Look, I appreciate all you have done for me but my pain is overwhelming at times. Don't judge a book by its cover. I may seem fine to you but I must tell you something. Even my blood hurts. Deep down inside I am nothing but emptiness. There may be no love left in me Adem."

"Valbona I am in no rush and I know that I want to be with you. I was content with myself until I met you but now I feel my spirit pulling me toward yours. I promise on my grandparents that there will be no pressure from me. You owe me nothing."

Valbona looked Adem in the eyes then slowly lowered her own as if in prayer. After a few long minutes she spoke into her hands that rested in her lap.

"Why would you want me? Why would you want a damaged person who will forever be in grief? Forever be another man's wife."

"It's simple Valbona. I'm in love with you. Right now those words do not require a response. Let's just see how things go. Let's not speak of this again. You will know when you are ready. In the meantime I am not leaving," Adem said.

"And are you planning to be a gangster? Will you take over the family business so I can lose another husband?"

"I have no interest in that at all. I am an artist. I am not a thug and he will know that if he doesn't know it already. I am not judging him but that is not the life that I have chosen. Not for me and not for my children," Adem said emphatically.

"Then yes Adem...you may court me but not just yet. That sounds like something from a movie doesn't it? Courting. We never used that word in the Bronx. You need some training Adem. But Adem please, we must move slowly. I'm not sure if I can deal with any more bad that life may throw at me."

Adem took Valbona's hand, kissed it lightly and led her into the house to speak with his mother and his *Babe*.

48

The day after the emotional meeting at the Marku estate, Hamdi called Gino on his cell phone to set up another meeting with the two Dons. Neither side had broken the ordered truce although the tension was extraordinarily high. The Bronx, or at least the Belmont and Morris Park sections, remained in virtual shutdown. Business was suffering badly and everyone was waiting for the next shoe to drop. One restaurant owner said it reminded him of how the Germans felt while they were waiting for the Allied Invasion. They knew it was coming but weren't sure where or when it would happen.

Hamdi threw a curve ball at Gino when he asked that they meet that afternoon again at four o'clock but in Italian-Albanian territory. DeLillo's Pastry Shop on East 187th Street a few stores down from Arthur Avenue. This was Gino's stomping ground as a boy. Every time he passed 604 East 187th Street he thought of his father and the entire family who worked in Uncle Bill Saggese's Half Moon Restaurant. This was where Gino knew he would get into the sales business. He worked the outdoor pizza stand for the restaurant from time to time. Gino's biggest problem was making the proper change. Pizza was fifteen cents a slice and he was too proud to make a fifteen times table and take his time with the money. At the end of the day his count was always off. Thank God calculators were invented some years later.

DeLillo's was just a few doors down from their sacred family restaurant. This was home, the only place Gino really ever felt at home. Why did Hamdi want to meet there? Gino trusted Hamdi but needed to take every precaution for the safety of Carmine Miceli Jr. If one renegade Albanian made a bad move the city would need the National Guard to stop the war that would follow. Gino accepted the time and place and immediately called a meeting at the Miceli townhouse with Carmine Jr. and Micky Roach.

At the exact moment that Gino was meeting with Carmine Jr. and Micky Roach, Hamdi Nezaj returned to see the Albanian Boss Ilir Marku. Hamdi had been approached by two associates of Grigor "The Czar" Grigorovich. Grigorovich was known throughout the Balkan and Baltic world as the brutal head of the Russian Mob in New York City. It seems "The Czar" wanted to have the honor of Boss Ilir Marku's presence at his daughter's engagement party at Tatiana Restaurant in Brighton Beach in Brooklyn in two weeks. He also wanted to have a sit down at any place of Marku's choice as quickly as possible. Immediately, if possible, with of course all due respect and security.

Micky Roach knew the Belmont neighborhood like the back of his hand as did Gino. With the Bronx Borough Command Mobile Unit less than forty yards away from the pastry shop and on the corner of E. 187th Street and Arthur Avenue, Micky could not imagine that any overt action would take place against his Don. That's just what disturbed him the most. It seemed too secure. Roach knew very well that these Albanians would kill their enemies while they were shaking hands on a wedding line in front of six hundred people, so to take a chance would be foolish and devastating to the family. Aside from not trusting the Markus to pull an end around stunt, all it took was one power hungry maverick who sensed that the Marku family was at its weakest point for an explosive attack that could take out Don Miceli and his Albanian counterpart. Micky's job was to see that this didn't happen.

Micky knew that he needed reliable manpower and a good strategy for a strong defense and counter attack. With the tight streets and difficult egress from the streets in the neighborhood Micky needed to think of every possible scenario that could happen. The Roach had just a few hours to formulate his plan and run it by Gino for final approval. He made sure that only the most trusted men out of all the Miceli soldiers were available for security detail. Over nine hundred Miceli men were available to choose from but Micky only needed fifty. Fifty men to take roof top positions, including the bell tower of Our Lady of Mount Carmel Church, pretend to be polishing their car, drinking espresso inside and outside of DeLillo's and their across-the-street competitor, Palumbo's Pastry Shop, window shopping, hanging out for hours in the damp and dank basements of the stores next to the meeting place and walking the streets looking for signs of potential danger.

Micky always relied on the best available firearms, from close range, blast-their-guts-out, to high powered sniper rifles that could shoot a fly. Every soldier had two-way communication with a squad leader and with Micky. This stuff was easy for a man whose criminal mind was nurtured from his birth in Sicily. All he needed to do was think about what he would do to get a bomb or a bullet into DeLillo's or on the street when the Dons arrived for their meeting.

Micky locked down a three block area to guarantee the safety of his Don and to assure that the meeting would happen without bloodshed. The police presence was a plus but no guarantee of comfort for the old Sicilian. How did he even know if the cops were all cops? How did he know that the Con Ed workers underground on Hughes Avenue were not some Albanians placing bombs in the sewers? What if the coffee or pastry was poisoned? What if the place was already wired or a bag was set to blow like that pizza shop he did on Castle Hill Avenue? What if Marku himself came heavy and shot Carmine and Gino like Michael Corleone did to Sollozzo and the Irish cop?

Micky knew one thing for sure. If someone wanted Carmine Jr. and or the other Don dead badly enough there was no way he could fully protect them. The best he could do was use his wit and instinct and try to reduce the risks...and be sitting at the next table to sacrifice his life if need be.

By one, two o'clock Micky Roach was ready to review his plans with Gino. Gino asked an old friend if he could meet in the empty party section of his restaurant for a few minutes. They met upstairs at Mario's Restaurant and the owner, Joe, served Micky and Gino the most delicious pizza and salad in the neighborhood.

After the security and counter-attack plans were unfolded by Micky, Gino recalled something that happened to him at The Half Moon Restaurant when he was ten years old. He told Micky the story and they both agreed to use this experience as part of their safety shield.

The meeting was taking place in a little under two hours and a few finishing touches needed to be completed before the powerful mob men arrived at DeLillo's. Micky left Mario's and headed for his own command center at Pasquale Rigoletto's Restaurant. Not many customers were having lunch these days because of the hysterical media coverage of the Italian-Albanian street war, so there weren't any nosy onlookers to interfere with Micky's plans and operation.

Gino headed for Our Lady of Mount Carmel to light some candles for all of the family and friends that lived in the neighborhood and had passed away before he went to wait for Don Miceli and Ilir Marku at DeLillo's. His gesture was more superstitious than religious as was the hundred dollar bill that he folded into the poor-box. Gino thought of the day he received his Confirmation in the church and how large it seemed to him then and how he thought what they were telling him was a nice story but basically bullshit. He would stick with the superstition in case any of the story was real. Gino was a gambler that always hedged his bets.

Carmine Miceli Jr. was the first to arrive. He came in a silver BMW 750i sedan with two bodyguards. There were two enormous black Cadillac Escalades behind him full of Miceli soldiers and heavy arms all under the command of Micky Roach. Micky met Carmine directly in front of the NYPD Command Vehicle as planned.

"Micky before I go in there I have to stop at Casa Mozzarella for my mother," Carmine said.

"Carmine, is this what you have on your mind? Cheese? *Madonna* you have a real *cappa fresca*," Micky said half laughing referring to a person with a clear head.

"Ay, are you kidding me Micky? If I don't bring back that fresh mozz and a few pastries to Mom, I'll never hear the end of it."

"Italian mamas and their sons. I will never figure us out Carmine," Micky said while checking out the rooftops and the men he put into position. All was quiet.

Carmine did his thing, spending $122 on cheese and specialty items at the delicatessen, and handed the bag to one of his men. He was munching on a piece of hot mozzarella when he left the store, made a left and headed for DeLillo's.

He was surprised by the amount of young kids eating Italian Ices on the sidewalk tables under the awning at DeLillo's. There were about twenty boys and girls from ten to twelve years old, some of them taking photos of each other eating the ices with their cell phones.

Nice kids, Carmine thought as he walked into the large pastry shop. He saw a familiar face. Gino was sitting at a table for four with a smile from ear to ear. Micky Roach was at Carmine's heels with the two burly bodyguards.

"Gino. What are you smiling at you nutty bastard?" Carmine greeted his new *consigliere* with a smile and a hug.

"Nothing Carmine. But you're right; I am a nutty bastard."

"When we were kids this joint was tiny. They must have blown out the walls," Carmine said.

"Watch that blown out talk Jr. You may give the Roach heart failure. The old DeLillo's was a few doors down. Like everything else in the neighborhood, you need to change or die. Just like us Carmine, we need to change or die."

"Yeah let's see what we can do to change things in our favor today," Carmine said.

"I think we will come out ahead. Let's see how things work out. In the meantime how do you like all of the bodyguards outside?" Gino asked.

"*Meenkia*, I swear I didn't notice one button on the street. I think I'm blind or Micky is slipping a little Gino."

"Did you see those kids out there? They are our bodyguards for today."

"What?"

"In the summer of 1961 I'm ten-and-a-half years old. My father tells me he needs me to come with him to the Half Moon. I heard those words and you would think he was bringing me to meet the Mick at the stadium. The Half Moon meant food, those small juke boxes on the tables, the guys milling around, it was the greatest place on earth for me," Gino paused to take a sip of lemon soda.

"So?" Carmine asked.

"So, it's about ten-thirty in the morning. No lunch crowd yet and he brings me into the old DeLillo's and gets me the large lemon ice and puts me on a barstool in front of the main door to the restaurant. He tells me no matter what I'm not to get up from the stool until he tells me it's okay. He promised another ice, this time chocolate and then some pizza or veal parmiggiano or who knows what. So one at a time these big Lincolns and Cadillacs pull up and these great looking men in suits and hats get out and come to the door of the joint. One guy asks me if I'm Louie Brown's grandson and gives me a quarter, one guy tussles my hair, one guy's cologne is so strong I gag on my ices. Some came on foot without a car but they have one thing in common. Even your father showed up and gave me a dollar, God rest his soul. They are all strong and powerful looking guys. My dad comes outside, he was serving these guys at the big family table in the back, he comes outside in his apron, goes next door, gets me the big chocolate ice like he promised and runs back into the restaurant. I'm in ices paradise. Now I have to pee after all the ice. My eyes are turning in I have to pee so bad. I look inside and these guys have platters of linguine and crabs that were put into the charcoal brick oven to bake a bit. The smell came outside like a cloud from heaven. These men are chowing down, talking, drinking lots of wine and the whole time I have to piss like a race horse." Gino sips his soda again.

"And?" Carmine asked.

"And my father comes out with a fucking pail for me to piss into. I can't even go inside to take a leak. I turn my back to the street and it was the best piss I ever took."

"Why couldn't you piss in the john?" Carmine asked.

"Very simple Carmine, I was the only bodyguard the bosses needed that day. No bastard was going to come in blasting or throw a bomb with a ten-year-old kid sitting in front of the door. It's not done. I'll never forget it Carmine, so I told Micky and he loved it. I went to the school yard and got all these kids, some Albanian, some Spanish a few Italian kids, and they will sit there until they have to pee. The more they hold it in the more stuff they get. Plus five bucks each. I told them we are doing a movie soon and this was a try out," Gino said.

"You are without a doubt the nuttiest bastard in New York Gino," Carmine said in awe of his old friend.

Ilir Marku came into DeLillo's with Hamdi Nezaj. Carmine Jr. and Gino rose out of respect and the usual greeting took place. Except for the kids the place was empty and one of the Miceli bodyguards stood at the door to tell anyone who wanted a biscotti that the place was closed for a while. The only other people in the shop were Micky Roach and the bodyguard. Coffee was ordered and the owner brewed the espresso himself. A dish of cookies was set on the table.

"Very good putting the kids outside Carmine. Smart like your father," Ilir said not missing the symbolic ring of protection.

"Thank you Don Marku, it's a long used trick in our world," Carmine said as he glanced at Gino.

"We have a lot to discuss Carmine so forgive my rudeness. I think we need to get to the business at hand," Ilir said.

"By all means," Carmine responded.

"I am here today to tell you that we will pay the sum of money annually as you requested. I do believe that we need to pay for our mistakes and I was blinded with rage. I should have listened to reason. I was wrong and we will pay." He paused with his hand on his heart.

"Thank you. And the rest of our proposal Don Marku?" Carmine said. Gino cringed inside as Carmine's impetuous personality came across a bit aggressive.

"Carmine, today I met with some people from Brooklyn. These are serious people. Very disturbed people who have no respect for our ways or your ways. They have only a tradition of violence without boundaries. They smell blood in the water like sharks. They asked to see me so that I would lead my people to join with them against you and the other families. Between what the government has done to your business and your own people losing what their traditions have demanded from them, there is much blood in the water, with all due respect. I spit on these people but I did not say no to them. I of course did not agree to join with these maniacs. I simply told them that I would consider their generosity and speak with my associates. I swear this to you as I sit here that I would rather give away my business than get into bed with these Russians."

Carmine started to speak and Gino smartly stopped him.

"Carmine, please let Ilir finish his thought."

"Thank you Gino. You see Carmine, for us to roll back our business to a time when we were trying to get a foothold here would be devastating to us both financially and emotionally. If I agree to what you are asking we will not be able to pay the restitution that we accept and that you rightfully deserve. Moreover, the spirit of our people, the *Shqiptarët*, the Sons of the Eagle, would be broken. That will cause bad feelings and destroy any peace that we hope for. If you take away a man's pride you destroy the man Carmine." Ilir paused again.

"Go on Ilir," Carmine said and Gino knew his young Don was learning.

"I propose that we work in harmony. That we do not ever again take what is yours without asking for and paying for our appetites. We keep what we have worked for and we join forces against these barbarians who will see us all dead if they could. Not only us do they want dead but our children and their children Carmine. This I say to you from my heart." By his countenance the Boss Ilir Marku was not going to have any part of a horse trade negotiation.

"I take you at your word Don Marku. I know from my father that you are not the kind of man to soil yourself with lies. In the face of this threat I think that I am the one now that needs time to think about this and speak to the other families," Carmine said respectfully. Ilir knew that the young Don had no choice but to join forces to keep the Russians from taking over their business. Carmine also knew this but just wanted to be respectful to his partners.

"One more thing my friends. I am soon to retire from this business. I have discovered that I have another son. A man whose mother was the love of my life before my marriage. I have been given another chance at life and I want to make every moment count. I want to spend time with him, to learn about him and his goodness. I will not ask him to be in our life gentlemen. I gave too much to this business to make the same mistakes twice. I will be seeking ideas from my close friends and associates both here and in Albania but they will know that whatever is agreed upon between us will be *besa*. Nothing on this earth will break that. My dear friend sitting next to me, Hamdi Nezaj, will also leave this life and run his business with his sons as he always has. With honesty and dignity and *besa*."

49

The meeting was finished. Micky Roach didn't have to protect and defend his Don. Carmine Miceli Jr. went back to his townhouse fortress on East 79th Street, in Manhattan, Gino went to see Joey Clams and C.C. to give them an update on the events of the day and Ilir Marku was heading back to his estate in Westchester to see his son Adem and discuss plans for the future. A future that he would offer to help Adem with and perhaps one day his family would grow and flourish in a legitimate way. He was also prepared to announce that Tenuta would be provided for here and in Albania where she would have a home near the sea. Ilir thought of his retirement spending time between his home in Scarsdale and his home in Tropoja. He had hope that he would see a few grandchildren and he envisioned those kids coming from Adem and Valbona, God willing.

The next morning Gino was feeling good about being back in his home in New Jersey. He had made arrangements for Ellen to return knowing that at least the *gjakmarrja* was over and they would be in relative safety. He wasn't thinking about the danger of being the *consigliere* for the Miceli family and the inherent dangers that went with that job.

Joey Clams was staying at Gino's home and started making arrangements to head back to North Carolina and the easy paced life that he was not certain he could stand anymore. C. C. also was staying with Gino and Ellen and was about to take an apartment nearby the Ranno home as Gino offered him a job as his driver and guy Friday. C.C. was thrilled as he was out of work for some time. His monthly military disability check just did not make ends meet.

Ellen had roasted her famous red peppers and was making a marinara sauce with her secret recipe fried meatballs, and for the men Gino opened some Tuscan red wine to celebrate being back home and starting his new career. Ellen knew that he was taking a job in "marketing" for a new Miceli venture. Gino thought it best to ease her into the truth when the time was right. He felt guilty about lying to her but felt it was necessary. Every lie people tell is necessary at the moment but Gino planned to tell Ellen whatever he could when he could.

"Ellen this place smells so good I think I may put off going home for a bit," Joey Clams said as the boys watched the Yankees beat the Orioles like a rented mule on the big screen television in the Ranno entertainment center.

"Ellen...did you hear what Joey said? He loves your cooking," Gino said as he fumbled with a bottle and a cork screw.

"Ellen? You know she's a little deaf, guys. Let me go up and see if she needs some help in the kitchen," Gino said.

A loud thump and the sound of running made Joey Clams and C.C. jump to their feet. Gino took off up the stairs but not before Joey grabbed him by the arm.

"Guns?" Joey asked.

"Closet, shells on top," Gino said and made his way to his wife.

C.C. went behind the wet bar in the room and came out with two knives used to cut cheese and salami. Clams opened the closet and came out with Gino's Beretta semi-automatic shot gun. The shells were where Gino said.

Gino saw Ellen on the kitchen floor and he ran to her just as a burst of automatic gunfire ripped through the walls in the kitchen. Three men in ski masks were in the house and they didn't come to shoot pool. They accessed the home through the outside deck on the kitchen level surprising Ellen as she was at the kitchen sink.

Clams went up one stairway and C.C. fanned out to the other so they could confront the attackers. Joey came up low into the kitchen and dining room level and blasted one of the masked intruders square in the chest, forcing him to unload his weapon into the floor. Joey moved quickly to the kitchen saying nothing while Gino was screaming that he was going to slit the mother fucker's throats. C.C. bum rushed another of the intruders and buried the sharp cheese knife into the back of the guy's skull. The would-be assassin dropped to his knees as C.C. picked him up from under his arms using him as a potential shield.

The third guy headed for the front door which was double locked. He fumbled for the lock when Joey Clams shot out both of his legs from behind the knees. The assassin went into a fetal position screaming in a foreign language.

"What the fuck is going on?" Ellen suddenly screamed out. She was knocked out from a blow to the back of her head by the intruders. Her skull was fractured but she was obviously alive.

"Stay put Ellen. Don't move," Gino said.

Joey Clams, C.C. and Gino ran to the foyer where the masked shooter was writhing in pain on the Terrazzo marble floor, his blood pooling in spots.

"You cocksucker. Who sent you fuck face?" Gino demanded as C.C. removed the automatic rifle from his grip and checked him for other weapons.

"Gino...back off right now," Joey said taking over.

"It's gonna be okay buddy. I'm gonna get an ambulance. Just tell me where you came from so I can help you," Joey said as he knelt down next to the injured intruder.

"Fuck you and your mother," the man said in a heavy accent, his mask still covering his face.

"Listen you Albanian prick I'm going to rip your fucking throat out right here," Gino said.

"Gino...go look after your wife. Get upstairs and call your people. We have to scrub this place," Joey said. Gino obeyed the command.

"Okay tough guy. Let's see how tough you really are." Joey put his hand out and C.C. handed him the knife. The injured interloper went on with a flurry of hate in his language.

Clams took the knife and buried it deep into the man's thigh twisting it clockwise and then counter clockwise. The guy screamed until his voice went into gasps for air.

"Once more? Or will you be a tough guy some more?" C.C. said as he hovered over the bleeding menace as he began sucking air.

"I came to kill one man. And wife. That's all I will tell."

"So you came from the fucking Jehovah's Witnesses pal? I'm bored with this. Who sent you? Live or die it means nothing to me," Joey said.

"Fuck your whore mother."

Joey planted the knife up and into the man's eye socket, killing him instantly.

Gino ran back to the foyer and the scene of the knife imbedded into the dead man's head. Gino became light headed from the surrealistic scene in his home.

"Now what the fuck did you do that for Joey? I just wanted that Albanian bastard to say Marku's name. And to think I trusted those fucks," Gino said.

"Gino, you need to up your dose of medication. These guys are not Albanian," Joey said.

"Not Albanian?"

"Russian, Gino. They are Ruskies. Listen to their accents. Look at their guns...Russian...so are their shoes...Russian. They're motherfucking Russians pal," Joey Clams said as he removed the knife from the dead man's eye.

"Marku was right. These are not people, they are real animals. They will stop at absolutely nothing. You, your family, your kids, your grandmother and everyone in their path. They have no sense of decency and honor. We're in for it now," Gino said.

"We sure are," Joey and C.C. said in unison.

At the very instant of the attack on the Ranno home Ilir Marku and Hamdi Nezaj were returning to the Marku estate after dinner at a dear friend's restaurant on East 58th Street in Manhattan. Club A is an excellent Steak House well known for their distinguished and sophisticated crowd as well as their fabulous food and great wine list. Ilir loved to see his childhood friend who owned the joint and listen to the piano man play while he enjoyed a quiet dinner with Hamdi. Hamdi on the other hand would have never stepped into Club A because they were not at all embarrassed to charge a hefty price for a great meal

Six bodyguards accompanied the two men to dinner, waiting inside and outside Club A trying not to be overly conspicuous. They believed correctly that in a restaurant as crowded as this one no one would be attempting to harm the Boss and his *kryetar*.

The Marku estate was well protected with ten additional bodyguards awaiting the arrival of Ilir and Hamdi who left his car in the circular driveway. Hamdi would be staying at the Marku home until he heard from Gino and the next meeting was set. There was no sense in making the trip back and forth to his home in Armonk when he could be needed for a sit down at a moment's notice.

Driving up to Scarsdale gave the two men a chance to talk more about their plans for the future.

"My friend, I trust that these Italians will do the right thing and understand that we are speaking from the heart. I don't think that they understand what *besa* means to us. They are in trouble from every angle and we may be the only real friends they have left. This generation of their business has little respect for the old world traditions of their fathers which may be their end before long," Ilir said.

"They don't trust in themselves Ilir, how can we expect them to trust us? They are in turmoil and you are offering them a chance to save their world. I don't think they see it this way," Hamdi said.

"It is ego. False pride will destroy them. Inexperience will be the spoon that brings the poison to their mouths. Gino is a good man, a smart man, but he is not from this life. He means well. He wants to help his friend who is also not ready for war with these crazy Cossacks. I'm afraid that if they make the wrong choice they will be swallowed whole."

"Ilir, I would not underestimate the Sicilians. We only see a small part of their world. They are very much like us. They have been conquered but never truly defeated," Hamdi reminded Ilir of the similar history of the Albanians and Sicilians.

"True. Only time will tell my friend. But that time is close to us."

"So what now? What are your plans for the clan?" Hamdi asked.

"I have only one plan left Hamdi. To see us out of this problem. To settle the territory and leadership of the clan fairly and to enjoy my life and the son I never knew."

"And what will Adem do for the clan?"

"Adem will make the clan proud. He is a talented man who will make not only the clan proud, but he will represent the best of the Albanian people. Believe me he will. But he will not be in our world. He will live his life his way. Hopefully he will be married and an entire village will be formed by him and his wife. I will help him where I can of course but I will not do it the way I have done everything else in my life. He will find his way without me for sure. A few well placed words and a few dollars scattered for his benefit is the most I can do for him. I will not lose another son and a chance to see my family continue because of my own stupidity," Ilir said as his car was driven to the exit on the Hutchinson River Parkway toward his home.

As the car carrying Ilir and Hamdi approached the large home the soldiers protecting the estate were alerted by hand held radio.

They stood in strategic positions around the property and flood lights were turned on to ensure that no one was lurking in the nearby shadows. The temporary truce with the Miceli family gave everyone a more relaxed feeling than the sense of danger just a few days before

As the cars rolled up to the estate's driveway and the guards moved toward the vehicles, a slow moving sedan rolled down the street. At first it looked like many of the rubber necking neighbors that were intrigued by the movement at the Marku residence. As the car passed in front of the driveway however, the back window and sunroof opened. In a split second automatic rifles appeared with their shooters firing directly at the Marku car. Three of the bodyguards were felled as the remaining men returned fire with handguns and Uzi's, neither of which are very effective in this kind of battle.

A second vehicle, a sparkling new minivan, approached the house from the opposite direction with the side door jammed open. In the driver's seat of the van, a masked assassin sprayed an automatic weapon at the remaining bodyguards on the Marku property while a killer in the back seat shot a rocket into the lead car, turning it into an inferno. One of the Marku men, well experienced from the war in Kosovo, ignored the shooting from the van and attacked the vehicle firing his Uzi. He hit both of the shooters in the back of the van, killing them instantly. The man with the rocket launcher was attempting to reload his weapon when his chest was opened and the other shooter in the front took two submachine gun shots into his face, splattering the driver with blood and bone. The brave Albanian jumped into the moving minivan to finish the driver. The vehicle crashed into a utility pole ending the assault.

All three men were dead as were five Marku men. Three Albanians were seriously injured.

As for Ilir Marku and Hamdi Nezaj, a quick thinking body guard had pulled them both from the vehicle and onto the ground in front of the house. A few scrapes and burns from the exploded car they were in was a gift in comparison to what happened to the car's driver, who was burned crispy.

The Boss and Hamdi were rushed into the house and into the safety of the basement. Mrs. Marku, the house women, and Valbona were all screaming hysterically but were ignored by the bodyguards that attended to their charges. The wailing of police and fire sirens turned the normally quiet hills of Scarsdale into a complete madhouse while the Marku home was bathed in orange light from the burning car in the driveway.

"Ilir, this could not be the work of Carmine Miceli. He would never attack you at your home...never," Hamdi said, his voice quivering from shock.

"I swear on my son's soul that if this is their work I will take my revenge on every one of them and their families."

The bodyguard who bravely rushed the minivan and stopped further damage to the Marku clan entered the basement with a souvenir of the attack. A Kalashnikov assault rifle, an AK-47, or what the Russians simply call a *Kalash*.

"What does this mean?" Ilir asked the bodyguard. He was in a state of confusion and shock, but with no fear at all.

"Mr. Marku, some of these men, the men in the first car escaped us. In the second car they are dead, three of them. Mr. Marku they were all Russians."

50

Joey Clams met with his son in the rehab center that was selected and paid for by Gino. Joey Jr. had gained a few much needed pounds and his eyes were clear for the first time in a long time.

"You know, this is probably your last chance to get your life back. I hope that you are smarter now," Joey Clams said to his son as they walked around the grounds of the center in Connecticut. Minnesota had been decidedly too far for Clams to visit.

"Pop, I feel a lot better and all I can say is I will try. I need to be here for a while and get my head straight. Then I can make plans for a decent life for myself."

"Joey I hope that this whole mess was rock bottom for you and that your words are not some game that you're still pulling," Clams said.

"I think I need to stay away from my friends and the Bronx. They teach us about changing people, places and things to keep sober. But I miss my friends and my cousins and everyone."

"Listen to me. Fuck those friends. I don't care what happens to them and you shouldn't either. This drug thing is too strong to beat when you stay in that world. I'm begging you to change into something better than you were," Joey Clams said as he stifled his anger toward his son.

"I'll do my best Pop. It's time for me to move on."

Just about a week later, on a sleepy Sunday morning in Tropoja, Albania, Mrs. Ilir Marku was in the large country kitchen serving breakfast to her daughter-in-law Valbona and her friend Adem. The Marku home overlooked a beautiful pasture replete with a babbling brook and an ancient stone bridge. The property was surrounded by a thick forest of pine trees and bramble bushes. Bales of yellow hay, food for the clan's livestock, dotted the landscape. Tenuta, Adem's mom was also in the house and was preparing the fresh orange juice, tomato juice, and steaming hot Turkish coffee for everyone. Some boiled eggs and a delicious fried dough *pettla* with honey were in abundance on the table. A CD of Adem singing Albanian ballads was playing softly in the next room as Adem lip-synced the words to Valbona when no one was watching.

On that morning in Lercara Friddi, Sicily, at the Miceli Family farmhouse, Ellen Ranno who was still recovering from the attack on her home and both Mrs. Carmine Miceli Sr. and Jr. and her young child were getting ready for breakfast. Mrs. Miceli Sr. was making cappuccino and preparing fried eggs and toast with Nutella as part of their breakfast. Her daughter-in-law Angela was dressing the baby and Ellen was listening to old Carlo Butti records on an antique victrola on the rear patio which was covered by a billowing canopy. The chickens in the back yard were scampering around and the two horses in the small corral were eating a mixture of oats and hay as they did everyday of their lives.

With their families safely ensconced in Europe, a meeting was held over 4,700 miles away that ended at two o'clock that morning in New York City. Carmine Miceli Jr., Gino Ranno, Ilir Marku and Hamdi Nezaj, along with representatives of two other New York Mafia crime families, an Albanian boss from Tropoja, a mafioso from Lercara Friddi, and a couple of major Albanian wise guys from Detroit finished a sit down in the back room of Club A on East 58th Street. The meeting lasted from early evening to plan their collaborative effort against their common enemy. The Italians learned a very important and very old Albanian proverb.

"Përgatitja dhe fati janë vëllezër." Preparation and fate are brothers.

There was no soft music playing, no pretty scenery, no trees, farm animals or hay. There were, however, a few familiar faces sitting at the bar. Micky Roach, C.C. Constantino, and Joey Clams Santoro waited for orders from their Don. Micky was in because it was the only life he ever knew. C.C. and Joey were in because their oldest friend Gino needed them. The next fight would test their nerve, their skills, and their loyalty. *La vendetta* and *gjakmarrja* are one and the same. The Russians needed to be dealt with.

CPSIA information can be obtained at www.ICGtesting.com
Printed in the USA
BVOW020849031012

301972BV00002B/2/P